Demonic Triangle

(Doomed Cases Book 1)

by

Joanna Mazurkiewicz

Copyright

Chapter One

I was staring at the long white stick, trying to convince myself that I was still dreaming. Two tiny lines in the small box had just told me that the test was absolutely positive and there was no going back. My heart began racing away, but this time the realisation of what was about to come hit me harder than any other time. I exhaled sharply and glanced back at about a dozen other white sticks that were spread on the bathroom floor.

Now I was suffering the consequences of my stupidity. Ricky, my best mate, had warned me to be careful countless times, but I chose not to listen. I never truly believed that I would ever be ready for this moment, and now it was the beginning of my end.

In the past three days I had taken at least twenty pregnancy tests and each one of them came back positive.

It was official—I didn't even have to go to the doctor—I was expecting a baby; there was a tiny creature growing in my stomach, a brand new life.

The father of this child was unknown.

My long-winded affair with the royal prince was done and dusted. Arthur and I hadn't slept together for exactly twenty-two days, two hours and seven seconds. He was away when I got fired, but that didn't matter. I didn't expect him to find me. I was only someone that filled his time.

What happened was in the past now. My new life was slowly falling apart. I had no job, no stable home, and on top of that I was going to be a mother.

The white stick fell out of my hand, down to the tiles. I slid down, covering my face with my hands, forcing myself not to cry.

Once I got fired from the royal court, I went through a partying phase. I had decided to travel for a bit and stopped in a few cities around the UK. I was sleeping around, first with random humans and then with even more random demons. Most of these past few weeks seemed blurry. I was high on magic, lost in sorrow and despair. Despite everything that I promised to myself, I had fallen in love with Arthur, the man that could never be mine.

Now I was regretting the fact that I ever thought working for the royal family could change my life for the better.

The space around me was dirty, dated, and bugs were crawling out of the sink. It smelt like someone had left a dead body in here and forgotten about it. My head started spinning, and before I knew it, I began throwing up. The darkness was creeping to the edge of my vision.

Ronan already knew what was happening. Now I finally understood that look on his face. He must have felt the shift of energies in my body, the new waves of magic.

Once I was done emptying my stomach, I sat back and took a few deep breaths, resting my head against the wall. Ronan had settled down in this small fishing village up north several years ago. We had been corresponding in the past, and a couple of days ago I showed up on his doorstep out of the blue, hoping that he could keep me safe for now. Ronan was the only demon that lived in this area, amongst retired humans and people that desired a quiet life, away from the crowded city.

A moment later there was a knock on the bathroom door. I exhaled sharply and told him to come in.

In the past twenty-two days I thought that I was invincible, that I could sleep around with anyone and not worry about the consequences. This was the only way that I could shut down the voices in my head, shut down the pain. Arthur's face faded away as I lifted myself back on my feet.

"What are you going to do, Maxine?" Ronan asked, staring down at me with his gleaming demonic eyes.

I couldn't feel my limbs all of a sudden. My energy was boiling inside me and my skin felt like it was burning. Maybe this had something to do with the fact that I was carrying a mongrel baby in my stomach. I needed to get used to the fact that I would be feeling like this for the next eight months and a bit.

"I don't know," I mumbled back, unable to think about the future. In my short life I never even considered being a mother; it wasn't something that ever crossed my mind. Work had filled most of my time, and then Arthur came along. I lost my head for him and fell into despair when it ended.

Ronan frowned and stepped aside, like he was letting me know that I couldn't keep hiding in the bathroom forever. This situation had to be dealt with, sooner rather than later.

"Maxine, if this child has even a drop of royal blood inside it, then your life is in grave danger."

His statement sent a chill down my spine, but I knew that it was true. The demonic world wouldn't accept the fact that Arthur slept with me willingly. The faction would believe that I had planned this from the very beginning in order to change the way mongrels were portrayed in the demonic world.

I got up and left the bathroom, knowing that I only had myself to blame for this. I didn't use any contraception. I wasn't even trying to be careful, so now I had it. The pregnancy was expected, and Ronan was right. If this child was Arthur's, my days on earth were numbered. Hell fully controlled royals. Any demons that had any kind of relationship with them were fully vetted beforehand.

An illegitimate mongrel royal baby would cause havoc on earth. The child would be taken away from me straight away and I would be sent down to hell. My options were limited, and I knew what Ronan was thinking, but I couldn't bring myself to even think about it.

There was a living being inside me and even though this creature could cost me my life, I wasn't prepared to kill it.

"Yes, you don't need to say it. I realise what might happen to me, but I have no idea who the father is. Before I got here, I went through a crazy phase," I told him, knowing that he most likely already suspected that.

The morning sickness had triggered my need to find out what was wrong with me. I never believed that mongrels could reproduce with humans. Okay, maybe I had been very naive, not thinking about protection, but my heart was shattered. I was ready for anything, just so I didn't have to experience this agonising pain day by day.

"That's why you're still drinking liquid magic? Do you know that this stuff is addictive? Besides, you have to start thinking about your options," he reminded me.

Ronan lived on the outskirts of the village, in an old cottage that he bought when he moved here after leaving his service at the royal palace. After I was nearly locked up by human police I decided to come here. Arthur had been deployed to Afghanistan a couple of weeks ago, and I needed a place to hide. There was a possibility that he hired someone to look for me, to find out if I was all right.

He could never know about this child, even if it was his. I was ready to sacrifice myself in order to protect him. My world wasn't his, and I needed to remember that.

"I appreciate everything that you have done for me, you need to stop judging me. I'm in agony and the magic helps. Right at this moment I don't know what I'm going to do," I said, wondering if there were any elixirs that could tell me who fathered my child.

"No, Maxine, we both know that there isn't such a thing," Ronan replied, reading my mind. "Get it together and start thinking about your future."

I began chewing my lips, dismissing everything he'd said.

Ronan and I met in one of the bars in London, when I was still a mouthy teenager with an attitude. At the time Ronan had a job in the palace. He was a butler for Princess Catherine. I tried to steal from him and nearly succeeded. Ronan cornered

me in the alley and told me that I didn't have to waste my potential. He offered to give me some lessons so I could tame my wild energy. We had been friends ever since. To this day I have no idea why he decided to give me a shot. Maybe he pitied me. A young orphan that never had a real role model.

I felt embarrassed that I didn't know who fathered my child. It could have been that red-haired human from the nightclub, or maybe it was that good-looking demon that outplayed me in the poker game. There was also that dark-haired bartender from an obscure pub around the corner from the Brixton tube station. I hated myself that I became so weak, so lonely.

My life had spun out of control.

After I rinsed off my face, I went back to hide in my room. Ronan had kindly offered me the spare bedroom that he'd used for storage in the past few years. We had a mutual understanding and I was truly lucky that I had a friend in Ronan. Everyone who'd ever spent any time with me knew that I wasn't very maternal, so my decision was supposed to be easy. Yet, I couldn't bring myself to ask Ronan to create that one potion for me that could solve all my problems. I still had a bit of time.

I shook my head and started counting the days from my last period. It'd been more than six weeks and I'd been so focused on my misery that I hadn't even realised what was going on. I sat on the bed, pulled my knees forward, and began to wonder about my future. This child was a blessing, but for me it was a death sentence if it turned out that Arthur was the father. Either way, my future was already doomed.

***

I didn't sleep much that night, well like most nights. Ronan was busy with his potion business. Humans from the village believed that he was an eccentric quack. He made friends over the years and people liked him.

Ronan was a full-blooded demon, part of Asmodeus faction, and he never embraced technology.

After being stuck in his remote cottage for days, I decided to go out and get some fresh air.

I kept thinking about Arthur, about our time together, about his dreams and aspirations. All my thoughts were about him and I was so desperate that I was ready to stalk him online.

The village had two pubs, a shop, and there was a coffee shop with internet access. I arrived here in order to forget, and instead I was prepared to cyber stalk someone that could ruin me.

It was strange knowing that I was now responsible for another being, another creature.

The sea breeze ruffled my long ponytail. I tucked my jacket tighter around my waist, feeling cold as I walked along the country road. The dramatic cliffs soared in the distance. My stomach was rumbling, but food wasn't on my list of priorities right then. I needed to find out what Arthur had been up to. I had to know if he tried to look for me.

Minutes later I passed two elderly ladies. They greeted me like they knew me, but I could read in their thoughts that deep down they wondered if I was the girl that Ronan was talking about a couple of nights ago.

I managed to locate the coffee shop, paid five pounds to the owner, and sat down with a stale scone in front of the laptop several minutes later. Mr. Gordon offered to show me a quick drink that I politely declined. I wasn't particularly tech savvy, but I knew how to use the computer. I didn't like technology, but this was the only other way of keeping up with the outside world.

I typed Arthur's name into Google and stopped breathing for a second. My palms began sweating as the energy stirred around me when an article about him popped up on the screen. The months of living like we were in a fairytale were finally over. Now I was sitting here, hundreds of miles away from home, stalking him online and telling myself that this was normal. After scanning the text a few times, I found out that Arthur was due to be back to London in three months, and that he was all right and safe. Part of me was relieved, the other pissed off that it came to this.

I had never been in love, well, I never thought that it was possible for me to get attached to anyone, especially a human, but it happened.

The endless nights that I had spent with others changed me, shifted my perspective of love. Sleeping around wasn't something that I wanted or planned, but when I was in someone else's arms, intoxicated on magical tequila, Arthur wasn't part of me anymore.

My throat was raw and I was heartbroken, but I chose not to drink anymore when I found out I was pregnant.

The owner brought me a warm cup of coffee ten minutes later. The internet was filled with information about royals in general. Apparently young Prince Georgie was partying hard in Dubai, not caring about his reputation at all.

I took a bite of the scone, hoping to tame my rumbling stomach for the time being, when another article caught my eye. I opened the page feeling the rising excitement. As soon as I started reading it, something inside me snapped and anger blinded me for a second. The source claimed that Arthur was planning to propose to Natalie Morgan as soon as he was back from Afghanistan.

My breathing became laboured and my limbs went slightly stiff. Arthur had gone out with Natalie on a number of occasions, and Princess Layla had always hoped that eventually they would end up together.

I shut down everything, knowing there was no point in reading on. The tiny voice in my head reminded me that he was never mine in the first place. This article was the final nail in the coffin.

I had to forget about him and concentrate on my future. The child was mine and I needed to make a difficult decision. I was ready to tell Ronan that I had made up my mind.

Chapter Two

I was pissed when I left the coffee shop, mainly with myself and mainly with the fact that I couldn't stop thinking about what happened.

I stepped outside and then started running. My feet didn't take me far. I had to stop several meters later and throw up on the side of the road. This time it wasn't the morning sickness but the fact that Arthur had managed to turn his life around and forget about me already.

It was time to stop feeling sorry for myself and fight through this misery. I couldn't bring this unexpected baby into this world. I never thought that I could cry over a man, and now here I was.

When I stopped being violently sick and was able to stay on my feet again, I started walking back to the cottage. My head throbbed with agonising pain, my vision was blurry. Everything about my existence felt shitty and pointless. The truth was that I wasn't capable of looking after myself, much less a newborn child. I had no stable home, no income, and I didn't know if I could fully commit myself to being a parent.

If Arthur only knew that there was even a slight possibility that he could be a father he'd condemn my plans. I shook my head, slapping myself hard. Yeah, I had to move forward and shut down the nostalgic voices in my head. This decision was mine and there was nothing that anyone could say that would change my mind.

Ronan came home around nine o'clock in the evening. The days were longer in the summer and I spent time sitting outside, trying to stay positive. I had been thinking about what to do next, long and hard, so after exhausting a few hours I welcomed him at the door.

I had to consider talking to Ricky too. He wouldn't approve of my decision. Well, he most likely would try to talk me out of it. I needed to remind myself that Ricky had stood beside me since we set up the business together, and his opinion meant a great deal to me.

"What is it, Maxine? I don't have the time for a chat. Mrs. Robinson is waiting for her parcel," Ronan said, passing me on the way to the kitchen. As usual he was in a hurry, but I had to tell him what I decided.

"Ronan, I'm ready to go through with what we discussed earlier on. I need your help," I blurted out, almost shaking. He finally stopped and turned around. His eyes were gleaming again, and there was a hint of relief in his expression.

"Be more clear, Maxine," he said.

"Termination. I need to not be pregnant, Ronan," I hissed, feeling so incredibly guilty and disappointed. I was a terrible person even thinking about abortion. Maybe one day Lucifer would get his hands on me, and I would get punished for all my sins, but right now I was ready for anything in order to stay on earth, to survive.

Ronan exhaled sharply and his eyes flickered at the corners. He approached me slowly and then placed his palms on my arms.

"What made you change your mind?" he asked.

"It doesn't matter. I've made my decision. My life is miserable enough and I'm not ready to bring a child into this world even if there is only a slight chance that Arthur could be the father," I said, lying to him and myself. It was much easier to decide after learning that he was finally happy in his own life.

"There is a way, but we have to use magic. Are you absolutely sure that you want to do this?" he asked, like he needed to torture me a bit longer.

"Yes, Ronan, I'm sure," I said. "So tell me when?"

"Tonight. We leave at midnight. Concentrate on your demonic energy because you'll need it. I have to be somewhere soon, wait for me in the cottage," he told me, grabbed a box from the cupboard, and left me alone again.

I wished that I could not feel guilty, but the voice of reason kept reminding me that I had to keep on living. Ricky was my friend and I was supposed to prepare him for the worst. Ronan didn't have a phone and my mobile was off. I wanted to be unreachable in case other demons tried to track me down.

My fingertips sparkled when I went up to take a shower. For a moment I stood in the water wondering what the hell was wrong with me. I made this baby, so it was my responsibility to take care of it. I couldn't simply kill it.

Soon my thoughts were interrupted by a foreign energy that rolled through my spine. There was a demon nearby and I knew for a fact that it wasn't Ronan. No one apart from Ricky knew where I was, so I automatically got suspicious.

I put some clothes on and opened the door, spreading violent energy around the cottage. After walking around for ten minutes strongly, I couldn't detect anyone. Maybe my paranoia had reached a new level or maybe I truly wanted to be found.

The stranger's energy stayed with me until Ronan arrived home. He didn't seem to sense anyone, so I didn't say anything. He'd lived alone for so long and now I had to adapt to his old eccentric ways.

"What should I expect tonight?" I finally asked when the clock on the wall pointed at eleven o'clock.

"Expect some pain. There is a special ritual that we have to follow, and only Sonia can produce such a strong potion," Ronan said. I sighed loudly and began asking myself if this was exactly what I wanted.

The physical pain, yeah, I could deal with that, but the emotional one was pulling me under the grave, disturbing my healing process.

"So who is this woman? I suspect she is a demon, right?" I asked, rubbing my hands over my old jeans. My gut all of a sudden was filled with heavy bricks and I felt even shittier than earlier.

Ronan changed his clothes and now was wearing mostly black. I felt on edge. Even my demonic energy seemed on alert.

"Sonia is extremely knowledgeable. She's a mongrel like you. Hell has been hunting her for as long as I can remember, so she moves around often," Ronan explained, packing odd-looking flasks into his bag. Well, that didn't sound great. I was supposed to trust a mongrel that had been on the run for God knew how long. At the same time I had no other choice. I couldn't keep this baby.

Maybe in the future I would feel guilty for the rest of my life, but right at this moment I had to think about myself and Arthur.

Half an hour later we left the cozy cottage and headed towards the coastline. I kept walking, assuring myself that this was the right thing to do. None of this seemed real, and I still hadn't spoken to Ricky.

Ronan as usual wasn't saying much as we passed his dearest fishing village in complete darkness. There were no humans on the streets, and somehow I was glad of that. I didn't need to speak to anyone.

My heart began thumping faster when we moved through the fields that were situated on top of the steep cliffs. The tide was in, and with every passing minute, I began doubting myself, contemplating if there was another way. The navy sky was filled with heavy clouds.

This small little creature inside my stomach felt like it was connecting with me already.

"She will be in one of the caves, and she knows that we're coming," Ronan muttered, when the path began moving down towards the shore filled mainly with stones.

I swallowed hard and told myself that I needed to keep going. Right now things were difficult for me, but that didn't mean that I couldn't be happy some day.

The tide was coming in and strong waves beat against the rocky shore. There were long steep cliffs on each side. In front of us there were just blocks of rocks, and I really wasn't sure where he was taking me.

As soon as we approached the end of the rocks, Ronan turned around.

"The strong tides shape caves on the outside, so we have to get slightly wet to find Sonia," he informed me. I didn't want to be here, but right now bailing out wasn't something that I was ready to do. Ronan moved his man bag to the other side of his shoulder and started climbing through the rocks along the cliff.

We didn't get slightly wet, we got soaked with seawater. The tide was going to be high this evening. Along the coast, as we climbed higher, finally reaching the cave that was shaped by strong current, dangerous rocks stuck out from each side. I saw a light as we moved closer. My demonic soul detected a mongrel close by.

Sonia must have used magic in order to create this space for herself. In the distance, any boat would notice the light, so this cave wasn't a particularly great hiding place, but her magic was possibly much more advanced. Sonia was using very particular spells, and this wasn't the best time or place to start asking questions.

By the time we both were inside, Ronan's breath was laboured. It was a hell of a trip, even for a tough older guy like him. I was freezing cold, ready to skip the introductions and just get on with the task. Ronan's expression was as usual unreadable.

"So you found me. Deep down I thought you wouldn't." The voice of a woman startled me slightly. She stood hidden underneath the rock. Sonia, the half demon that Ronan told me about appeared to be in her late forties. She had long dark hair and sharp Nordic features.

Ronan released some of his protective energy, and I tried to relax. The demon that stood in front of me was supposed to help me get rid of the problem. She had red

eyeshadow above her hazel eyes, wide cheeks and narrow lips. She was dressed in ordinary clothes, old jeans and a long sleeve dirty shirt.

My instincts reminded me that my options were limited. I couldn't risk bringing the mongrel baby into this world, the tiny creature that could possibly have royal blood in its veins.

"You forgot that I know this area better than anyone," Ronan stated, dropped the bag, and embraced Sonia in a strong but friendly hug. I scratched my head, wondering what the hell this was about, but kept my opinions to myself. They obviously must have known each other from the past.

"How are you doing, my old friend?" she asked, once they were no longer embracing. "And who is the scruffy half demon?"

"Hey, I'm standing right here," I barked, and her eyes gleamed. Okay, so I was wet, my clothes were dirty, and my hair all over the place, but still she didn't have to be rude.

"Maxine, this is Sonia," Ronan introduced us, ignoring his friend's comment. "She's here because we need your help with a particular case."

I wanted to laugh that he called my misfortune a case, but Ronan had lost his sensitive nature when he stopped working for the royals.

I looked around the cave, seeing that she must have slept in the corner on some old clothes. The cave was lit with candles, and there were flasks, herbs, and some dead insects on the small table. Sonia seemed settled here. I didn't know her story, but Ronan mentioned that she was hiding, and living like that only confirmed it.

"You're expecting a mongrel baby," she said, walking around me. Her energy was powerful, rising fast and linking with my own.

Cold shivers crawled over my spine when she mentioned the baby. I had no idea how she knew, how she suspected that I had slept with a human.

"Yes, I am and my situation is complicated. Ronan mentioned that you can help me to get rid of it," I said, already hating myself for it, for treating it like an unnecessary burden. God, I was terrible. Her eyes gleamed even more, and she smiled.

"Well, that's my expertise, but I don't think that you're fully convinced you are ready for it," she stated, like she was reading my mind.

"I can't keep it," I insisted, feeling even more conflicted about everything.
"Does the father know?"
"I'm not quite sure who is the father," I added, wanting to be done talking about it.

I felt like this was a job interview.
"Ronan, take a seat," she said. "I have to prepare a certain potion. If she is sure,

then we can proceed."
My stomach made a funny jolt filling with dread. Ricky would have talked me out

of it, but there was no time. I had a feeling that Sonia wasn't planning to stay in here for long.

She went to the table and started mixing stuff, mumbling formulas that didn't make much sense. Images of Arthur and all the other men that I had hooked up with in the past began rolling through my mind.

I started pacing around the cave, aware of the rising power that circulated around, growing with my heartbeat. If someone had said several months ago that I would be sitting in the cave on the outskirts of some remote village trying to find a way to get rid of the baby that I was carrying inside, I wouldn't have believed it. Now it was my doomed reality.

I knew that I wouldn't be able to look myself in the mirror once the deal was done.

"The potion is done. Now you just have to drink it and forget about it. The magic will do what it is supposed to," she said. I looked at her then, realising that the moment had come. I stood up ready to make a decision, ready to kill an innocent human being.

Chapter Three

The seconds rolled by and I still wasn't saying anything. Sonia was holding something in her hand, a stone of some sorts. Earlier on she placed an empty cup on the wooden table that was now steaming with strong magic. The smell of rosemary and other rare herbs wafted through the cave.

I couldn't believe that I just had to drink it and the whole problem would go away in a heartbeat. This wasn't something that I anticipated. Sonia's eyes were penetrating, and she was seeing through me, seeing that deep down I wasn't sure if I was ready.

Back in London everyone that had ever known me understood that not many things could break me. I had worked for royals, I had protected them, and now I was just about to fall apart.

"There is a formula that you have to whisper while you drink it," Sonia added, dropping the stone into her pocket. Ronan was aware that I was undecided. He released some calming vibes towards me, telling me that I could go back to normal as soon as I drank the potion. He obviously wanted me to go ahead with this abortion.

The prince and I were done, so I had nothing to worry about, and I couldn't be a hundred percent sure if the child was his.

"And that's it? What will happen to the fetus?" I asked stupidly already knowing the answer. Deep down I still needed to absorb all the details. Going through pros and cons didn't give me any confidence. I had to save myself, and giving birth to this baby could send the whole of hell into havoc.

And if the child was Arthur's, my future was shaky at best. Sleeping with a royal wasn't a crime, but creating a half-blooded royal could cause a lot of problems to authorities in hell.

Sonia shifted her weight to the side and pursed her lips. Obviously she didn't like that I was hesitating. I wished that I'd brought a strong drink with me. Ronan came here with me, introduced me to this woman. That one drink could make me normal again, so what was I waiting for?

"The magic will destroy the fetus, you will throw up a few times, possibly bleed too, but tomorrow morning you won't be pregnant," she informed me, then went to the table and picked up the drink for me.

This time I took the cup, feeling violent magic scorching through me instantly. The potion was powerful.

I thought about Arthur once again. We had talked about children, and I knew that at some point he wanted to be a father. Maybe in different circumstances we could have created a real family, but I had to remember that as long as he was a prince this was impossible.

I held on to the magic, squeezing the cup harder. The time stretched, and my thoughts started racing again. This was simple, but the pain was greater. It spread everywhere, burning me like a fresh wound.

The energies stirred inside me and I wished that I could be somewhere else.

"Right, I don't think your girl is ready to get rid of this child, Ronan, and you know how much I hate wasting my time," Sonia barked, taking a step towards me.

Tears welled in my eyes, but I refused to cry in front of them. What the hell was wrong with me? I came here to kill the creature that would have a tough life anyway, but I just couldn't go through with it.

All the tiny voices in my head were screaming at me that there was no other way, that from now on I would have to keep living with this secret forever.

"Maxine, I thought you decided, that you had gone through your pros and cons?" Ronan asked, sounding angry all of a sudden. I clenched my teeth, knowing that he genuinely wanted to help me, but right then I couldn't pull myself together.

I finally lifted my head, swallowing the tears away, and placed my hand on my stomach.

"I can't do this. I'm sorry, but this child will have to be born," I stated, knowing that it was my sacrifice. Ronan and Sonia most likely thought that I was stupid, but I wasn't ready to become a monster. Arthur would remain my long-lost love, forever.

"A weak soul. Mongrel children are very challenging, dear, so you really have to think about this. And please don't think that father will help you in any way. Human men aren't ready for that kind of news," Sonia stated and Ronan narrowed his eyes at her, like he disapproved of what she said.

"Maxine is not quite sure who fathered her child," Ronan said.

"Well, you might sense it later on. As the fetus becomes more active, the mother can glimpse memories from the past," Sonia explained, sounding bored. It was obvious that she never had kids. She seemed cold and detached.

My head hurt as memories about Arthur resurfaced. Now I had to come up with a new plan. After all, I wanted to keep this child, not even knowing if I was capable of raising it.

I had to get out of here and speak to Ricky. There was no way that I could get back to London, unless …

"Just a word of advice," Sonia interrupted my train of thought.

"Yes?" I asked, realising that either way I needed to stay with Ronan for another eight months and a bit.

"Stop thinking that it might work out with the human. They are the weak link within demonic society. You're on your own. The sooner you realise that, the stronger you will become."

"Thanks, I'll keep that in mind," I added, then turned around ready to disappear. I didn't wait for Ronan. He had to respect my decision and let me get on with it. We were friends, and he was ready to help me earlier on. I left the cave, moving through the rocky shore, petrified that now everything could turn against me.

Was I weak?
Maybe, but I couldn't go through with this abortion.

I couldn't become a woman that was too scared to face the consequences of unprotected sex. It was then or never, and I chose to risk everything for someone that wasn't even born yet.

When I came back to the cottage it was just after one in the morning. Ronan had chosen to stay with Sonia. They obviously had other matters to discuss, and their relationship was none of my business. I went over everything, and I told myself that I had made my choice. I had options, but instead of thinking about what was next, I took my phone and dialled Ricky's number.

"Wow, Maxine, I thought you said that you wouldn't be in touch? Is everything okay?" he asked as soon as he answered the phone.

I took a deep breath and squeezed my phone, cutting the blood circulation to my fingers. My throat felt tight, but I had to tell him everything. He was the only one that could understand what I was thinking.

"I tried to have an abortion, Rick. Ronan took me to this female demon, but I couldn't do it," I said, getting straight to the point. There was a silence on the other side of the phone.

"He talked you into it, didn't he?" Ricky asked throwing accusations straight away. My voice was lost, but I had to keep going and tell him exactly what I was planning.

"No. Ronan only did what I asked for. I was stupid, thought this would solve everything, but eventually I backed away," I told him. "That demon female

mentioned that I might figure out who the father is later when the baby will be more active."

"I've heard about it, but that won't change the fact that you're going to be a mother, Maxine. What if Arthur is the actual father of your child?"

I rubbed my forehead, wanting to stick to everything I planned to tell him. Yeah, I was following my emotions earlier on, made a rushed decision, but in the end the child had to have a good start in life.

"I will find someone that will take care of it, Ricky, possibly adoption. We both know that I'm not mother material. I can barely take care of myself."

"It's different now, but once you hold this creature in your arms your perspective will change. Don't jump hoop yet, Maxine, think about it," he muttered and I sensed that he wanted to say more, but he was hesitating.

"What's wrong, Ricky? Is it the business?" I pressed, really missing him and the agency. After I got fired from the palace we lost a lot of clients, but Ricky was smart. He could get everything back up and running in no time.

"Arthur came to my place a few times before he left for Afghanistan."

My heart made a happy dance in my chest, covering the fact that earlier on I was slowly dying, thinking that I would never see him again. The sudden pain came back like an arrow, piercing through my heart.

I didn't say anything, waiting for him to continue. There was probably more. Well, it looked like he cared a little.

"He wanted to know what happened to you. He got violent a few times," Ricky continued, sounding normal. He would never betray me or reveal my location. We

had an understanding, and I knew that I had to dismiss Arthur's efforts. He was far away right now, thousands of miles away in a foreign country. "The guy still loves you, and I don't know, maybe you should have tried talking to him."

I hated when Ricky got emotional.

"Don't try to make me feel better. We are done. My whole career is ruined. It's better this way," I insisted, remembering how humiliated I was standing in front of the Queen and her entourage.

"He showed up drunk, and hurt. For the first time I felt bad for the guy. He genuinely had no idea what happened."

My mind was spinning, but I kept telling myself that Ricky was wrong. Arthur knew that I got fired from my post. We were done fooling around and I had risked enough. It was time to stop thinking about that and concentrate on my unborn child.

"I don't care. This would never work anyway. Ricky, I'm staying here until I give birth. No one can know, do you understand?"

"Don't treat me like an idiot. You're like my family, Max, and I'm behind you a hundred percent," he added, like he was saying that he would help me take care of this child, but that was highly unlikely.

"I know that, but I'm scared and lost."

"Don't be. You're Maxine, the toughest and most unbreakable woman that I ever knew. You will be fine," Ricky said, pumping me with positivity. I smiled to the phone, thinking that this was what I needed. I hung up several minutes later, realising that he was right. I could do this. I could be a mother despite the odds.

***

Several weeks had passed since my conversation with Ricky, and I stayed hidden, not doing much at all. After some time I told myself that I had to show Ronan a bit more gratitude. He took me into his home while he tried carrying on with his own life, at the same time looking after all my needs. It was a big ask especially for someone who didn't like people very much.

It was odd being pregnant. I was sick all the time until the first trimester had finally passed. Every day I kept staring at my stomach, wondering what I would do when my due day arrived. My demonic energy shifted, and I had been lighting stuff up randomly pretty much all the time.

Being a half demon I couldn't go with the standard adoption, and on top of that I was stuck in this small village with no way of getting out. I was afraid of being recognised, even being as far away from London as possible.

Ronan kept shaking his head every time he looked at me. I was getting heavier and the months began disappearing, but my pain remained.

I still remembered when I felt the baby's movement for the first time. I was overjoyed with the fact that I didn't drink that potion.

My days were filled mostly with reading and staring out the window. Ronan asked me not to hang around in the village any longer, especially when I started showing. Everyone knew Ronan, he had a quite a reputation in the village, and he just didn't want people to talk.

It was two weeks later when I woke up late at night with the awareness that Watchers were close by. This never happened to me before, and I never thought that they could find me in a place like this, but five seconds later I was standing on my feet ready to run.

The baby was kicking continuously and the fear scorched through me instantly. It was clear that they had tracked me down and it was time for me to disappear.

Suddenly images of a man from my past assaulted my mind. In that moment I finally suspected the true identity of the baby's father.

Chapter Four

I shot out of the bed and ran downstairs, knowing that my time was limited. The Watchers couldn't have known that I was hiding here. They must have been patrolling this area off chance, hoping to find a demon that wasn't supposed to be living amongst humans.

I paced around the kitchen for a moment, thinking about what to do. I didn't have the time or strength to use any charms, so I had to disappear. Panic pulsed through my legs. Baby was very active, moving swiftly inside my stomach.

Ronan was out; his bed was empty. There must have been a reason that Watchers showed up here in the middle of the night. Maybe I had made a mistake trusting him, but at the same time I didn't want to believe that he could sell me out like that.

No one apart from Ricky and Ronan knew that I was here.

I shivered with cold when I opened the front door and stepped on the grass barefoot, glancing around. In the past few months I tried to stay on form, and running was the only exercise that allowed me to feel free. Now I could rely only on my legs. I started moving through the forest, thinking about Ricky and the agency.

The Watchers' intense energy collided with mine. They were aware that I was close, and they were summoning me over to them. There was a possibility that they were working for someone that wanted to find me. No one apart from Berith himself had any power over them, but these days everything was possible.

They were aggravated that I wasn't responding, most likely already aware that I was trying to get away. My heart was jackhammering in my chest. I was slow and vulnerable.

My feet were moving and that tiny voice in my head kept telling me to stop running and try to reason with them. Maybe in any other circumstance I would have tried that, but right then I didn't want to take any chances. The Watchers would have sensed that I was carrying a mongrel baby inside my womb. Then the uncomfortable questions would follow, and I wasn't ready to reveal anything about my past.

I was moving fast through the bushes, circulating between the trees, my breath laboured. The energy surfaced all over, making me slightly dizzy.

Where was Ronan when I needed him the most?

After so many years he was still the only person apart from Ricky that I trusted with all my heart. I didn't believe that he had anything to do with them. There had to be a traitor, someone that wanted to see me in hell.

Sweat dripped down my face. I stopped for a second and listened in. I heard voices behind me. My lungs were burning and the forest seemed to be getting darker and wilder.

A year ago I probably would have escaped easily, but right then I was eight months pregnant and already exhausted.

My demonic energy boosted my strength a little, but my body indicated that I had to stop and rest.

The Watchers wanted to use their energy against my will. I was most likely the only other mongrel in the area, and by running I had given them a reason to chase after me.

Moments later I stumbled, missing a protruding rock, and falling facedown on the ground. Burning pain shot over my leg, but I ignored it. I instantly touched my stomach, making sure the baby was all right. I thought that the chase was over, the Watchers were too close, when something else, or rather someone else caught my attention.

There was a woman standing by the tree, staring back at me. She had a basket in her right hand. I pushed myself back on my knees, breathing hard. Her dark eyes moved over my silhouette, stopping on my stomach. The Watchers were closing in on me.

She must have sensed them too because suddenly I felt her energy circulating around me. Hell, I had no idea what she was, but for sure she wasn't a demon. Even in the darkness her features were extraordinary, her magic reviving.

"We need to get close to each other. They won't be able to sense you this way," she told me. I hesitated for a second, wondering if I could trust her. In the end of the day I had no other option, so I obeyed her. I couldn't carry on running.

I dragged myself off the ground, and then she came closer. I didn't know what happened after that, but she covered us both with her dark cloak, whispered some words and leaned down to me.

"Don't move; they won't be able to notice us. My magic will protect us."

I wanted to argue, but the Watchers' energy surrounded the place all of a sudden. Paralysing fear spread through me quickly, tightening my throat. A moment later two Watchers emerged from the trees in their true forms. Their snow-white wings were impressive, shining in the darkness.

One of them was tall and slender, and his blue eyes moved over the space, stopping right on me.

That was it. I was going down. There was no way that this woman could make me suddenly invisible, but I forced myself to stop breathing for a few long moments.

"I lost her demonic soul," he stated. I nearly screamed holding my stomach when the baby kicked hard. It obviously didn't like me in any distress.

The other Watcher looked around; he was disorientated.

"She must be close. She's just a mongrel," he said, dragging his hand through his hair. "Let's move. We can't lose her."

The taller one shook his head, and a moment later they carried on walking through the forest.

I couldn't believe it. Somehow they weren't able to see me. This was impossible. The woman's arm was on my back and her magic felt unbelievable. The Watchers had disappeared, but we stayed under her cloak for few more minutes until I could breathe normally again.

"Thank you ... I can't understand—"

"I'm a warlock. My magic is different than the magic of any ordinary demon," she said, smiling. Only then I realised that she must have been right. I had heard about warlocks, but I never believed that they still lived on earth. It was dark, but I could still see that she had long red hair and wide green eyes.

"Thank you, if they had found me, I was as good as dead," I explained, wondering what she wanted in exchange. There weren't many warlocks left on an earth populated by demons. Ricky once told me that Lucifer began hunting them down years ago when they were powerful.

"I sensed your fear miles away and your child's fear too," she said. "I was picking up some herbs, hoping to keep away from any demons and humans."

I stood up and felt like my legs were going to give out at any second. She caught my arms, sending me a sharp wave of energy. It was a spike that I needed, but at the same time I hated being so weak and exposed.

"I will walk you back to the safe place," she informed me.

"They weren't supposed to know that I was here, and my friend wouldn't betray me like this," I explained, feeling confused. I had no idea if it was safe for me to go back to Ronan. What if there were more Watchers waiting for me there?

"You're trying to protect your baby, that's understandable," she said, and her eyes gleamed with joy.

"It's complicated. I've left behind my whole life and in the end I'm still a coward," I said, thinking about the cave and

Sonia. I had wanted to kill it, just because I was willing to protect someone that wasn't in my life anymore.

"I'll walk with you. The Watchers are trying their chances. Sometimes they patrol these remote areas. I messed around with their sense of direction, so they won't be able to track us down."

I called out my demonic power, and her words instantly calmed the baby down. Every part of me indicated that I should start running, but on the other hand, this creature had just saved my life. Maybe I was simply paranoid. The Watchers weren't here for me; they were passing this area, and then they must have sensed me. Everything was suddenly very clear.

"All right, you're right. I should go back to the cottage. My name is Maxine, by the way," I said. She gave me a warm smile and took my arm.

"Matilda. I was married to a demon once, and when I'm around others I tend to conceal my true nature," she explained. "I live in this area, alone."

"So you're truly a warlock?" I asked, just to be sure that my own senses weren't misleading me.

"A widowed warlock, yes," she admitted with another smile. "Your baby is going to be due soon and you're scared, confused about its future," she pointed out like she was reading my mind.

We started walking thought the woodlands. It was probably very late, and Ronan was most likely looking for me.

"Isn't that obvious? This pregnancy wasn't planned, for sure," I said, thinking about Arthur again. God, I really needed to get a grip and stop believing that we ever had a real shot.

"I always wanted to be a mother, but sadly warlocks aren't able to reproduce," she said unexpectedly. "I don't want to be insensitive, but what's your story? Why are you hiding here?"

I wiped the sweat off my forehead. We were alone, and I wasn't sure if it was safe for me to talk about my past, but she seemed genuinely interested. After all, Matilda helped me get rid of the Watchers, so there was no point being secretive. Eventually they would have figured out who I was and then I would've had no other choice but to leave with them.

I started talking then. I didn't know why, but I started telling her about my stupid decisions, about what happened when I got the job in the palace. The past nine months were tough. I was isolated and lonely. Maybe from Ronan's perspective I was putting myself in danger, trusting a stranger, a warlock, but this felt natural.

Then I told her about Doomed Cases, about Ricky and Arthur. The baby was moving, but in a calm manner while I was telling her about getting dumped by the royals.

"Well, that's a hell of a story, Maxine," she concluded as we reached Ronan's cottage. She was right: there was no sign of Watchers anywhere near, but Ronan himself was waiting outside.

"Where the hell have you been? I came back an hour ago and your bed was empty," Ronan shouted when he saw me. A moment later he saw Matilda and he released some of his energy.

"Calm down, this is Matilda, she's hidden me from two Watchers that were snooping in the area. I woke up sensing them, and panicked," I explained.

"A warlock, well, that's unexpected. Please come in before Maxine goes into labour at my front door," Ronan muttered, shaking his head. It was dawn when the three of us sat down at the table with a warm cup of tea.

"I work for myself these days, run a pottery business in the middle of the forest," Matilda explained after Ronan warmed up to her a bit more and explained that he was out hunting earlier on. "Maxine is lucky that you're helping her. Her situation sounds complicated."

"She should have gotten rid of that child when she had a chance. It's a grave risk. If the child has royal blood, then her time on earth is going to be truly over."

Ronan didn't have to repeat that. I already knew the consequences, but in the end I couldn't kill this little human inside me. Soon I needed to make a decision.

"This child grows inside her womb for a reason. Maxine made the right choice. You can't condemn it. Mongrel or a human, it doesn't matter. It's a blessing," Matilda stated quite fiercely.

"You're a warlock and you have no idea what will happen to her or this child if it turns out that the royal is the father."

"Ronan, please, this is not the time. Matilda saved me and that's the bottom line. Let's talk about something else," I warned him, getting tired of his arguments. I made a commitment to myself and now he needed to accept it.

"We both know that you won't be able to keep it, Max. Adoption is the only way forward and you haven't found anyone suitable. This child will bring you down to hell!"

Suddenly my hormones were raging and I wanted to cry, but Ronan was right. I had been isolating myself in the past few months. Soon I was going to be holding this child in my hands knowing that I wouldn't be able to look after it.

An awkward silence stretched for a moment. Matilda was staring back at me. It was strange that I couldn't sense her emotions. I had never met a warlock, but it was clear that they weren't at all like humans. I was suddenly curious about her powers.

"I will take care of it," I mumbled, feeling less and less like myself, the tough and strong mongrel.

"Maxine, we just met, but I believe in destiny. I would be willing to look after your child. Once you give it away for adoption you will never see it again. Deep down we both know that you are not ready to give it away to strangers."

Ronan and I looked at Matilda with sudden disbelief. A bunch of ice cubes cascaded down to my stomach, because in that moment I realised that she was right. I wasn't willing to give my child away, despite everything that happened in the past.

Chapter Five

This whole thing seemed completely surreal. She wanted to take care of my child. I was sitting at the table staring at the woman I had just met, thinking that she couldn't have been serious. From the very beginning I knew that arranging a legal adoption was going to be tough. Giving away my child to complete strangers was something that I never thought I'd actually go through.

"Don't be absurd, woman. Maxine will know who fathered her child at birth, possibly later. She needs to get ready to forget about the infant as soon as possible," Ronan said, shaking his head.

I opened my mouth to say something, but then changed my mind. Matilda kept staring at me intensely, and even though I couldn't tell what she was thinking, I knew that she wanted to help me.

"Maxine doesn't want to give her child away, Ronan. She's tormented. My own life is empty and I would be honoured to look after it until Maxine figures out what to do. I don't expect you to make a rush decision."

Ronan pursed his lips and one of the flasks on the window exploded. Okay, so he was determined to put his point across, being the stubborn old man. Seconds later his thoughts came through. He was telling me that I was risking too much. I needed to remind myself that he was only trying to look after me.

This woman was a warlock and trusting her like that was a mistake. Most demons didn't even realise that warlocks existed. Ricky had told me that a few of them lived in London, but I never had a chance to face any of them. Their past was filled with mystery, but I wanted to trust Matilda.

I had thought about adoption long and hard, but deep down I still wasn't sure. Humans wouldn't know that the baby was special, but later the magic would interrupt their lives.

"Matilda is right, Ronan. I don't know what to do and this new option sounds reasonable," I finally said, playing with the ring on my finger, the ring that was supposed to symbolise my love for Arthur.

Matilda tossed her red hair behind her and touched my hand. I wanted to pull it away, but that didn't happen. Somehow the warmth that spread through me suddenly eased the tension inside my body.

Ronan and I felt the Warlock's magic circulating around and maybe I was crazy to even consider this, but after all, I didn't know what else to do.

"Adoption is the way forward, Maxine, and no offence, but we don't know anything about this woman," Ronan pointed out, making a face.

"None taken. I understand that you're both reluctant, but I'm happy to spend some time with Maxine until the baby is born. This way maybe you can get to trust me."

"Do what you want, Maxine, but don't run to me crying after this doesn't work out. I'm washing my hands," Ronan stated, finally getting up from the table. The sun

was rising on the horizon and I rubbed my hands over my face, trying to pull my thoughts together.

This child was a blessing, but it was also a curse if it turned out that Arthur was the father.

"Stay with me a few weeks before my due date. I'm not saying yes just yet, but this is the best solution of them all, Matilda," I told her, pushing images of Ricky out of my head.

He could easily talk me out of it, but I had at least six more weeks to fully commit myself to this plan.

"I have been living alone for the past five years, putting a lot of hours into my business. It would be an honour for me to take care of your child. All my family is dead, and my husband is in hell. It's a new purpose, something that would make me happy," Matilda said and then got up too.

I didn't say anything else, thinking that maybe this whole thing was unbelievably stupid, but deep down I trusted her already. Warlock or not, I knew that she had a good soul.

We exchanged some details and I walked her to the edge of the forest. We talked a bit more, trying to get to know each other better. Matilda left an hour later, assuring me that she would be back.

I went inside the cottage feeling conflicted and lost. The child was kicking and my internal voice was telling me that I couldn't take it back to London and I wasn't willing to give it out for adoption.

Matilda was my solution, possibly a miracle sent from hell. It was either that or leaving everything behind and disappearing. The problem was that I wasn't ready to vanish just yet.

***

No one else visited me, and the Watchers didn't show up again. Matilda's magic must have worked, and I was suddenly very glad that our paths had crossed. A few weeks before the due date I was planning to relocate, but now this was almost impossible.

Ronan believed that I was too vulnerable to move around and he wanted me to stay put, as far away from the demonic community as was possible.

Matilda came back four weeks later and after some gentle persuasion Ronan agreed to let her to stay over in the cottage. I was lucky that my and Ronan's paths crossed years ago. Deep down I knew that he had a kind soul.

I had never had any friends. Ricky had been part of my life for as long as I remembered, so it was going to take me a while to get used to having someone around me all the time.

Matilda talked about her life, letting me into her world slowly. She was taking her time. She probably sensed that I didn't trust many people. I wasn't sleeping well, with thoughts about the past and Arthur keeping me up most of the time.

In the last two weeks I learnt from Matilda that warlock's were able to produce extraordinary power: they could manipulate fire and human thoughts. Matilda was particularly good with potions and remedies. Demons had been afraid of them, only because they were afraid of their powers. Matilda had married her husband for love, but his family betrayed him.

He was taken down to hell when he tried to protect her from other demons and she had been hiding ever since.

I didn't know how, but we connected emotionally and spiritually. Matilda was kind, caring, and she taught me to stay positive.

As the due date approached I grew more conscious about what my life would be after the birth. I spoke to Ricky again and some of the news from London caused me further aggravation. Arthur had gotten engaged to Natalie Morgan. Ricky didn't want to talk about him, but eventually he had to tell me that the future king was finally over me.

Then, during one evening at least ten days before my due date, my water broke. I went into labour two hours later completely unprepared and petrified. Ronan was out sorting some business in the village, so I had to rely on Matilda. My energy went berserk, igniting various things in the cottage. Ronan had to use special potions to keep my powers in control. I couldn't touch anything, my fingertips were in flames. The contractions were getting stronger. Everything changed an hour later.

Around five a.m. I started screaming at the top of my lungs, experiencing the worst pain in my life. I thought that labour wasn't going to be that hard. Millions of

women went through it, often more than once, but I couldn't stand the agonising pain.

"Maxine, I'll use a little magic to help you relax." I heard Matilda's voice close to me.

It didn't work, because the pain was unbelievable. Sweat was dripping down my face and I was ready to rip that child apart. I just prayed for it to stop hurting. I didn't know how long I was in labour, but at some point Matilda told me to start pushing. Then I heard Ronan in the room too. He must have sensed my distress, so he came back.

Images of every man that I'd ever been with started moving in front of my eyes. Matilda was talking to me, and I kept screaming until the pain pushed me to release some violent vibes.

Tears mixed with sweat, and then more rippling pain. This whole thing lasted for what felt like hours, but somewhere in between my screams, pain, and sweat I finally heard the baby cry.

Everything suddenly stopped, and I experienced an explosion of colours, warmth and joy. Time ceased and nothing else mattered anymore.

Matilda had tears in her eyes and suddenly there was this tiny creature on my chest, covered with sticky white stuff. It was the most beautiful baby that I had ever seen and it was mine.

"There she is—your daughter," Matilda whispered, wiping her tears away. I was exhausted, ready to shut down my energy, but I couldn't physically move. The world stopped as I stared down at something so special and so precious.

My mind was spinning out of control, and I swallowed hard, wondering why on earth I ever wanted to get rid of this beautiful tiny little girl.

God, the pain didn't matter then, well, nothing mattered. Then she stared at me and images from the past began assaulting my mind. I felt her heartbeat, her tiny limbs on me. She was sending me images, revealing the identity of the father. This wasn't something that I ever expected or prepared myself for.

I opened my mouth and kept touching her, making sure that she was still real.

This little mongrel baby informed me that the future king, Prince Arthur, was her real father. This was beyond amazing and scary at the same time. In that moment I knew that my life was never going to be the same again.

"It's true then. My dear lord, Maxine. She's connecting with you, right?" Ronan asked, appearing next to me.

The sudden joy shifted into disappointment and anger. Either way, with or without this new knowledge I still had to give her away. I loved her instantly and unconditionally.

She was stunning, but there was royal blood in her veins and that turned her into a cursed child. She needed someone that could give her all the love and devotion, something that I wasn't able to provide myself.

I wiped my tears and pushed myself to look away. This was the worst feeling in my life. Sudden despair filled my lungs and I couldn't catch my breath. The pain was suddenly unbearable, worse than I could have ever imagined.

"Take her, Matilda. You were right. I want you to look after her for me. I don't know if I ever will be capable of being her parent, but for now she's your daughter."

Matilda understood. She touched my face and lifted the baby. She was going to be her guardian from now on. I was broken, knowing that she would be away from me, possibly forever.

I looked away knowing that there was only one thing left for me to do. I had to go back to London and try to start over—without her. Ricky was running my business and he needed all the help he could get. There was no point in me hiding anymore.

I would go back, carrying the burden of the most dangerous secret on my shoulders—a secret that could drag me back to hell if ever discovered.

Chapter One

"Do not be afraid; our fate
Cannot be taken from us; it is a gift."
— **Dante Alighieri, Inferno**

My phone kept vibrating annoyingly in my pocket; it hadn't stopped ringing since I left my tiny flat half an hour earlier. I tried to ignore it for as long as I could, but I knew that it was Ricky subtly reminding me that I was yet again running late. I was going to work, making my way through the cold and wet, gloomy streets of Brixton. Keeping my eyes open to my less-than-safe surroundings, I was careful of the people around me, sometimes passing busy-looking humans on the streets who were definitely up to no good, but I was still smiling through my sleep-deprived state. Last night people kept pouring me drinks, and my cards were awesome, so I didn't want to leave early and lose the chance to win some cash back. I didn't regret anything, even when I woke up with the biggest hangover in the history of mankind this late morning.

Around halfway through my journey, the heavens ripped open and rain started pouring from the sky. It wasn't a light drizzle. In a matter of seconds my good mood disappeared and I was completely soaked and even more pissed off by the fact that I didn't own a fucking umbrella.

It was around half past four in the afternoon and the fact that February had been dragging for God knew how long was making me feel even shittier about myself.

I was glad that I didn't put any makeup on today; otherwise the rain would have made me look like a tribute act for the band Kiss. I had another couple of streets to walk through before I would reach the office, so when my phone began vibrating for the tenth time, I turned to the left and walked inside an old townhouse with a broken lock. Ricky was relentless, so I had no choice but to call him back. I'd given Ricky dozens of reasons to be worried about me in the past, and now he was most likely just checking to see if I was still alive.

The building stunk of mould and mildew. There was no way that I could afford to buy a new mobile just yet, so I had to keep it away from the rain. Ricky had his ways to track me down and I didn't want to put myself further in the shit with him.

"What?" I snarked when he answered his phone.

"Where the hell are you, Maxine? Three candidates already left. You were meant to be here at three thirty, dammit!" Ricky said—well, more accurately roared into the phone. Great, I didn't need to have him on my back tonight.

I bit on my lower lip and forced myself not to roll my eyes. I'd completely forgotten that tonight I was supposed to help him interview our first full-time assistant. Over the past couple of weeks Ricky had been telling me that we needed to expand, that we weren't coping, but it appeared that my very own dark inner demons had screwed with my head. So much that I had mixed up the days of the week. People had been telling me that I had to start writing things down. Yeah, really? Like I was going to run around with a notepad in my hand.

"I'm on my way. Chill, and please stop yelling at me," I said, wondering why I'd agreed to this in the first place. He could easily interview people himself; he didn't need me to hold his hand. Besides, I really wasn't too keen on spending money on an assistant. The bottom line was that I had to get my shit together and at the very least start arriving at the office on time.

There was a silence on the other side of the phone. Ricky was breathing loudly, and I knew he was pretty pissed off.

"Max, I'm worried about you. You promised to be on time today," he said, and a hot boiling guilt filled my stomach. I hated when Ricky was so caring; he knew that I was trying hard to climb above the surface of pain.

"I'm on my way," I mumbled into the phone.

"You played poker last night, didn't you? Are you hungover much?" he asked sarcastically, already knowing the answer anyway.

Ricky Donovan was the biggest womaniser amongst his own faction so it surprised me that he had time to give a damn about me. Then the tiny voice in my head reminded me that we had been friends and business partners for many years, and we'd always looked out for each other, even during our toughest times.

When I was battling a hangover I was more sensitive to human emotions, and tonight every couple of meters the stench of pain, the caress of happiness, and waves of sadness kept invading my body, hitting me hard. I couldn't block these intense vibes, taking it all in and suffering the consequences. On the other hand, I had to numb the pain, forget about her screams for at least for a few hours. Last night was one of those times.

"Ricky stop nagging me. I'll be in the office. It's bloody raining and I'm soaked and you're not helping," I complained, running my fingers over my forehead. My skin was burning, and that wasn't a very good sign. There was the possibility that another demon was nearby, and not a very friendly demon.

Ricky swore loudly, most likely to himself, and I heard him shuffling paperwork all over his desk. "Maxine, this is getting ridiculous. It's been a year—longer than a year. Gambling and drinking won't erase your shit. Get it fucking together and act like you're actually a fully fledged grown up for once. We are a team!"

That comment struck me like a bullet, and I had to hold myself steady for a good few seconds. Ricky could be insensitive at times, although deep down he was just damaged like I was. He shouldn't have reminded me that I was still broken, that my soul had been nearly ripped away from my body, that I'd nearly lost everything.

"We both know that I do care about you and the business so shut your bloody mouth. I'll be there soon. Just use compulsion to keep the humans there," I snapped through my gritted teeth and hung up, feeling like my anger was getting out of control, and that was a bad sign. I felt bad about arguing with Ricky. He only looked out for me, and it was my fault for being late. After all we were running a business partnership.

Two bulky men passed the building that I was in, stopped, and glanced in my direction, probably aware of sudden demonic energy, the inhuman power. The problem was that most humans could sense that something was wrong. They might have been weak, but they weren't stupid.

I closed my eyes quickly and took two deep breaths, swallowing the violent fury and remembering the reasons I'd made that difficult and painful decision twelve months ago. It was never really a choice. It was my only option and I had to do it alone; he didn't deserve to know the truth.

I shivered with the cold and put my hood over my head. When I came out of the building, I shoved my mobile into my back pocket, picking up my pace. I headed for the office, knowing that it wasn't wise to keep Ricky pissed for too long. Sometimes he acted more like my overprotective brother than a business partner. I reminded myself that I loved him dearly; he was the closest thing to a family member that I ever had and we both needed each other.

Twenty minutes later I would have made it to the office like I had promised. Yes, after passing a couple more streets I would have been sitting next to Ricky, listening to some chick babbling about working in a team and trying to forget about the fact that my hangover was dragging me down the road to destruction. The problem was that something happened between Green Lane and Parkway Road, something that forced me to use my power.

I chose a shortcut, using the back alley that separated two housing estates. In hindsight it wasn't my wisest idea. A split second later I felt gut-wrenching fear that literally knocked the breath out of my lungs, and then I heard a loud, petrified scream. The scream resonated within me; after all, half of my DNA was demonic, my mother had hooked up with a full-blooded demon and nine months later she had given birth to me. Because of this I was able to read most human's minds, but only to some extent— images, feelings, sometimes a few words. Tonight I knew instantly that someone was in trouble, and that was part of the problem of being a mongrel (half demon, half human) —my abilities were always pushing me to do shit that I didn't want to do.

I breathed in the fear that got attached to my soul and then I tried to exhale, as the energy rushed through my system.

For fuck's sake, why me and why the hell now? Will I ever be able to just walk through the streets without getting involved in someone else's shit?

Okay, so maybe I was a little bit harsh, but with this hangover from hell I wasn't ready to play hero, plus capes were just a bad fashion choice. I wanted to concentrate on my own problems for once. On the other hand I couldn't live with myself if I didn't do something to save this human in trouble.

I shook my head and crept closer to the back of the building, feeling my demonic side being drawn to the crippling fear of death. On top of my oversensitivity to human emotions I also had exceptional vision. It was a drizzly, grey evening, and visibility was poor. The streets looked like they were taken straight from a black-and-white Hitchcock film, and in that gloomy alley humans wouldn't have seen anything.

I noticed two unfriendly-looking demons surrounding a petrified human woman. They were part of the Asmodeus faction, most likely ready to drain her of any and all lust and innocence. The price for that kind of thing was high and many useful potions could be produced from this human's innocence. Rage burst to life inside me, setting my blood on fire. Shit like this was not cool in the human world. Being half human gave me empathy, and what they were about to do to this girl was akin to rape. Those two bastards knew it, but they were ready to dismiss the rules just for a few coins of favours in the underworld.

Sometimes certain members of demonic factions liked pushing their luck. These two assholes were clearly far away from their designated district and they were breaking the code, attacking an innocent human. My head was banging like hell, but despite that, I had to get involved. I couldn't just leave her there on her own. She didn't deserve to lose all her innocence as well as her passion and lust, then be left to die.

"Such a strong energy … vicious and intense. She will please Asmodeus and we will be rewarded," rasped the larger and hairier demon, brushing his repulsive gnarled fingers over woman's neck. He had a lot of tiny scars on his forehead and a tattoo of a skull on his arm. That seemed a bit obvious, but I wasn't too sure if the tattoo was given to him by the head of the faction or he had it done in one of those fake studios.

The second demon was shorter; he looked like he had spent more time on earth. He wore nicely fitted clothes and his thick black hair was in an approximation of a human style but smeared with too much gel. My exceptional eyesight never let me down, and I knew that these two demons were looking to draw out the episode just for fun.

"Please let me go. I don't have any money on me," the woman squeaked, like a dying bird.

The hairy demon laughed and shifted closer. He grabbed the woman's throat and lifted her a couple of inches above the ground. I'd never seen a demon go to this extreme for something that he could buy on the black market. This woman, whoever she was, had no chance of pulling away. Those two were probably ready to take away her soul too.

The good side of me, the one that wasn't lazy or selfish, reacted. I moved from my hiding place, releasing the energy that had been brewing inside me for weeks feeding the flames of my fury. I knew that there was always a price to pay for magic, for using my abilities to their absolute demonic extremes, but I couldn't worry about that right now.

"Oh, boys, I suggest you step away from that lady right away. Don't you know that no means no? I'm sure it isn't the first time a girl turned you down. Besides, we both know that breaking the rules topside means Lucifer himself will fry your arses in the pits!" I shouted, creating a wave of protection around me. It was one of the tricks that I was taught by Leviathan's men, converting human fear into my own energy. By the time the two of them turned around, I had a Sherafine elixir in my right hand. Maybe it wasn't totally necessary, I could deal with them without it, but I was going to enjoy using it on a member of the Asmodeus faction. A girl has to get her kicks somewhere, right?

"Ted, look at this. A dirty mongrel is sticking her beaky nose into our business," the non-hairy one stated, and his eyes gleamed with an unknown energy. Shit, that's what I thought. These two were running around London getting high on lust, hurting innocent human women for fun. That was why I hated hell. Asmodeus couldn't even keep an eye on scumbags like them.

"You have two seconds to stop what you're doing or you will get hurt. Really, really badly. And I don't have my first aid kit with me," I said, as sarcastically as I could, letting them know they had a chance to leave. The uglier and wider demon licked his lips greedily and smiled. I had an advantage—my eyesight—I could see better than them, than anyone.

Unfortunately the other demon joined his mate, and for a good few moments both of them laughed loudly, holding their quivering fat bellies. One of them shot a fireball in my direction, trying to scare me, thinking that he was skilled and gifted. I moved my body sinuously to the side, flexed my protection shield and absorbed the ball. My energy escalated, streaming out of my pores. Every single hair on the back of my neck rose.

I jumped in front of the uglier one and threw the Sherafine elixir that disabled him completely, then tossed off a swift roundhouse kick straight into the other's jaw, knocking him good and proper to the ground. I expected a battle, a true scrappy street fight. What I got was strung-out demons too high to fight me. This was easy, almost too easy, but on the other hand, no other female mongrel had a black belt in Tae kwon do and years of experience in the security industry.

The woman who stood plastered to the wall let out a hysterical whimper when the earth underneath my feet started shaking. I felt the strong rising heat that made my toes curl and caught a whiff of a burning sulfuric smell. The much hairier demon was on the ground moaning in agony holding his neck; the other demon lay where my last uppercut left him, pretty much knocked out—not dead, but close enough. I walked up to the woman, covering her with my body. My lungs contracted against the smell, as the earth opened up and bright yellow and red light spread everywhere. The woman was screaming now and I was sweating like a pig, trying to fight the urge to jump into the pit.

I glanced down, seeing the large hole in the middle of the alley filled with hot lava that melted away parts of the pavement. The heat was unbearable, and I felt strong burning on my back. An incredible force whizzed through the air, ruffling my hair and pulling me away from the woman.

"No … you bitch, I won't let him take me!" roared the skinnier demon, crawling away from the hole, suddenly conscious. He was bleeding, most likely wounded by my attack. The human's heart was jackhammering so fast that I was scared she was going to have a heart attack at any second, and that wasn't something that I had anticipated.

A thrilling and intense energy began dragging the two demons down to the hole. My leather jacket was melting into my body and that strong urge to jump too was messing with my half-human mind. Within a few seconds, both demons got sucked inside the pit. The whizzing noise was strong, pushing and pulling things around the alley. A split second later there was a loud blast, and then silence descended all around me, sucking the rest of the oxygen out of my lungs.

Everything was back to normal when I opened my eyes again and took a long, deep breath. Demons were gone, the hole too. I had no idea what happened, but no one apart from Watchers was able to open the gates of hell and there were none around. I was most certainly sure that I was the only supernatural being within a hundred yards.

Now I was stuck with a woman who had witnessed and felt everything that happened. That really complicated things for me. Now I was not only late, but also exposed. Fuck my life.

Chapter Two

"Remember tonight... for it is the beginning of always"
— **Dante Alighieri**

"What happened? How ... who—?" The girl stuttered, glancing from where the hole was and where the two sleazeballs disappeared, to me with my half-melted coat and singed hair.

I had to calm her down somehow, but I didn't know where to start. There was a possibility that Watchers were going to show up at any second. They were responsible for preventing humans from knowing about the demonic world. Even though I had enough adrenaline in my system to run a marathon, my head was still pounding. I just couldn't catch a break. I needed to forget about my doozy of a hangover and get my sorry arse out of here as soon as possible. The woman was losing the plot, mouthing words that didn't make any sense. Humans just couldn't comprehend anything outside of their little bubble of reality and that there was something other than them in the world. Still, I felt sorry for her. Despite her obvious shock and fear, there was something in me that didn't want her to be removed by the Watchers.

"Look, you've had a mind fuck. I know it's all confusing right now. I'll explain everything in a second, but we have to keep moving," I said, pulling her upright to her feet. The dreaded shadows of the city were making me agitated. The Watchers were in the area, probably looking for the person that opened up the gates. A chilling dread hung over my head. They also took care of mongrels and demons that threatened to expose themselves to humans. If they caught me, the uncomfortable questions would follow, and I couldn't afford to be stopped now.

Somehow I managed to hobble several meters dragging this chick without falling down. I was trying to gather my thoughts. It was difficult enough with the blisters on my back healing and my hangover, but the demon side of me was howling to be released, scratching at my impulses to get back to see if the gate would open again. My whole body throbbed painfully and I knew that I was going to suffer tomorrow morning. It'd been a couple of weeks since I last trained, since I worked my muscles to that kind of extent. In my line of work it was easy to dismiss the pain, but I wasn't used to it like before.

The noise from the alley should have brought attention from other humans, but I had been right all along. No one in this damn city paid attention to other people anymore.

"The light…I felt so warm…those men were sucked right into the ground," the woman kept saying over and over again. I had to drag her down the pavement just for a few moments to catch my breath, trying to keep a good pace. Lugging my sorry arse and the girl was pretty taxing. At least it hadn't stopped raining yet. Watchers didn't like rainy weather because they couldn't track the magical fingerprint as easily in the rain, plus some weird shit about frizzy hair. You'll never meet a demon that isn't a little bit vain.

Ricky was going to lose his shit with me. I had no idea how much time had passed since I spoke to him on the phone. There was a strong possibility that all the candidates had already left, and my business partner would be sitting behind his desk, cursing me out and making a voodoo doll. Okay, so this time around I had a good reason to be late, and maybe I shouldn't have stuck my nose into someone else's business, but these arseholes weren't going to stop with one innocent human. They were marked by a Watcher, so they were probably convicts on the run, who knew?

The woman became very vocal all of a sudden, attracting too much attention to two of us. We were in a crowded street now and I had to do something. Other humans were staring. Some guy with a dog asked me if my friend was all right. I waved him off and pulled her around the corner.

"Hey! Hey! Calm down, crazy lady, you're safe. The men ran away. I kicked their butts and called the police. You don't have to worry anymore," I said, placing my palms on her cheeks.

As the warmth of my energy reached her face, she stopped mumbling all of a sudden, staring at me with her wide blue eyes. I hated fiddling with human minds or emotions. If I wasn't careful I could easily read their desires and tap into their deepest secrets. Sometimes I was too scared, in case I accidentally crossed that line that I let them see beyond the charm. I hated when my own privacy was invaded and had serious issues doing this to her, but right now the woman could get both of us into trouble. I had to calm her down.

I swallowed hard, seeing a little blond girl in her thoughts, and then her fearful eyes shifted, and she smiled. I was aware that tonight I had used too much energy. I didn't have time to worry about the consequences right now, but I could feel the cold chill in my bones. The future didn't look bright and the price for magic was always high.

The woman flinched, glanced around and narrowed her eyes at me when I backed away from her.

"Who are you?" she asked, and then cocked her head to the side. "Wow! Your eyes are so beautiful, so dark. I swear I think your pupils are almost purple."

I scratched my head wondering if I might have accidentally sent too much energy into her and damaged her mind. That was impossible. I was gentle and she seemed strong.

"You were attacked in the alley, but it's okay now, you're safe. I scared the bastards away. They tried to mug you," I explained, tossing my long dark hair behind me, confident that she would believe me. The woman opened her mouth but didn't say anything. She looked down on her clothes that were wet and giggled nervously. I stood in front of her, puzzled, worried that I had done something wrong. I knew my limits, I knew that I was skilled, but maybe today, for the first time in my life I'd gone too far.

"Oh my God, really? I don't remember anything. Thank you so much." She leaned back and sagged against the wall. "It's like I have this big black hole in my head," she said, looking confused.

"That's okay, it's probably shock. It will pass," I assured her.

Then she threw herself at me with what had to be the world's most awkward hug. I went stiff almost instantly. First of all, this woman was a complete stranger, and second of all I wasn't used to anyone touching me.

"Thank you. You probably saved my life."

"Yeah. Yay me. All right, I think that's enough now," I said, pulling away from her. "You don't have to worry. They were probably junkies after your money, but they didn't manage to take anything anyway."

"I'm so glad that you came to my rescue. My name is Emma, by the way," she said, smiling widely. "I shouldn't have taken that shortcut, but I was running late for a job interview. Bummer, I must be like two hours late now."

It started raining heavier all of a sudden. I grabbed her elbow, not even thinking what I was doing.

"Come on, I know a place where you can dry off."

She nodded and we both started running through the streets. Twenty minutes later we reached my office. By the time we entered the building we were both dripping wet, but Emma was oddly recovered and somehow excited.

Ricky was right; I was weak enough to fall back to my old nasty habits. Magical tequila had shut down all thoughts about the past and made me happy for a while. No matter how heavy the secret weighed on me, tequila managed to carry it when I filled my belly with it. Plus tequila was way cheaper than therapy.

Emma didn't seem to have an off button. She would not shut the hell up and kept talking all the way upstairs. She mentioned her white cat, her daughter, and the fact that she should have left her house early to get to her interview on time, a sale on at her favourite shoe shop, her favourite teacher in high school—on and on she went.

When I barged through the door of Doomed Cases, my own supernatural detective agency, I was exhausted and cold. Ricky slammed his fists on the desk as soon as he saw me. His normally perfectly symmetrical face was twisted in a rage, his tie was on the table, and two buttons of his shirt were open.

"Two freaking hours, Maxine. You said that you were just around the corner. All the candidates left. Are you fu —"

"Oh, hello, my name is Emma. I'm so sorry for being so late. I came across some difficulties on the street when this lovely lady rescued me out of what seemed a mugging." Emma cut Ricky off, shoving me to the side and shaking his hand enthusiastically. Ricky was a full demon, born to the Beelzebub faction. He was cast out from the underworld when he was caught sneaking out to the world outside and doing some dodgy business with other mongrels. He was bloody handsome, always well presented with an immaculate dress sense, but tonight he looked like he was just about to explode.

I held my hand up to him to stop any further rant he was about to vomit at me and scratched my head thinking how I could explain in front of Emma, eyeing her with confusion. For a split second I wanted to tell Ricky that he could shove this whole business up in his arse, that I was done, but somehow I restrained myself.

"Emma? As in Emma Carter? The five o'clock slot?" Ricky questioned my newly acquainted crazy human, suddenly forgetting that just a second ago he was ready to whoop my arse for being two hours late.

"Ricky, I got held up at the back street, when two freaks —"

"Maxine, shut the hell up for a second," he snapped at me. "And meet our new assistant, Miss Emma Carter."

His sudden anger vanished, and his eyes gleamed with amused curiosity. My clothes were sticking to my body and I was dreaming about a hot bath. I seriously didn't care who Emma was right now.

Emma had streaky black mascara marks under her eyes, but she looked ecstatic. Ricky couldn't be serious; this random woman wasn't here for an interview. I didn't believe in that kind of coincidence.

"New assistant... but... but I haven't been interviewed yet, and I was late ... so very late," Emma stuttered, staring at Ricky in utter disbelief. I needed to sit down. This was too much for me to handle, even for one crazy evening like this.

"It's all right, Miss Carter, you're hired. I don't have to introduce you to my business partner, Maxine Brodeur, as you have already met. Please come in tomorrow at twelve with all your paperwork, so we can add you to the payroll," Ricky shot away.

"Man, can I have a word with you?" I said, finding my voice. My business partner was acting crazy. He knew well enough that we couldn't hire a human.

"Oh, thank you, Miss Brodeur, I'm so happy. This couldn't have turned out any better. I have been searching for a job for weeks. Thank you so much for rescuing me from those nasty men and the fire ... yes, there was a fire. I saw something strange, like lava—"

"No, there wasn't any fire, Emma. You're still confused," I cut her off abruptly. "Come back tomorrow like Ricky said. You hit your head pretty hard, so I suggest you have yourself checked out at the hospital."

She should never have remembered the pits. I'd cleared her thoughts, implanted a different memory.

There was no way on earth that she could handle our supernatural cases, our caliber of clients. This was against our code of practise. Ricky was playing with me, and promising this woman a job was cruel.

"You're both so lovely, and did I tell you that you have beautiful eyes? This one time I went to a beauty salon to do my nails and I swear to god the woman was special, she changed the col—"

"Emma, thank you so much, but we would like to see you tomorrow. Just go home and rest all right?" Ricky interrupted her this time around with his forceful tone of voice. "Let me walk you down."

"Oh of course, silly me. I'm sorry to blab so much when I'm nervous, but you really are beautiful, Maxine, with those purple irises," she added again, beaming.

I waved my goodbyes and slumped down behind my desk, rubbing my face with my palms. The human was right—I was a freak of nature. My eyes were bizarre: at times they were brown, other times almost purple. To anyone from outside I wasn't just an ordinary human being with a pale complexion and dark colourful highlights.

Before when I had a stable career working in security, I used to make an effort, wore proper clothes and even put on makeup most days. Now after a year from hell (no seriously, real Hell, fire and brimstone and all that bollocks) I tended to wear the same hoodie and old jeans for days before I even considered doing the laundry. If my client didn't like my appearance, then they could get lost. There were plenty of mongrels and demons in this shitty city that needed my help.

Ricky showed up several minutes later, looking perfectly happy.

"Right, now you can tell me what that shit show was really about. You can't be serious. We both know that we can't take her on," I said, putting my legs on the table. The water from my soaked jeans began dripping on the paperwork.

"It's a done deal, Maxine. I already gave her the job. Emma is going to be our new assistant and if you'd gotten here earlier on, then maybe we could have picked someone else," Ricky said, folding his arms over his chest. The bastard was good looking, well groomed for a man and a demon. He knew that he was an asset to the agency, always bringing in new clients.

"Well, two demons from Asmodeus's faction cornered her on my way here. They were planning to drain her lust and innocence. I had no other choice but to help her," I explained. I seriously needed a drink and nothing else would cut it but tequila. I most likely looked terrible but felt even worse. My clothes were soaked and singed, and that crappy taste in my mouth wasn't going away anytime soon. "Besides, we both know that we can't take on a human. She already witnessed enough tonight. Clients won't like this and on top of that she is—"

"Cute," Ricky finished for me, smiling wolfishly. "She is the sweetest human creature that I ever met, and she will do just fine. Besides, you already messed around with her mind. We need her. The cases are a mess and we might have an audit next week. Lucifer is sending his people to find out if we are following the protocol."

I sighed, feeling a dull pain in my head. I was completely broke, and I was late with my rent. Last night I blew all my available cash, so now I wasn't in any position to argue with Ricky. I had to let this one go.

The odd thing was that, although she chattered away, I kind of liked the human that I just saved. It was hard for me to like anyone these days, but she was so happy and genuinely excited about a job. My mind was now sober enough to be aware of the images and feelings I wanted to hide so that they danced right in front of my eyes and I desperately needed a distraction. Someone that could help me pull myself back from the torturous misery. The world around me was changing, and I had been slipping down in the past six months. I had to get my shit together.

Emma was like a small weak candlelight in a moonless night. She seemed to have no idea the world that she had grown up with wasn't real, that there were other creatures walking amongst normal human beings. Maybe that was the reason I felt connected with her—she had the purity and innocence of a happy mind that I lacked.

Two years ago, I was the happiest half demon in the world. Everything was working well for me, until it all fell apart.

"Stop overthinking this, Maxine. You will be working with the human. It's time to shift things around here. You know I've tried to help you, to push you forward, but it seems to me that you want to stay unhappy, broken and sad. You have a business to take care of, bills to pay and people that rely on you. Tomorrow you will be here at two o'clock in the afternoon, and if that means I have to come to your crummy flat myself and throw you out of bed, then so be it. Now go home, cure your hangover, eat something and don't even dare go out drinking tonight," Ricky said, getting into my head. God, I hated when he was so insensitive. "I mean it, girl, pull through or I'll personally make your life difficult."

After his speech, I opened my mouth to argue. I wanted to remain my stubborn, difficult self, but honestly I couldn't raise the energy to give a shit. I jumped off the table and walked towards the door not saying anything at all. Maybe for once I was willing to admit that he was right. I'd never fucking tell him, the vain demon bastard.

Chapter Three

"There is no greater sorrow
Than to recall a happy time
When miserable."
—— Dante Alighieri

I woke up the next day feeling fresh and well rested. For the first time in a long time my head was clear, my body didn't ache from a restless night, and there was no eyeball-shattering hangover. It was strange to see this fucked up world in its true colours rather than hidden by my Ray-bans. I may have woken with my body straight, but I still had my mind and spirit to get right. I wasn't one of those women who could hand myself over to fate or faith. I usually found my mind in the bottom of my spirit. *Tequila won't solve your problems but it's worth a shot.* Yeah, I had a logo T-shirt; don't judge me.

I had spent my whole night watching trash TV. Even though my mouth was dry and nothing seemed to slake my thirst and despite the fact that I was desperate for a drink, somehow I managed to stay in my flat. The darkness came as usual, torturing me with the whys and the what ifs, but I had to remember that life wasn't easy in general and my melancholy and sadness wouldn't last forever. I could have made a different choice in the past, but then I would have to deal with the consequences of my actions.

I lived in the worst part of Brixton, because it was the only place I could afford these days. From a very young age I had been left to take care of myself, so money had never been an issue for me. Only about eighteen months ago I got myself into a lot of debt with unpaid rent and utilities. Things were complicated. Ricky had tried helping me out a few times, but eventually he couldn't keep settling my debts for me. Most of the time, I acted like I didn't give a shit about anything anymore. I was a shadow of my former self. I was just a sad drunken creature. The work was still important, but not like before. Now it just helped pass the day rather than being my raison d'etre.

"Get it together, bitch. No one will ever take care of you but you," I said to my own reflection in the mirror.

The pep talk helped a little, not much, but it was time to stop feeling sorry for myself and get on with life. The gambling, well, I kept telling myself that I had it under control. I'd played cards since I was fifteen years old. I used to be really good; however, over the past twelve months I had lost more money than I had coming in and that wasn't good. Ricky didn't get it. I needed poker to fulfil my empty nights; I needed to be around people to take my mind off life, socialise without actually being involved with people I may have to pretend to give a shit about. Just so I could push through the dark cloud that hung over me. Money didn't matter to me anymore; I didn't want to live to work rather than work to live.

After this silent and stupid contemplation I took a shower. First one this week by the smell of me. It was a new day today and I was going to make an effort. I had no one in my life to impress so usually I didn't bother to make myself look decent, but I had to start somewhere with this mind, body and spirit shit. I brushed my hair and put a bit of makeup on. Shockingly I started to recognise the old me in the mirror.

My rent was overdue by two days, but my money box in the drawer was empty. I couldn't ask Ricky for a loan. I didn't need another lecture from him about responsibilities and shit like that. I had to figure this out myself, and fast. Mrs. Patel was going to have to wait. I was hoping to meet a new client today, the one that Ricky had told me about a few days ago. A quick injection of cash would be helpful, and everyone in the city knew that I always took a deposit on accepting a case. I dreaded to think who they were and what they wanted from me.

In my line of work I mainly dealt with demons. Vain assholes who thought they were the centre of the universe, and because I am only a half demon or a mongrel I am at their beck and call. It's a complicated system that they live by when trying to decipher the underworld. Seven head demons represent seven factions that are responsible for keeping order on earth and in the underworld. Lucifer was still the master of the hell and he was the most powerful. There was also Mammon, Asmodeus, Leviathan, Beelzebub, Astroth and Berith. Each one took care of their own affairs, yet still answered to the government in the capital.

Humans had no bloody idea that there was another world out there, that heaven and hell truly existed. Demons had been living amongst the general populous for generations, a lot of the time breaking rules and mating with humans. Lucifer hated the fact that there were so many mongrels on earth, orphans like me born with demonic DNA. We'd always been treated like second-class citizens, with not many rights, but a lot of responsibilities. Although no one really cared when we got romantically involved with humans. Our protocol was less strict in comparison to full-blooded demons. Below demons there were other creatures too, dark and twisted souls that lived in the pits. Berith, the demon in charge of all the entrances to the underworld and the Watchers hadn't been doing their job in keeping order in the ranks. Berith faction had always been weak, and most of his demons liked sneaking out up to earth to seduce women. They liked partying hard. That was why there were so many other beings walking on the streets attacking innocents and causing havoc amongst humans.

Two years ago when I was getting tired of my job in security I discovered a gap in the market. Many mongrels battled to remain anonymous, struggling to fit in since we didn't really belong here on earth or in the fires of hell. We were innocents with tainted souls. If a crime occurred, it usually brought out our demonic nature, or if there was an issue involving another demon, human police couldn't help us. Most mongrels didn't get a very good start in life. We weren't important, and the factions we belonged to showed no interest whatsoever in getting us out of trouble. So that was where I fit in.

It was an easy decision: I had skills and resources, so I applied for a loan. Two months later the office of Doomed Cases officially opened up. Ricky was one of my first clients. His ex-wife rinsed him from all his money and disappeared. He wanted me to go after her and didn't care to mention that she owned a pet, a chimera that nearly ripped my face off. It wasn't like you could distract a fire-breathing ten-foot mix of lion, eagle and snake with a chew toy, unless of course his name was George. It was a difficult case, but I had gotten his money back, all of it. We became friends after that and soon enough he wanted to invest in the business. I was skeptical at first, unsure if I wanted a partner, but he managed to convince me. It was difficult to run a business when I had a full time job, so I chose him to take over the management.

I felt odd leaving my apartment at one in the afternoon completely sober and well rested. I pulled my tangled hair off my face into a bun and pulled my leather jacket closer together. The freezing cold weather wasn't helping my mood and I felt like I didn't belong anywhere, like I was just an outsider. Part of my demonic soul craved an escape, but mongrels weren't allowed to enter the underworld, unless they were summoned by the head of a faction or the Watchers.

I ended up running to the office hoping to improve my mood. Two years ago I used to run every day; now my form wasn't that great judging from my impression of an asthma attack. When I got to the office I saw that a new desk had been delivered and Emma was sitting behind it. Suddenly events from last night hit all at once. After two weeks of drinking magical tequila my memory recall was in pieces.

"There she is, our bad arse Maxine. Surprises just keep on coming today," Ricky shouted, clapping when I looked around the room. The rent in this part of London was expensive, so we didn't have much space. There were two other small rooms at the back separated by the kitchen. Ricky was the paperwork guy. I had never spent that much time in the office. Most of the time I was out in the streets.

"Hey," I said, greeting them both.

"Maxine, it's good to see you. Ricky has explained everything and the job sounds perfect. I can't wait to get stuck in." Emma beamed, knocking the pen pot all over her desk, and then going red instantly. She wore a bright pink dress, with a thick black jumper thrown on top of it. I had never paid attention to other women, but her style was loud and flashy.

"Really? Already."

"Yes, Maxine, Emma is very keen. I just gave her a general overview of all the cases that we have been working in the past and she seemed very open-minded about the whole 'not everything is as it seems' thing," Ricky said, looking positively elated at this. He must have gotten Emma up to speed with the world around her. I had no idea how he was going to deal with telling her about the other world, but she needed to know what she was getting herself into, even if that was against the rules.

"All right, I'll be in my office making some phone calls," I said, not quite sure what to make of this whole thing. Everything was going to be fine, as long as he didn't shag our new assistant. It was against office policy to fraternise with fellow employees, a policy that I had just made up.

"Take your time, darling," Ricky muttered after I opened the door to my room. My eyes instantly fell on the large and thick brown envelope that was on my desk. Shock froze the air in my lungs when I recognised the bright red wax seal on top of it. I would recognise that crest anywhere. The lion with the crown. A tendril of panic seized me, and my blood thudded in my ears so loudly I thought I was going to throw up at any second now.

The pain from last year, the emotion and that deep fear rippled through my entire body. I grabbed the envelope and flew back to the front office, ready to tear it apart. The royal seal felt like it was almost burning my hands. There was no reason for them to get in contact with me again. I was done with them, with him. Someone must have made a mistake sending it to me, to this address. Everyone had paid the price for what happened, and I was forced to do something unforgivable, something that drained me of my ideals, my hope and everything that I ever believed in.

"Ricky, how did this letter get on my desk? Who delivered it?" I shouted, shaking the envelope in front of his face, like it was cursed. He saw the seal almost instantly and paled.

"Max, I have no idea. The postman left everything on Emma's desk. No one was in your office," he replied, and his eyes started to glow. Too late, it was too late. I had to open it. There wasn't any other way around it.

I took a few steps back, knowing that I was going to have to break the rules in front of the human, but that was on Ricky's head. He took her on, so he needed to deal with the consequences. If she wanted to work here, she needed to get used to weird shit like this.

I threw the envelope up and I kept it suspended in the air using my abilities. The royals could go to hell for all I cared. I cut myself off from that life a year ago, but this symbol amplified my pain, reminding me how much I suffered. The plain manila envelope slowly began to glow and the heat in the room rose until it started to burn with ruby red flames. I wanted it to turn into ash as quickly as possible. I'd also like for it not to have shown up on my desk, but that ship sailed. Twelve months ago I promised myself that I would never deal with royals ever again. They destroyed me, crushed a part of me that I'd never get back, and made me the person that I was today. A shadow of my former self.

"How are you …" Emma was stuttering, standing up, her eyes wide open. Ricky was pacing around nervously. The envelope was burning, but it seemed like the paper wasn't changing colour at all. This was impossible.

I used my abilities to intensify the magic so the heat and flames would do their damn job. Small beads of sweat appeared on my forehead, as panic slowed down my heartbeat. Suddenly the world around me was blurry and I was using all my powers trying to destroy this damn letter.

Several minutes later I collapsed on the floor and the thick, brown letter landed next to my hand. The edges were intact, and the royal symbol was shining with red colours. I had no other choice but to read the letter that was sent to me.

"Max, are you all right?" Ricky asked, walking up to me. He knew that I didn't like being touched by anyone, so he didn't even try to lift me up. My breath was laboured when I lifted myself off the floor. My heart was beating, but there was no blood feeding it through my body. I felt dead from inside out.

"The flames, it didn't do anything to the paper. How… how is this possible?" Emma asked, looking from me to Ricky. There was a lot that we needed to discuss with her, but now wasn't the right time.

"You have to read the letter, Max. It's probably from the head of the faction," Ricky stated.

"No, it's been a year. Those bastards have no right to send me anything. I work for myself," I growled, slowly losing my temper. The memories flooded my mind. I had been used by them, by him. This wasn't acceptable.

"Max," Ricky warned me. I knew that he was right. The letter was indestructible. No matter what I tried, I couldn't destroy it. My heart jackhammered between my ribs when I picked it up and opened it. I felt like that past year didn't mean anything, and as I started reading the letter I realised that I would never be truly done with them.

The deepest part of me knew that the royal family was part of my life forever and there was no escape.

To Miss Maxine Brodeur,

I regret to inform you that an incident occurred last evening at the palace. This incident has caused much consternation, and as such I am working closely with Lord Chamberlain who is keeping me apprised of this situation henceforth. Instruction has been given by the queen herself to resolve this matter as soon as possible.

It is my regret that we have not been formally introduced and I apologise for this unsolicited letter. I have heard a great many things of you and your loyalty to the Crown. I must impress upon you with the utmost sincerity that the royal family is in urgent need of your services. The Doomed Cases establishment has of course been on my radar for some time now, but I never thought that I would have need of your services.

I am sure you can appreciate that this matter is strictly confidential and you are under obligation to answer to me, as I am a head of Lucifer's main faction. The press must not know, and I need to remind you that you must remain professional at all times.

We require you to come to the palace immediately and look into this very sensitive matter. The human police have been notified, but I believe that this issue requires being overseen by someone from "our" world. Someone who can investigate this further and liaise with members of our royal family. Miss Brodeur, I have been advised that you would be the only person for the job, as you know the protocols and exacting standards of the palace. May I also remind you about your demonic responsibilities and serve consequences of noncompliance or disobedience.

Yours

Master Rodriquez

"What does it say?" Ricky asked, placing his hand on my shoulder. My judgment was clouded, and I was breathing, but the oxygen wasn't getting into my lungs. They were summoning me to the palace. This couldn't be happening. Not after a year.

"The case, we have a case at the palace and we have to go now," I whispered, knowing that this was the price of magic. Last night I saved Emma and today I was going to pay the biggest price in my life. I was going to see him again.

Chapter Four

"The more a thing is perfect, the more it feels pleasure and pain."
— Dante Alighieri, The Divine Comedy

"But... what if a client comes in?" Emma asked, looking apprehensive about being left alone. "I won't know what to say. I only just started a couple of hours ago."

I couldn't think straight. My stomach felt like it was filled with heavy bricks. Ricky looked torn and that was a first for him too. My power was on the verge of blowing this whole building up like a firework display. Sometimes my own abilities surprised even me. By the age of eighteen my magic was fully developed, dispelling the belief that there was a difference between mongrel and demon powers. I was able to gather energy from around me and use it for my advantage. I could sense people's emotions and fears, understand other demons.

"Just improvise, take their details and tell them that we'll get back to them," Ricky told her, shuffling through the papers on his desk in the other room.

I was balling up the royal letter in my palms, trying to calm down, but my heart hammered in my chest way too fast. I didn't want to go to the palace and meet the new seer. That part of my life was behind me. I knew what could happen if I ignored the letter. Ricky was in a better position than me. He was a demon with a complicated past, but he didn't grew up in an orphanage like I had. On top of that Emma had witnessed the whole incident with the letter, but she was taking this whole thing better than I expected. Ricky must have used some calming powers to ease her anxiety, but at the end of the day she was still here, so we had some sort of progress.

"Ready?" Ricky asked, picking up his coat. I nodded, but deep down I was ready to throw up or enter the underworld of my own accord.

Suddenly my past and my present collided and the weight of it sat on me like a ton of bricks. I had tried so hard to keep the two separated as if I were two different people. The old me and the new me. I had forced myself to compartmentalise as much as I could, but to be face to face with my past was going to cripple me. I had spent two years as head of security for the royal family and last year I ended up on the streets, cursed and completely torn apart.

Ricky's car was parked at the back. I didn't own one. I had too many debts and there was a strong chance that I was going to get evicted from my flat in a week or so.

"Can we stop at the liquor store? I don't think I can go there completely sober," I said, my voice trembling as I cracked the bones in my knuckles.

Ricky didn't say anything at first, just started the engine of his Mercedes. He had to be fucking worried how things were going to pan out. Nothing good could come from this case, nothing at all. My business partner knew my history with the royals. He was the one that attempted to rescue me when I was drowning in pain.

"No, Maxine, you're going to walk up there with your head held high and deal with everything professionally. Alcohol only clouds your judgment and that royal bastard has to see that you're doing just fine without him," Ricky told me, driving into the main road. "You have risked your life in order to give someone else a chance, a vulnerable creature that didn't get the choice if she wanted to be brought back to this earth or not. Get it together, Maxine, and stop pretending that you need alcohol to function. You're better than that."

My mouth was dry, palms sweaty, and uneasy energy ran through body. I couldn't allow Arthur to see me weak or to see that anything had changed, that I had changed. We hadn't seen each other for over twelve months. I was hoping that he wasn't even in the palace. Rodriquez, one of Lucifer's demons, was obviously new, he must have just been assigned to this post. I had no idea how he managed to get into the royal court in the first place, passing through the Chamberlain's office. He must have had significant connections in the underworld or he was more than just an ordinary demon.

The afternoon traffic in London was terrible, it took us over an hour to get to Buckingham Palace. Then we had to wait another half an hour by the gate as the guards were going through our ID's and getting authorisation to let us pass. My energy was charging down my arms, causing havoc inside my system. Even after a whole year I still had dreams about him and sometimes wondered if he ever thought about me at all. I had always been seen as this brash, sarcastic, independent mongrel—the woman who could protect anyone, but inside I felt weak, completely falling apart. My well-guarded past had finally caught up with me.

Finally at around three o'clock in the afternoon Ricky and I were sitting on the bench outside Rodriquez's office. I was breathing harder than I should, glancing around the familiar space, the long corridors and rooms that I used to check when I worked here. It was so familiar to me, so why the hell did I feel so anxious?

A second later, a slender human stepped out of the first room to our right.

"Miss Brodeur? Mr. Donovan?" he asked, like he wanted to be sure that we were who we said we were. Ricky nodded. "Follow me please."

I noticed that there was also an unmarked police car outside. Whatever happened must have been serious. There were way too many people hanging around the palace for this to be a minor concern. The royal family had plenty of different residences in the country. Deep down I was hoping that Arthur was stuck somewhere remote, like Balmoral.

We stood up together and walked through the huge entrance that separated the West and East Wings. I had almost forgotten how large and silent this building was. At the time when I worked here it seemed majestic and regal, but now it felt cold and austere. All the rooms reminded me of what I had lost. Memories flooded my mind, threatening that fragile part of me that was supposed to hold it together.

We finally stopped in the part of the palace where most of the staff worked, in front of a pair of large, highly ornate, gilt red wooden doors. The slender human knocked and then we all entered.

"Mr. Rodriquez, they are here," he announced. There was an older demon sitting in a tall wooden chair behind an equally aged and carved desk, writing something down on the paper in front of him. His powerful energy radiated from him beaming from every part of his body so his status and power were understood. He didn't react to our presence, not even when his assistant left his chamber.

Having been born into the modern world, I was used to technology, but demons were grounded in tradition. They liked it old school. They didn't use computers and got used to handwriting all their messages.

Standing in front of him was torturous, waiting to be acknowledged—I really needed a goddamned drink. The tension that filled the room quickly became unbearable. I could tell that Ricky was becoming impatient and felt disrespected that Rodriguez was ignoring us. My nerves jangled through my body; I was desperately trying to breathe normally, but struggled with the anxiety that I felt.

"Finally we are meeting *the* Miss Brodeur, the famous Maxine, the mongrel that caused such turmoil in the royal court twelve months ago," the demon said, lifting his head and resting his eyes on me. He reminded me of a wild lion, with his longish blond hair and brown beard that covered most of his face. He was dressed in a sharp black suit, but his eyes were the most striking feature of his whole appearance. It was difficult not to keep staring at the wide golden pupils that shimmered in the dim light. He must use charms to make himself look more ordinary for his day-today duties around the royal court because his eyes looked inhuman.

An icy shudder crawled over my spine as I shifted my weight to the side, trying to act like I was unaffected by him. I was so glad that I decided to look half decent today. This demon was powerful, linked to Lucifer himself, and he knew my story. He had an advantage over me and that wasn't helping me with my anxiety at all.

"Yep, that's me. You summoned us here for a reason, so please get straight to the point. I have plenty of clients that are waiting for me to get back to their cases," I said, ignoring his comment. This wasn't the time or a place to get into a discussion about my past.

My own energy rolled over my limbs in warning, momentarily weakening my core. I felt him trying to reach out to my demonic soul; he wanted to assess it. Even if he was higher in the faction, it was bad form to reach out like this without permission. Nosey old bastard! He was curious to see what was so special about me, but I had kept my wards intact, preventing him from discovering my secrets. Some demons could read others, but I learnt from a very young age how to keep my mind closed away from anyone's business.

He stared at me intensely for good few moments as if to unnerve me, before he said, "The queen's grandson disappeared late last night. The family is worried, but will not want to involve the police just yet. This needs to be dealt with as swiftly and discreetly as possible," he said, averting his eyes from me to Ricky. "My name is Rodriquez, by the way. I'm the head of Lucifer's faction inside the palace. I have been asked to make sure that our royals are looked after, that there is no interference from our world."

More likely to spy on them, I thought, forcing myself not to snap.

"The queen has a few grandsons. Which one in particular has gone missing?" Ricky asked, sounding inpatient. Arthur was one of the queen's grandsons, but I had a feeling that he was safe and sound. I had no idea why I still cared. He was the cause of all my problems, partly because I was too weak to say no.

"George, the youngest. There are reports that he had been acting out of character over the past couple of weeks, disappearing for long periods of time, causing arguments with his aunt. Some staff reported that he was possibly high on drugs, but I believe that he might have been under the influence of potions or strong elixirs. The Metropolitan Police have sent a detective who is going to work with you on this case. Her Majesty has insisted that you adhere to the old school rules. I'm sure you understand that means we have to be careful not to be exposed."

"It sounds like you have your own agenda. If humans are involved, then why do you need us? Surely your staff or the queen's guard can work with the police, just as well as we can," I pointed out, knowing that humans were restricted by rules and procedures and that they would delay everything. I had to have a free hand. There were plenty of people in the palace that I didn't want to face again. Arthur was one of them.

Rodriquez frowned and pinned me down with his stunning eyes.

"The demons in the palace are tied up with other things. I heard that you're the expert, your reputation has preceded you," Rodriquez explained, sounding irritated, probably because he couldn't read me, my wards were that strong. "Besides, this isn't just an ordinary kidnapping. A very powerful demon is involved…possibly even a few demons. There are some traces of potions, elixirs in Prince George's room. In addition, he was taken when all the guards were in the palace. Some of the staff raised the alarm when traces of his blood were found on the floor this morning."

"Maybe you should call someone else. We are pretty swamped as it is, Mr. Rodriguez, and I would think that the royal family would rather stay away from me. Our recent history is such that we are not on the best of terms last time I checked," I said, as everything was slowly overwhelming me.

That precious secret had been burning my soul day by day. I had vanished from the face of the earth for a good six months, and only Ricky knew where I had been. When I returned back to London, I wasn't the same person. Part of me died, so I used any distraction possible to hide my pain. Mostly I turned my love of cards into a nightly ritual, poker and magical tequila that numbed everything, the excruciating pain that I had to live with from then on.

"No, Miss Brodeur, unfortunately there isn't anyone else that will do. We have to find Prince George quickly, before word in hell spreads. His aunt—Princess Layla—asked specifically for you. Lucifer requires your services, and you must do it discreetly," Rodriguez explained sharply.

He was right, I couldn't say no. I was only a mongrel, and I answered directly to the head of the faction. Ricky was cast out and I couldn't let them summon him back to the underworld. His life was in London, amongst humans. This was the price that I was now paying for screwing up, for believing that I could be happy too.

I chewed my bottom lip nervously, thinking about my options. The problem was that I didn't have many. Ricky seemed pissed off too, probably thinking about other pending cases that we were working on. We both had been cornered and I couldn't risk arguing with Rodriguez. If he wanted to, he could make my life very difficult.

"Fine, we'll need three thousand pounds as a down payment, weekly stipends of an additional thousand pounds to be paid directly into our account and the rest can be settled once we find little Georgie. That's the standard rate. That way we will dedicate all our precious time to this case," I said, certain that we couldn't back away now. The deal was done. Lucifer wanted me to take care of the problem, and we needed to get paid.

Rodriquez's left eye twitched, but he didn't say anything. He simply opened the drawer and then started putting bundles of cash on the table. A moment later I was holding an envelope full of money in my hand. Maybe I wasn't going to get evicted after all.

"If the formalities are settled then let me take you both to George's room. Detective Zachary Quinton has been put in charge of the human investigation. Princess Layla has already spoken with him, so he's aware that he will be working closely with you," Rodriquez explained, getting up. His demonic power filled the room, knocking some air out of my lungs. Ricky was slightly pale. Obviously he felt it too. It was easy to be affected by his domineering energy that stuck to ours like glue. Part of me always wished that I was born a full demon, just so I had more control over what was going on in my life.

"I work alone, Mr. Rodriguez," I said, reminding him that humans were only going to slow this whole process.

"Detective Zachary is one of the best. He cannot be ignored, so you must compromise, Miss Brodeur," Rodriquez stated, and I bit my tongue forcing myself not to come back with some snarky comment. As far as my experience went, the human police were useless. They did very patchy work, using old school methods that didn't work anymore. At least I had contacts, people that I could rely on. I didn't need some arrogant human to follow me around.

Ricky was surprisingly quiet. I could tell he wasn't too keen either on us fully committing to this case, but the money was a motivating factor.

The walk to the other side of the palace was long and exhausting, mainly because every room reminded me about my time with Arthur. The prince's quarters were on the third floor. I didn't need a tour. I had been in George's room a few times before, mainly to check if he was all right. He must have been staying in Buckingham Palace quite a lot lately. I didn't understand why, as he had other apartments around London. This just didn't seem right.

Princess Layla was standing outside the door. She was talking to a tall dark-haired human. She glanced at me, pursed her lips in a thin line and gave me a courtly nod. It was obvious that she hadn't forgotten my illicit affair with her nephew; that ice-cold look reminded me that I wasn't particularly welcome here.

"I'll take you straight to George's room. You can get acquainted with Detective Quinton in a moment. We can't waste any time right now," Rodriquez said when I was ready to stop and speak to the woman that I used to work for.

"That won't be necessary, Bill. Maxine knows the palace like the back of her hand. I'll take it from here," said the voice behind me that I instantly recognised.

Suddenly that tough, harsh Maxine that kicked ass turned into a scared little mouse, a creature that couldn't even turn around to face the man that broke her heart.

Chapter Five

"The devil is not as black as he is painted."
— **Dante Alighieri, The Divine Comedy**

Prince Arthur, the son of tragically dead Princess Catherine had cleaved my heart in two. Our affair was enchanting and intense. I never believed that I could be stupid enough to actually fall for him. Maxine Brodeur, half demon and half human was never planning to commit herself to a relationship that broke her soul. In her code of conduct, she promised herself to never get involved with her clients, but Arthur became an exception.

"Arthur, I've got this. Your aunt asked for Maxine, and she has a lot on her hands. All the evidence needs to be processed thoroughly right away," Rodriquez said, kind of getting between me and the prince. I didn't want to turn around; I wasn't ready to face him after such a long time.

Two years ago I was a different person. I had a life that was full, a job I adored and people whose company I enjoyed. Then Arthur came and used his charms to sweep me off my feet. Two years later and I am the antithesis of that girl.

Right then, the same warmth that I felt when we met for the first time overshadowed the fact that I had a job to do in the palace. Nothing seemed important enough when he was around.

"Actually my aunt wants to have a chat with you, Billy man," Arthur said, more forcefully. "I can deal with Maxine. We have so much to catch up on."

Rodriguez exhaled, looking from me to Arthur, probably calculating if it was wise for him to leave us alone.

"All right, I'll be right back," Rodriquez said, giving me a sharp look that probably meant not to forget that I was here for a reason, not because of the prince.

Ricky was taking notes, probably nosing for some sort of clues. He was in my head too, telling me to take it easy, to calm down. I wasn't listening. All the promises and the wall that I had built up over the past year were razed to the ground the second I heard Arthur's voice.

I took a deep breath and slowly turned around and faced him. My heart stopped functioning. All the people in the background, the voices in my head were insignificant. My human side was compelled to melt, to feel that same warmth around my heart.

For a human, Arthur was exceptionally good looking, tall with a wide jaw and lips that I had acquainted myself with thoroughly on many different occasions. His eyes were pale green, almost grey. His hair was longer than it had been; a dark shade of blond, it had that just-fucked quality to it that made you want to run your fingers through it. I remembered the texture of it in my hands. It looked like he stopped cutting his hair around the time that I stopped working for the royals. At times when I had a chance to use the internet I stalked him online. It was sad really, but somehow this kept me sane during the most miserable time of my life.

I swallowed hard as his eyes took in my appearance. The tiny sparks of my demonic power zoomed between us. The heat rolled over me, igniting the fire in my stomach.

There was no point pretending: I wasn't over him. The past twelve months, the time that had passed meant nothing.

"Hello, Arthur," I said, putting on that strong and confident tone of voice. "Please show me what happened here last night."

I don't even know why I said it. We hadn't seen each other for over a year and I should have at least asked him if he was all right. That awkwardness between two people that used to love each other was still very apparent.

He smiled and winked at me, stepping closer. The door to George's main room was open, but I wasn't able to move. My feet were glued to the wooden floor, heart beating frantically in my chest.

"Your wish is my command, Flower," he whispered, leaning closer, as if no time had passed. That nickname brought back all the intense feelings that we had shared with each other over and over again. When we started spending more time together and our connection became stronger, Arthur gave me a silver ring that was supposed to always remind me of him. The ring wasn't special; he said that he found it in the cemetery when he was visiting his mother. I still wore it—even now I was moving it over my finger, remembering all the days when I felt like I couldn't carry on without him. Arthur said on many occasions that the ring wasn't worth anything, but for me it was the most special gift I'd ever received.

I needed to regain my focus and assess the crime scene. There was no way I was going to focus with him following me around, asking awkward questions about the past twelve months.

Ricky appeared at my side, pulling me away from Arthur.

"A demon was in this room, but I can't detect to which faction it belongs. Some of the blood was already swabbed off the floor and sheets. I will collect what I can." Ricky spoke in a hushed tone, his voice tight.

Arthur was watching us. I had no idea what to expect, but the prince didn't seem angry or resentful. After all, I had just vanished and never said goodbye. I always assumed that he knew why I did it. "Are you all right?"

"Fine, I'll be fine," I answered with a lie.

A familiar enigmatic energy began sliding inside, connecting with the demonic part of my soul. That and the intense wave of lust scorching through my entire body was a very bad combination. Ricky nodded and began moving around, collecting the evidence that we could analyse later.

George's room covered the square footage of a small apartment. The high ceilings gave the room a feeling of grandeur and made it look larger. The old sash windows overlooked the main courtyard outside, and a stream of sunshine flooded into the room. There was a modern kitchen and a bathroom on the other side. A large antique mahogany bed stood in the middle of this majestic space. The bed was rumpled, the sheets were tangled, and all around a burning, acrid smell infused the air. The stench burned the inside of my nostrils and made me slightly dizzy.

I needed to find some physical evidence, a connection to a demon that had taken George.

"How are you, Flower? It's been a year. You disappeared and my heart bled longing for you," Arthur said when I stopped by the bedside cabinet, hoping to take a closer look at the black powder that was spread over the wooden surface. He looked down at my hands. "You're still wearing it. That could only mean that you have been thinking about me."

He was lying to me. He had never tried to find me. I would know if he had. When word in the city was out that I was back, he ignored it.

"I don't imagine it was too painful for you especially since Natalie was there to console you. I congratulate you on your engagement, Your Highness," I snapped back, unable to sound anything but bitter about it, ignoring the painful comment about the ring.

The truth was that Arthur had seduced me. He had gone to a lot of effort to make me his and I kept playing his game, stupidly believing that no one would find out, risking everything for him. His engagement to Natalie Morgan was the final nail in the coffin. Once I found out, I stopped stalking him online, stopped reading stuff about him in the papers. We were done and our affair long forgotten.

He shoved his large hands into his jeans pocket and his enigmatic smile faded. I swear to God, I thought I saw a hint of sadness in his eyes, but no. He couldn't have been torn up by the fact that our affair was history now.

"You know that my hands were tied back then. I searched for you after you left, Flower, but you vanished. No one knew what happened to you. I never meant to—"

"Please stop it. Don't bring up the past. I was asked to come here to investigate George's disappearance. If I knew that you would be here, I never would have agreed to it. We have nothing to discuss. I'm just an ex-employee and you're the future king," I told him, imagining how it would feel to hold him one last time.

Humans were cruel, but love even more so.

I reached out after taking a small plastic bag from my jeans pocket, hoping to gather some evidence, but then Arthur grabbed my wrist. His tight grip twisted and he forced me to look him in the eye. His touch awakened something inside of me and I thought I felt something that I never thought would come alive again. Absolute Love. The longing for the small life that I left behind, that I had to give up.

I felt everything he was feeling at that moment. Sadness, lust, and disappointment that he hadn't fought hard enough for me. He had broken the rules, and I was forced to leave my post.

"Oh, Maxine, Flower... I have missed you so much. The Queen Mother and everyone else...they fucking pushed me into this engagement. We had something, and I had—"

"Found anything yet, Flower?" another voice interrupted. Arthur let go of my hand and I stepped away. A tall, good-looking guy was standing next to us. He must have overheard Arthur call me Flower. I hadn't really had a chance to take a good look at him earlier on when he was talking to Princess Layla.

Now as he was in front of me, I was taken back by his appearance. He was almost as tall as Arthur, with thick black hair that curled over his ears. I suspected that his human mother or father was from the Middle East by his caramel skin and angular features. His deep brown eyes were framed by a row of thick black lashes. His strong jaw was peppered with that sexy day-old stubble that you see on male models, enhancing his good looks, and his mouth, lord have mercy—his mouth was curled up into a sexy smirk displaying his kissable lips to perfection.

I cleared my throat, pretending that I didn't hear his remark and that his face didn't just knock me on my ass.

Arthur narrowed his eyes at the stranger, looking pissed that we had been interrupted.

"As a matter of fact, yeah, I did find something, but we haven't been introduced, so you are who exactly?" I said, ignoring the tingling of heat low in my belly, the warmth that turned me on.

Many people learned of my affair with the future king, but nothing had been leaked to the press, so royals were lucky in that respect. My career, my life, everything would have been over then.

Ricky was watching me from the other side of the room, shaking his head. I was having trouble concealing my emotions and he was reading me very openly.

"Detective Zachary Quinton, and you must be Maxine," he said introducing himself, eyeing me up and down like a predator, with that annoyingly sexy smirk on his face. He was very confident, whip smart and obviously convinced that I was going to slow down his investigation. He wasn't concerned that he interrupted a royal conversation just a moment ago. A delicious unexpected shiver passed over my spine as his eyes rested on my breasts, longer than was appropriate.

"I don't think we have been formally introduced. My na
—"

"His Royal Highness Prince Arthur," Zachary cut him off. He used a sarcastic tone of voice that suggested he wasn't that impressed by the future king that stood right in front of him. Both men shook hands and the tension escalated.

"Arthur is fine. I hate the official titles. I was just updating Maxine on everything that we know happened. She knew George well." Arthur started blabbing, moving closer to me, like he wanted to mark his territory. I didn't know what the hell was going on here. Suddenly I felt like the prize steak, ready to be consumed by two hungry predators.

"I'm sure you were, mate, but I doubt very much that you can help. I want to go over some facts with Miss Brodeur, without interruption if you don't mind," Zachary shot out. My jaw dropped. I couldn't believe he just called a prince "mate," at the same time winking at me. This guy needed to learn some manners.

Arthur narrowed his eyes at him, probably ready to come back with some smart remark, but he hesitated.

"Maxine, find me before you leave. I need to speak to you," he said, only loud enough for me to hear, then muttered, "Detective," to Zachary and walked away. I stood in the same position completely baffled. I had never witnessed anyone speaking that way to Arthur.

On the other hand, Zachary had this domineering, alpha, take charge aura about him. He obviously wanted to come across as someone who wouldn't be intimidated and focused on the job at hand. Maybe that was his thing.

He wore a heavy leather jacket, with dark trousers and cowboy boots. He didn't look like a cop and I was ready to hold all the judgment back, but then he opened his mouth again.

"So you and Prince Charming? How very lovely." He chuckled, curling his lips in a smile. My blood rushed into my ears, and anger rolled over me in a violent way. Okay, so he was a wanker too. It took me only one second to figure it out.

I took a step up towards him, wanting to use my energy to wipe that arrogant smirk off his handsome face.

"Listen to me, Detective, I'm not here to be arm candy and no one is getting into my pants. I was summoned here to investigate the disappearance of Georgie, so I suggest you forget about what you think you may have heard and tell me if you have anything we can go on," I said, standing way too close to him, but at that point I didn't care. I could have come across as intimidating if I wanted to. A wave of his cologne brushed over my nostrils. I liked that musky, very masculine and woody smell.

"Flower, I'm here in my official capacity as a copper. Whatever you do with Prince Charming doesn't concern me. I work best on my own, but this case is unique ... so I've been told, so much so, that it requires a woman's magic touch. That's supposed to be your expertise, Flower."

I was ready to stick my hand between his legs and twist his balls so he would stop testing my patience. I had no idea if anyone was watching us, but right then I was broadcasting very angry and very twisted demonic vibes.

"My name is Maxine, by the way. Rodriquez called me because I'm the best at what I do, so I suggest you to drop that chauvinistic attitude. We are going to have to work together and if you pay attention you may learn something," I told him, not backing down.

He didn't back off like I expected him to, and his proximity felt suddenly intimidating... and somehow hot. Deep down in my stomach I felt something that I thought I would never again experience standing so close to another man.

No, he is just another human with a cocky attitude.

"I work alone and only alone...but I suppose you can tag along," he smirked. "The young prince here was taken against his will. There is evidence of a struggle as seen by the pillows on the floor, the upended books and the water glass on the floor. It's baffling that the intruder managed to pass the guards with the amount of security the palace has. We need to study the CCTV carefully and start interviewing witnesses pronto, Flower."

"We will see about that, arsehole," I muttered, exhaling sharply. I made up my mind. I didn't bloody like Detective Zachary. No— correction—I couldn't even stand being around him for another next minute.

"What was that, Flower?" he asked, when I was walking away.

"Rodriquez has my number. Call me if you're ready to cut the crap and work with me on this case; otherwise don't bother," I replied. "In the meantime, I'll be around here, trying to find George on my own."

I don't know why I had to flip like that, but this guy made my blood boil. There were other humans in the room, and I had to tone it down. My fiery attitude wasn't going to get me far.

Zachary was watching me from the same spot where I left him. I didn't have to glance back to know it. He made me curious and possibly even a little hotter under the collar. Still, his bad boy cop attitude wasn't impressing me.

"What have you got?" I asked, joining Ricky, who was sweeping the sample of what looked like bits of demonic elixir. The demon that took George was most likely a male. Not many female demons knew anything about potions or elixirs. It had always been a male-dominated industry. I liked learning new things, so I'd started reading books filled with potion recipes so I could brew them. It took me years to master a couple that were very challenging, but eventually I was able to prepare a few without anyone else's input.

Ricky looked at me first and then diverted his eyes to Quinton.

"Supernatural charms. The prince was hooked on a few various ones. His blood is filled with it," Ricky stated, looking at the tiny dots of liquid that he managed to put into a flask. "I don't like how that human is looking at you. What the hell did you just tell him?"

"Nothing really, but I should have told him to stay out of our business. It seems he can't play nicely and share his toys." I sighed. "He is our new partner in crime. Detective Zachary Quinton, the arsehole."

Chapter Six

"Love insists the loved loves back"
— **Dante Alighieri**

There was a lot of grey powder sprinkled around George's bed that I didn't recognise and Ricky had found an unknown potion in young Prince George's blood.

Somehow I couldn't believe that the intruder was that sloppy leaving all of this evidence for us to find. Something had happened in this room, and I had a feeling that the whole kidnapping might have been staged, that someone knew that the royals would panic and call the police.

I studied elixir books that weren't available to other demons and mongrels, not on the earth at least. Ricky had quite a collection; some of his titles were stolen from the underworld library. He never told me who owned them, and I didn't ask. It was safer not to possess that kind of knowledge. The energy in George's room was still a mystery to me, but it was something to go on. Zachary kept watching me when I walked around assessing the smells, texture, and obvious signs of any demonic encounter. He didn't try to talk to me again, but he kept that annoying smirk plastered on his face.

There was no time to challenge his ego. I wanted to make sure that I hadn't missed anything. I was obligated to find George. Lucifer's head of the faction was on my back and my movements were limited. The supernatural world wouldn't take too kindly to the fact that I had broken the rules that had been decreed years ago in order to protect humans from the truth.

An hour later Ricky and I had enough to start our investigation. Zachary had disappeared some time ago, and my anxiety shot up reminding me that Arthur wasn't done with me yet. He was most likely waiting for me somewhere by the entrance, and I couldn't allow him to drag me back down the path of destruction, especially in front of his aunt, Rodriguez, and Ricky. They all knew that we had been involved, and they all knew the reason why he came.

I had money now, so this evening I could go out on a bender to put off thinking about all the feelings that had been dredged up today by seeing Arthur. After so many losses, I finally had a chance to win back some of the cash I'd lost, and the cards were on my side. Arthur needed to be wiped out of my memory forever, and if that meant I had to get wasted, then so be it. That was for tonight though, right now I had George's case to work on.

"Miss Brodeur," Rodriquez shouted after me, when we were leaving. "Have you managed to ascertain anything yet?"

For some reason his attitude was making me nervous. There was something odd about the way he carried himself, the way he looked at me. He was using his own abilities to pass through my wards, and that was extremely worrying. Maybe he was put in charge of this post to make sure that I wouldn't screw Arthur a second time around. I had no idea if Lucifer knew about my involvement in royal affairs, but whatever was going on I knew I needed to keep on my toes about this demon.

"Strong, unidentified potion was used to knock George out. We also found grey powder all over his bedside table. We are going back to the office to analyse everything further," I explained. "By the way, I don't think I can work with Quinton. He has his head farther up his own arse than seems humanly possible."

Ricky laughed, and I was annoyed that I let Detective Zachary Quinton get under my skin. There was no way we were going to agree on anything, especially how to take this investigation forward.

"I'm afraid that you have no choice, Miss Brodeur. The royal family wants you to work closely with his division. I have been told that he has exceptional contacts on the streets and he is very skilled … even for a human. He will be in touch. I don't doubt that."

"A skilled human?" I repeated, shaking my head with disbelief. "He is a stubborn chauvinistic idiot that has the manners of a shit-flinging baboon. And whilst were are talking about this, let's clear something up—if the royal household hadn't fired me in the first place, George would still be here."

I was too angry to wait for Rodriquez's response, so I started walking away. Rodriguez could easily ruin me, but right now he needed my help, so I could afford to be a little disrespectful. Ricky caught up with me a second later. Anger and fury had boiled my blood. I had to get it together.

"What the fuck was that about, Max?"

"Nothing. You know that I like working alone," I replied, walking faster than it was necessary.

"What did Arthur want?"

We were only a couple of meters away from the exit, and I wanted to tell Ricky everything, but first I needed to get out of here as quickly as possible.

"Max … hey, Max wait."

"Crap, crap, crap," I said, as the wave of emotions forced me to stop. Ricky cursed loudly when Arthur caught up with us, just by the exit. The prince obviously had trouble understanding that I didn't want to see him, that we had nothing to talk about.

I took a deep breath, dismissing the storm of emotions that suddenly pumped through me, and turned around.

"Yes, Your Highness? What do you want?"

He smiled, and those cute dimples appeared on his cheeks. Why did breakups always have to be so difficult?

"Can we talk alone?" he asked, leaning in like he wanted to kiss me. No... no, he wouldn't dare, not in front of all his guards and my business partner. "How are you doing Ricky?"

"Ecstatic, Your Highness, but I'm afraid we're in a hurry. We have pressing matters to attend to," Ricky stated quite clearly, using his own demonic energy to convince the prince to leave me alone. I couldn't let Arthur drag me back just because I couldn't keep my hands off him.

Arthur quite clearly still wanted me. I read his emotions, his desires. He didn't understand that after a year I was still picking myself up, still trying to forget about the pain that I experienced back then.

"Ricky, give it a rest would you? This shit is starting to irritate me. Max, you owe me a conversation. This will be quick. Please, Flower?" he pleaded, using that tone of voice that cracked my stone cold heart. It wasn't just the way he was looking at me, it was also the fact that the strong fiery pull was still there. The lust brushed my face, neck and cleavage. I had turned my life upside down for him, almost traded my existence for something that I could never share with anyone.

"Fine, two minutes," I snapped, pissed off with myself and the fact that Ricky's magic wasn't influencing Arthur like it was supposed to. I glanced back at Ricky, who looked frustrated. The guards were watching us, some of them were mongrels. There weren't many in the palace, but a few that I had trained remained.

Arthur walked to the side, hiding us behind the pillar. My pulse was thrumming so quickly that I couldn't control it anymore. I had never been lucky with the opposite sex. I always prioritised my work over everything else, but when I started working for the royals things changed.

Arthur's blond hair fell sexily over his eyes as he glanced around, moving closer to me. The heat of his human body was doing something to my demonic scarred heart.

"What do you want, Arthur?" I asked, blocking the images of us making out in the dark corridors. This wasn't one of those moments.

"You know that I don't love, Natalie. After you left I was a wreck. I couldn't believe that you would disappear on me like that. I have been trying to forget you, to move on, but it's impossible," he was saying, using his left hand to caress my cheek. His touch was healing, calming, and I wanted to close my eyes and jump back to the past. I would have made different choices back then.

Then my mind assaulted me with images of the time after we were caught. I remembered the moment when I stood in front of the Queen Mother confessing to my sins, to the fact that I seduced her grandson. She wasn't the only one there. His aunt, uncle and George. They all looked at me with disgust and repulsion. It was the most humiliating moment in my life. It didn't matter then that he had promised to love me for as long as we lived—our special ring was worthless. I had betrayed the royals and the members of the public, by putting the future king in danger.

"No. You have no right to say anything to me. You did nothing to save me, to defend me. What happened then closed the door on us. It's in the past. So stay away or I swear to God I'll hurt you," I snapped, stepping away from him and inhaling the crisp air.

Ricky must have felt my anger and resentment. A calming delicate breeze ruffled my hair and I was praying that no one had been listening in. From early on I learned that the palace was filled with secrets and people that would do anything to keep spying on me and the prince.

At the time when everything exploded I'd wished that I had died or had been sent back to hell. I was willing to do anything to save myself from the pain I felt back then.

Arthur's pupils dilated, but he didn't back away. He was broadcasting his feelings so openly, while my heart was wounded, broken and torn. Despite everything, he still loved me. I hated knowing that he wanted to bring me to his chest and ease the pain, I hated the fact that I could feel his torn emotions. That's why I was cursed, that's why it was so difficult for me to move on.

"Maxine, please. I made a mistake, a terrible mistake. You mean everything to me. We don't have to be so distant. I'll break the engagement. Now that you're back," he continued saying, pleading with his heart for me to give him another chance. "The hospital, the children at the ward. Does this mean nothing to you?"

Tears forced their way to my eyes. I couldn't believe that he was playing on my emotions like that. The memories were still too raw. Arthur became a patron of a children's hospital in London a couple of years ago.

When I was responsible for his safety I used to accompany him there with other guards. Over the period of time, I became involved, playing and bonding with kids that no one visited. Arthur became attached to a few. He donated extraordinary amounts of money to the whole ward and he felt personally responsible to visit them.

The hospital, the room filled with lonely kids connected us, and while I was there I was able to sympathise with the pain that some of the children experienced—since I'd grown up with the same kind of loneliness. It was our moment that no one could take away, the moment when I felt truly fulfilled and happy. After I vanished from London to deal with the consequences of my action, those memories of the hospital impacted my future decisions. I left my hiding place torn apart, knowing that I was possibly crushing yet another life.

I was ready to shake my head and walk away, but Arthur grabbed my face so lovingly that I instantly changed my mind. Then he kissed me, his hand cradling my neck.

In that moment I lost all the resolve I had built up over the past twelve months. His lips reminded me of everything that was ever lost to me, the passion, the longing for his soul. My body turned into an inferno, blood rushing through my veins wildly. When his tongue connected with mine, I moaned, as our love exploded. I had the tendency of over-broadcasting my demonic powers whenever Arthur was around. Sometimes my emotions affect humans too. They felt everything, the ecstasy that scorched between us, the heat of the moment. His touch was liberating and I instantly wanted more.

The kiss didn't last long and it didn't matter how good it felt. I forced myself to remember the betrayal and the pain so I was strong enough to break it, to push him off me.

"No. You have no right, Your Highness. What had been between us is done. You did nothing, said nothing, so now you have no right." I raised my voice, not caring for the world that every security guard, even the demonic ones had just heard me.

I forced Arthur to obey me, to stay where he was, and then marched back to Ricky, who looked disturbed.

"Let's move now," I barked, and he only nodded. I knew he wanted to tell me a lot of things, but there was no time. I didn't look back, but I knew that Arthur stood behind the pillar, unable to move, and he was fighting with himself to go after me again.

When we were outside, I took a few deep breaths, shoving my thoughts and desire to the back of my mind. That damn hot kiss made me lose my head, but only for a moment. That was why I was so reluctant to show up in the palace, to get involved with royal affairs again.

It was hard to admit, but I missed the thrill that the job used to give me, and I damn well missed Arthur.

These days I was living day-to-day, killing creatures that escaped from the underworld, solving murders, and finding missing people. Most of the time I didn't know how I managed to survive for so long, nearly drinking myself to death. This wasn't the life that I signed up for, but somehow I couldn't change it.

"Are you all right, Maxine?" Ricky asked, most likely for the fourth time since I got in his car and I still hadn't responded. We were leaving the royals behind. I arched my head up, trying to forget about the pain that kept rippling through me, that I was so suddenly aware of.

"I'll be fine, once you drop me off at The Broken Shoe. It's five o'clock, after all," I said, wondering if George was still alive. For some reason I had a feeling that we were gonna have to move heaven and earth to find him.

"No bloody way. We have a job to do and a new human in the office. You're not losing all our money tonight just because you made out with Arthur again," Ricky snarled, driving faster and scaring the shit out of me. "Maxine, you're a fucking badass motherfucker, not some pathetic heartbroken mongrel, crying over someone that you could never have. "

I hated being in the car. It was one of my many phobias and Ricky was driving way too fast.

"How do you know what he was trying to do?" I asked, dejected.

"It was obvious. Your emotions were running wild. That spoiled brat's got some nerve cornering you like that. The quicker we solve this freaking case, the quicker you will get away from that royal bullshit. Right now we need to get back to the office so you can forget about what happened." When the car stopped at the traffic light Ricky looked back at me and added, "Although, Arthur wasn't the only one in that room that got slightly hot under the collar."

I looked away, pretending that I didn't know what Ricky was talking about. The silence was supposed to indicate that I had no opinion on Ricky's crazy theories.

"That hot shot detective was eyeing you from the moment you showed up. He was aroused, Maxine. I felt it."

"Zachary Quinton is just a chauvinistic, arrogant prick," I muttered, thinking about the way I felt when he was treating me like I was beneath him.

"Like I said, Arthur wasn't the only person that got a bit of lust up. That bad boy detective got your engine running too, Maxine," Ricky added, sounding very amused all of a sudden.

I turned away from him and exhaled sharply, knowing that he was absolutely right. Detective Zachary Quinton was an arsehole, but for some reason I was attracted to him.

Chapter Seven

"O human race, born to fly upward, wherefore at a little wind dost thou so fall?"
— **Dante Alighieri, The Divine Comedy**

I was in a terrible mood when we got back to the office after being stuck in traffic for two long hours. Apparently the roads were blocked due to an accident. The first thing we saw was Emma pacing around looking stressed. She exhaled with relief when she saw us.

This day couldn't get any worse and I really needed a strong drink.

"Thank God you're both here," she said. "Some guy was here. He didn't want to leave. I was so scared that he would murder me and throw my body into a river."

"No one does that these days, hon, trust me," I said.

"What guy? Did he say what he wanted?" Ricky asked, using his abilities yet again to calm her down. He really needed to stop messing with her head. We couldn't afford to check her into a mental institution just yet, and she had already seen too much.

In certain circumstances humans knew about the other world, but only if their minds were strong enough to handle that kind of news. Things like that were mostly handled by Watchers. A demon that wanted to reveal our world to a human needed to apply for a certain relief licence. If the head of the faction said no during an official hearing and the human already knew everything, the Watchers would erase the human's memories and the demon in question was punished. I really didn't want to be in that position with Emma.

"He didn't tell me his name or what he wanted other than you, Maxine. He was tall, dark, looked like a gangster. He said he wanted to speak to you. He promised to come back," she explained, waving herself with the stack of paper. "He was very handsome with these dark penetrating eyes."

She muttered the last sentence in a hushed tone when Ricky had turned around. Emma didn't waste much time when we were out. She was no slouch. There was a stack of files on the floor, and the first drawer of the filing cabinet was organised. She had gotten through a couple of years of a mess already. Ricky had mentioned that some members of a faction would come down to audit us to see if we were following the protocols of operating in the human world discreetly. At least some aspects of our business had been taken care of for now.

"What else did he say?" I asked, wondering if this was about my debts. One of the demons had given me a few months to sort the cash out, but he never dared to come over to my place of work before. I needed to make tonight count and finally win my fair share back. It'd been too long.

Emma smoothed her blond hair and fixed her human eyes on me.

"He said that it was good to finally put a face to the picture and he will see you tonight to discuss the case," she stated, sounding confused.

I slammed my palm over my desk, feeling like my blood pressure was already up.

"Quinton was here," I snarled, when Ricky looked at me, putting all the evidence on the table at the back. "How did he find us so quickly? We were supposed to be invisible to, you know, *other people*?"

"I have no idea, Maxine, and we haven't got time to dwell on it. We need to find the person responsible for the mess in the palace. We don't want Rodriquez on our backs … especially not now," Ricky muttered, probably not wanting to use the word "demon" in front of Emma.

"You take care of the evidence and call me if you find something. I need to go out, talk to my old circles, find out if anyone has heard anything," I announced, ready to disappear.

I really needed a drink to get my thoughts back in order. Ricky knew that I didn't like spending too much time in the office. I was most effective when I was out on the streets. I wasn't expecting Quinton to show up in here. He obviously didn't like wasting time. Besides, if George was still in the city, then I had to hurry up and track him down. Royals represented pure human genes. Many mongrels believed that drinking their blood would make them more powerful than a fully developed demon. I didn't think this theory was accurate, but demons liked spreading untrue rumours. The bottom line was that every member of the royal family was a hundred percent human and there was nothing special about them.

"Max, I think you should stay here tonight. We have a lot to go through. Besides, Quinton may come back," Ricky said, sounding more and more like my nonexistent mother. "I had dinner plans with a lady friend, but it looks like I might have to cancel."

"Ricky, I'm not going out playing. You know that I hate sitting at a desk. Let me see what I can find out in Hackney and report to you later on or tomorrow, all right?"

I don't know why I was lying to him. We both knew that at the end of the night he could find me in The Broken Shoe. Maybe it was easier that way, pretending that I was being conscientious and responsible. He smoothed his jaw, looking from me to Emma.

"Fine, but leave half of the cash in the safe," he said, slightly less hostile.

Okay, I got it, he didn't trust me and he had good reasons for it. I had proven to him on a number of occasions that I was a lousy partner. I marched back to my office and took half of the money out. We had a small safe secured with charms at the back. Things were different two years ago. We had an understanding. Ricky ran the agency and I did what I wanted. That was before I fucked it all up and nearly bankrupted the whole business.

Maybe, sober for once, I should go back home to see Mrs. Patel and pay the rent. She had tried calling me a couple of times already, but I didn't have a chance to return any of her calls. Mainly because I didn't know what I was going to say to her.

Once I hit the tequila I couldn't control myself, didn't know when to stop. It was easy to admit to all of it now, but when it came to my poker I loved the thrill of the unknown. I never knew what would happen in the next round, if I was going to get good cards or not. Either way, the game helped me to think of things other than my past.

Emma had cleaned my office too and left a pink notebook on the desk, with a thank you note. I could tell her emotions were unsettled and that she wasn't certain if she was cut out for this position. We couldn't keep messing with her thoughts and we could apply for a licence once we presented our case to the head of the faction. She was strong enough to take the truth, to know that humans weren't the only creatures living on earth.

I spent the next half an hour going through some of our ancient texts, hoping to find something on that strange grey powder, but I couldn't focus much on the text. Ricky had locked himself away in his room, so I slipped away after an hour, telling Emma not to expect me until tomorrow. Most of the time I was a night owl. Mornings were tough, and I'd never gotten up earlier than ten a.m., even when I worked for the royals.

Outside, I headed straight to the underground. Ricky loved his Mercedes, but I preferred to use my legs or public transport. But it was hard to block out human emotions, especially when I was surrounded by crowds of people. From a very young age I kept hearing things that were depressing and sad. Humans had never-ending problems, issues that they constantly worried about. Sometimes it was exhausting to coexist in this world, but I had to blend in somehow.

On the tube, I mercifully found an empty seat and closed my eyes, settling in for the journey. I gave myself permission to spend this time to think about my day and how it felt seeing Arthur, which led me to remember everything I'd tried to forget. Concentrating on my past, I shut down the multiple voices in my head.

It was my first time in Buckingham Palace and I was bloody nervous. I didn't know what to expect. I had worked in security since I was eighteen years old, protecting rich kids and important demons that escaped from the underworld.

Now I was stepping into a completely different world. Graham, one of my clients who owned half of the banks in the city, had sat me down one day and proposed a deal. He thought that I was wasting my time working in commercial security, that I was talented enough to do something much more ambitious.

I felt kind of burned-out anyway, spending many years working myself to death, waiting for something else but never knowing what. I was bored, ready to leave London behind and start somewhere else.

Graham had heard that the royal family needed a new head of security and he had promised to send my resume to his contact in the palace. I had to be interviewed like anyone else, and get ready to go through millions of security checks and present my medical records. It was standard procedure, but I was up for a challenge and kind of excited.

The security guard by the gate had kept me waiting half an hour, and when I was eventually let through, the thrill of excitement shot over my spine. The whole place was amazing, and I couldn't stop *wondering if I would adjust to this new role. Graham had to make several phone calls and I was going to owe him big time, but I knew that working for the royals was the opportunity of a lifetime.*

Some human in a tight white shirt made me wait outside a long twenty minutes, before a tall demon called me inside his office. There was no one else apart from me, and once I got inside my nerves started slowly paralysing me.

A member of Beelzebub's faction was sitting in front of a large antique desk. He was young, very young, probably in his early twenties. These days nothing shocked me anymore, and I knew that despite his appearance he was most likely very powerful.

"Have a seat, Miss Brodeur. My name is Edward Johnson and I'll be conducting the interview today," he stated, then smoothed his tie. He had short brown hair, wore designer glasses and a very expensive suit. My CV was in front of him. I recognised the font that I changed a couple of days ago. "Tell me, why do you think that an ordinary mongrel like you should be put in charge of royal security?"

I shifted on the chair, feeling attacked. That little fucker had some balls treating me like I was beneath him, but I needed to remember that this wasn't just a job, but a huge step up the ladder. He most likely wanted to see if I was going to lose my temper.

"I have six years of experience working in commercial security. I have a black belt in karate and a grand master belt in Tae kwon do. My demonic abilities are fully developed. I have protected demons, rich

kids, and managed the entire security staff of one of the biggest clubs in London. Taking care of the security staff of the royal family will be hard, but I'm ready to take on the challenge," I said, knowing that all of this was on my resume, that my achievements weren't overall impressive.

"I get it, but this job comes with many different responsibilities. Your main focus will be on Prince Arthur and he is going to make your life difficult. So far he has fired three excellent candidates, simply because he didn't like them. He doesn't care about the protocol or the press. The faction wants to protect him from 'our' world and dangerous demonic influences. We have tried to pair him up to humans, but so far none of them have worked out. It's time to change that."

Wow, so maybe it was a good thing that I was half demon after all. Apparently the head of the faction needed to have full control over the future king. That was interesting and kind of worrying.

"I'm ready for a change. I have spent way too much time on the streets. I have been waiting for this kind of opportunity for years," I stated.

"Good. I like you, Maxine. Your resume is very impressive and your background doesn't bring any major concerns. The future king should be satisfied. You also need to remember that you will be managing other guards, men that haven't worked with women before. Do you think that would be a problem?"

I started laughing then. He was right: I was only twenty-four, and most of the time men didn't appreciate getting orders from a woman. I had worked hard to build up a reputation for myself. Men weren't a problem for me as long as they treated me with respect and as an equal.

"No, it's never a problem," I told him. "I have worked as the only woman with men for over six years."

I didn't know if the interview was going okay or not. The demon in front of me kept asking me other questions, left the office for several minutes, and then an hour later he was giving me a tour of the palace.

All this baffled me, but I assumed that it was just a standard procedure. Deep down I was very disturbed that a demonic faction was working for the British monarchs. Presumably Lucifer didn't like giving humans a free hand, and he needed to keep an eye on one of the most important families in Britain.

"Graham was right. You're going to do well in here," Johnson stated after he introduced me to most of the security staff. I blinked rapidly, wondering if I had heard him correctly.

I was just about to ask him what he meant, when we both heard loud whistling, and a moment later a tall, blond guy appeared greeting us with the most delicious smile.

I left the tube station at Hackney Downs, remembering how extremely excited I'd been at being presented with that kind of opportunity. I was going to be a head of security and I would protect Prince Arthur himself. Two years ago this sounded like an unbelievable break for me. I was so naive then, badass but very naive. I had no idea that this job would ruin me forever.

I was fresh and young then, maybe a little inexperienced in certain aspects of my life, but ready to take on any challenge. My life seemed simple, and it was—until the moment I met the Prince himself.

Edward and I both turned around at the sound of the whistle. The man that approached us was definitely human with a lot of charisma. His emotions were calm and he seemed relaxed. He was dressed in jogging shorts and a white T-shirt.

"Ah, there is Arthur himself. Let me introduce you," Johnson said, smiling tightly. My jaw dropped. I had never paid attention to the royal family, so back then I didn't know what the future king really looked like. I wasn't expecting to meet the prince himself.

"Ed, what a surprise. I've just been out on a run," Arthur said, eyeing me with curiosity. He was sweating a lot, but I liked his messy look, the curiosity and gleam in his green eyes. This man was trouble.

"Your Highness, allow me to present you with your new Head of Security," Johnson said, throwing me completely off guard. "This is

Maxine Brodeur. I was planning to make the proper introduction tomorrow, but since you're here—"

"Maxine, pleasure to meet you," the future king said, getting to me faster than I expected and extending his hand for a shake.

He was much taller than me, his shoulders broad and muscular. For the first time in my short life I was speechless, staring at this man in total amazement. He smiled wider, and then suddenly a wave of desire flipped over my stomach. When our hands touched, I felt the zing of electricity that suddenly ran between us, connecting my demonic soul with his human emotions.

"It's good to meet you too, Your Highness," I managed to say, unable to take my eyes off that man, that human. We were staring at each other for a good few seconds, still holding each other's hands, and with every passing moment my heart beat faster.

I should have known back then on that corridor that my life was never going to be the same again. I should have predicted that meeting the prince would break my ordered life to pieces, that after a year in the royal court I would have to hide in order to protect the secret that could never be revealed.

Chapter Eight

"Into the eternal darkness, into fire and into ice. "
— **Dante Alighieri, The Divine Comedy**

I didn't go straight to The Broken Shoe. For a good half hour I walked around contemplating what to do. Soon the craving for a drink won and I entered a different pub near Hackney an hour later. The Broken Shoe was hidden between the small alleys in Brixton, and it served a different caliber of customers than the one I had chosen tonight. I was hoping to speak to one of the guards from the palace. He had a tendency to hang around here a while back. The pub was called Six Bells and there was a mixed crowd in here: a few drunk humans, mongrels and a demon who sat at the back with a pint of beer.

Matt was one of the guards that I personally hired almost two years ago. I knew that he liked drinking in Six Bells, mostly because that was where he met his ex-wife; he was a nostalgic kind of guy. Also he was the best person to talk to about the night that George disappeared. He knew most of the staff and I hoped that even after a year not much had changed.

I glanced around, slightly apprehensive to see two Watchers sitting in the corner and eyeing the crowd in front of them. Their presence was worrying. They only appeared if a creature from the underworld was on the loose, or if a human accidentally had learned the truth about the demonic world. They also dealt with demons that didn't stick to the rules. This wasn't good, but I shook my head, wanting to ease my paranoia. The bottom line was that they weren't here for me, well, hopefully not. I was getting paid to track George down and I was certain that I would have something after talking to Matt. The past was the past, and there was no point dwelling on it.

"Hey, Mattie boy, how are you this fine cold evening?" I asked, situating myself next to him. He looked at me, releasing a huge smile, and then scanned me up and down with his deep brown human eyes.

"And who the devil let you in here? The one and only Maxine Brodeur," he said. "I had a feeling you might show up soon enough."

"Well, you know me. I don't like wasting time," I replied and nodded to the barman to pour me some tequila. I knew that this wasn't what I was normally used to, but the spirit was enough to shush my troubling memories. "You're the perfect person to tell me everything that I need to know."

Matt was lean and built up like he had taken too many steroids. He had deep circles around his eyes, a square jaw, and he was completely bald. He was divorced with teenage kids, and after many years of failed relationships, he still hoped to find the right woman.

"I didn't see anything last night, if that's what you're after," he said, getting straight to the point, and then he took a generous gulp of beer.

"That's disappointing. I was hoping that you might have actually seen at least something?" I asked.

"No, we all got the call around midnight, but by that time the young prince was already gone. I've got no idea how the intruder even got into the palace in the first place.

There were guards stationed almost everywhere and no slackers sneaking off."

I looked at the gold liquid in front of me, aware that it'd been two nights since I had tasted it.

"To be honest, I don't really want to talk about last night. Tell me who George has been hanging around with lately. Any questionable individuals?" I pressed, and swallowed my first shot of tequila. The alcohol burned my throat, but the sensation afterwards felt damn good. *Mama was home, baby.*

"The usual—spoiled kids from Chelsea. There had been some arguments with Princess Layla too. George wanted her to stay out of his business. You know, the same domestic stuff as usual."

I asked the barman to pour me another shot of tequila, and once the alcohol started burning through my veins, I began relaxing. The stress from earlier on faded and my torn heart became stone cold again. Hell, drinking was my escape from agonising pain, from feeling like the loneliest person on this planet.

"There is more though, isn't there, Matt? It's not just the usual problems at home," I said, pretty much aware that he knew more than he wanted to say. Whoever the hell was in charge of the security these days must have been keeping all the guards on a short leash. The rules were simple: all the staff that worked for the royal family had to sign a nondisclosure agreement, but Matt owed me more than a few favours. I didn't want to bring this up right away, but I needed to know what young George had been up to. Something wasn't sitting right.

Matt finished his pint. I had all night, and I wasn't planning to leave empty-handed.

"I heard that the prince had been seen in the company of some redheaded chick. An older one. Boys were saying that he didn't want to leave her side," Matt said, barely in a whisper. "I don't know how much of this is true, but they were seen kissing and holding hands."

"A redheaded woman? Had anyone seen her with him before" I questioned, thinking that maybe George had lost his head for some cougar. There was nothing strange or suspicious about that. Who knew? Maybe the whole kidnapping was staged.

"Well, I know for sure that she wasn't one of his usual girls. None of the guards had ever actually seen her, but his friends had talked about her a lot. Besides, young Prince George was a prick. He wasn't like Arthur," Matt said. "If you know what I mean"

I nearly spat the alcohol all over the bar. That name made me feel suddenly very angry. I needed to get out of here and get back to Brixton with this new lead. The woman must have meant something to George or maybe I was reading too much into it. Women were always likely to become less moralistic, shall we say, when they were around young royal bachelors. There was also a possibility that she was a demon, trying to take advantage of our young prince.

"Okay, that's pretty much all that I needed to know, unless there is something else you want to tell me?" I asked, hopping off the stool. The alcohol was working, finally untangling my emotional downfall.

"He is missing you, Maxine. Natalie doesn't fill the hole in his heart that you burned with yours," Matt said unexpectedly when I turned around, ready to leave. I stopped abruptly. My stomach rolled with warmth, but I pushed it away. Matt was just a guard, but he obviously knew more about royal affairs than I expected.

"What are you talking about?" I asked, my voice small.

"A year ago when you left, he went into total meltdown trying to find you. Got himself into a lot of trouble with the police and guards."

I wasn't expecting to feel so shitty about my whole life when I entered this bar. Arthur didn't give a fuck and Matt was lying.

"Well, it looks like he sorted himself out quickly enough," I muttered.

"Barely. He still talks about you to other guards, to staff. He hasn't forgotten about you, Max," Matt added, but I couldn't listen to this anymore.

I glanced back at him and then walked away until I breathed in the cold February air. My chest heaved with pain reliving the worst day of my life. Matt had no idea what he was talking about. Arthur's grandmother made sure that we would stay apart, and he had never tried to find me.

I needed to get out of Hackney and pour a whole bottle of magical tequila down my throat to kill the guilt. I was forced to leave something behind, something that connected me to Arthur on a whole new level. I looked down on the ring that he had given me and shook my head, forcing the tears away, wishing that I could tell him the truth about my disappearance. Wishing that this pain would go away for at least a moment.

It took me another hour to get back to Brixton, and by the time I was walking through the streets of my neighbourhood it was ten o'clock at night. I hated living in such a sprawling city. The public transport was a nightmare, and on top of my ridiculously high rent, I wasn't even covering all the bills.

I turned right, losing myself in the narrow alley that eventually would take me to The Broken Shoe, my favourite local pub. My stomach was burning, and I had to play tonight, before I did something really stupid. Deep inside there was an unbearable craving for the most precious thing that I was forced to leave behind, someone that had changed my life forever.

That night I was sloppy, and my thoughts were racing, so I didn't even notice that I had been followed. A grown human male was creeping behind me, and by the time I felt him it was too late. Seconds later I was slammed against the brick wall by a large, muscular man that wore a strong, kind of familiar aftershave. I'd had a couple of drinks a while back, but no one had ever surprised me in such an unexpected and violent way.

"Hi, Flower. I think such a delicate creature like you shouldn't be walking around the streets alone ... so late at night," said the voice that I vaguely recognised. There was something wrong with my excellent eyesight tonight, but it only took me couple of seconds to figure out who had managed to successfully corner me in the darkness.

"You have two seconds to get the fuck away from me before I smash your face against this brick wall," I snarled, and felt his heat rising fast. Yeah, I just let Detective Zachary Quinton manhandle me. On top of that, he was getting turned on by the fact that I was pissed and not in my usual control. My vision suddenly sharpened. He was staring at me with those dark eyes filled with curiosity, roving over my parted lips. We only met for what—two seconds earlier on, but I really wanted to kick his arse right about now.

"Shut up and listen to what I have to say. I don't like when someone interferes in my business and you're doing exactly that right now, so I want you to quit. The streets of

London are ugly, filled with too many unexpected surprises," he said, moving his face closer, almost brushing his lips over mine.

My stomach made a flip, as the unfamiliar wave of lust heated up between my legs, causing havoc in my torn demonic soul. There was no way that Zachary was simply just an arrogant son of a bitch, an ordinary human. His energy was pushing his thoughts into my mind, and he narrowed his eyes like he wanted to see past the anger and fury. I didn't have time to get overwhelmed. I wasn't going to just stand there and listen to his threats.

His grip was powerful, but it was dark and he couldn't have predicted my next move even if he was a demon after all. I twisted my right leg around his and then tossed him over to the side while he lost his balance for a split second, but he didn't fall down. My inner strength gave me some advantage and I lifted my leg, smashing my boot into his pretty face, throwing him on his back several meters away. For a human, well, I had to agree, he was strong, but he must have forgotten that I had spent six years mastering my fighting skills. I wasn't just some girl that he could mess around with.

I was sitting on him before he had a chance to take another breath, and I was bloody surprised to feel the hard bulge in his crotch. It looked like Zachary was not only an arsehole, but a sexual deviant too.

"Now, you listen to me, Detective. You obviously have no idea who I am and what I'm capable of, but you can shove your demands where the sun doesn't shine. I'm on this case whether you like it or not, and trust me, it will take a lot more than your muscles to get rid of me," I said, wondering why I was so pumped up with positive vibes and why the hell I liked sitting on top of him. Crap, this was supposed to be straightforward.

He smiled at me, and I frowned. There must have been something really wrong with my focus that night, because he shifted underneath me. He used his knee to kick my exposed back, easily punching the air out of my lungs. I was slammed back on the ground, seeing stars, possibly for the first time in my life.

My energy surged down through my aching body, letting me know that this human was going to kick my arse. For some reason, I was losing my usual focus and before I even realised, he was sitting on top of me. The heat that exploded between us was sudden and fiery. When I finally managed to open my eyes, his face was inches away from mine.

"I asked nicely; now I'm telling you to stay out of my way, Flower. You might be tough and shit, but there are things in this world that you don't understand," he growled, staring at me with his gorgeous eyes. His attitude really pissed me off and I wondered why our paths hadn't crossed before. Zachary obviously thought he was some tough motherfucker with a badge and a big gun.

I started laughing, partly because I wanted to cover my explosive feelings, and partly because he was broadcasting his desire for me loud and clear. My reaction made him angry and he narrowed his eyes at me in confusion.

"You really chose the wrong person to mess around with, and the most stubborn one. Get off me before I do something that I regret later," I whispered, not even knowing why I was so adamant about proving my point. It was hard to judge what his deal was and why he was so determined to keep me away from his investigation.

"Flower, you wouldn't hurt me even if you wanted to," he said, lowering his eyes to my cleavage. That short moment of distraction gave me an advantage. I extended my arm and then punched him as hard as I could. Okay, maybe this wasn't ladylike, but I was done with his bullshit.

When I was standing on my feet, looking down at the hero detective who was now bleeding, it kind of hit me that I never felt better, sort of like myself from two years ago, before Arthur shattered me. It was refreshing.

"How about we make a deal? Down the road there is a pub where I like playing poker. You beat me and this case is yours, but if I win we will work together on this case. What you say, Detective? Have we got a deal?"

He glared at me, touching his bloody nose, and I smiled widely when I heard him mutter, "Deal."

It was going to be a fun evening ahead.

Chapter Nine

"Lost are we, and are only so far punished,
That without hope we live on in desire."
— **Dante Alighieri, The Divine Comedy**

I must remember to keep some money for rent.

I must remem …

"All right. Let's get this over with before I have to arrest you for assault." He interrupted my train of thought, getting off the wet ground. I glanced back at him, kind of curious and angry at the same time. I sensed something deeper in him, a softer side of his domineering personality that I was yet to discover.

"The pub is just around the corner, and for someone who claims to know these streets I'm surprised that you're being so ridiculously impatient," I said, rolling my eyes.

"Flower, just spare me the small talk," he snapped back. I had no idea why he was pissed off. He was the one that attacked me. Maybe he was used to getting things done his way. So far he only revealed that he wasn't happy working alongside a woman.

We were both silent until we entered the old, secluded pub on the street corner. From any other person's point of view, the building didn't look particularly appealing, but I had built a relationship with the owner over the years. There were a few humans at the back, clutching their hands around their pint glasses and glaring at us from the distance.

Paul, the barman, nodded to me, not looking too pleased with the customer that strolled in after me. Yep, it was odd to see a stranger in here. Paul used to be a Watcher, part of an angelic faction that guards the gates of hell. One night he left his post unattended, lured by a beautiful demon from the Asmodeus faction. Several hours later, he was found naked, stripped of all his abilities, and then cast out from his post, sadly never gaining his powers back.

"The usual, Maxine?" Paul asked, placing the glass in front of me and eyeing Zach with his demonic eyes.

"Yeah, three shots straight away. I have a game to play," I said.

"Vodka for me," Zach muttered, then grabbed a napkin and wiped the blood underneath his nose. Once Paul poured our drinks, I didn't need to wait for an invitation. The shots in front of me were special; Paul spiked it with a dash of elixir that he made especially for me. The combination of demonic magic, rare herbs and blood of a poisoned dragon meant to heal a broken heart. At least I kept telling myself that. I was an addict, but after finishing a bottle, I could still function the next day. That was part of the problem.

Zach ordered a beer chaser and went to sit down at the table by the window.

"Why on earth are you hanging out with a human, Max? He's a cop too, you know," Paul asked, leaning over the bar and eyeing me intensely. I took a new deck of cards from my pocket and started shuffling them around. "And what happened to his face?"

"Unfortunately for me, he's been assigned to a case that I've also taken on, and we had a disagreement," I blurted out, aware that Zach hadn't taken his eyes off me. A shudder tickled over my spine. I could still feel the heat from earlier in my veins, but I had yet to determine if it was the way Zach was looking at me or my conflicted emotions.

Paul acted like a human, and most of the time he didn't like bringing up his past. After so many years in London, he put on a bit of weight, and he had aged. His soul was still young, but for a human he looked like he was in his mid-forties.

"I sense trouble, Max. That man is filled with resentment. He holds a grudge. Maybe he lost someone or he killed an innocent human," Paul said, looking over my shoulder. "And he desires you, but he doesn't want to admit to it."

My jaw dropped slightly as I stared at Paul, wondering why the hell he had to make me uncomfortable. My opinion about Zach's feeling was divided: I wasn't too sure if he wanted me or if he was acting that way in order to get rid of me. Paul was right—Zach's soul had been tormented by some kind of tragedy from the past. Maybe that was the reason he seemed so detached.

"Well, that's too bad. I have to work with him either way; otherwise I'll be in trouble with the underworld. Young Prince George went missing late last night. He might be in the underworld, who knows? Or with a demon. Things are kind of complicated. If you hear anything you'll let me know, right?"

Paul's green eyes twinkled with confusion. He just didn't care for royals at all.

"I'll keep an ear out for you." He nodded back to Zach "I don't like him, Maxine. I'd stay away. He is trouble and we both know that you don't deal with trouble well," Paul muttered, putting the bottle of tequila on the bar along with a clean shot glass.

I grabbed it, ignoring his comment. He started sounding more and more like Ricky. Why did everyone feel the need to give me advice on how to live my life, advice that I didn't want or need?

"Thanks, Paul, but I'll be all right. Just keep the drinks coming," I said with a wink. I grabbed the whole bottle and went back to the table where Zach was sitting. I threw the stack of cards right in front of him.

"So let me get this straight. I win and you will move aside, you won't interfere in my investigation?" Zach asked when I poured some tequila into my glass. His eyes were lidded and travelling over the tight old T-shirt that I wore today—eyes so different from Arthur's. Fuck, I needed to stop thinking about him.

"Let's play, unless you want to lay out your whole life story for me?" I said, winding him up a little too much. His eyes twitched like he noticed something in the bottle. Paul was careful with his elixirs, mixing shit like that with human spirits was dangerous.

"I'm certain, Flower, that your life story is much more interesting than mine," he said, smiling. Sweet mercy; that smile bloomed burning heat in my stomach, and he had cute dimples on each side of his gorgeous jaw when he did eventually laugh. Exactly like Arthur's. *This was pathetic.* I really needed to stop comparing him to Arthur. Maybe I should have gotten rid of the ring, then I wouldn't have to be assaulted with painful memories whenever I thought about the opposite sex.

"Too bad you aren't going to hear about it tonight," I snapped back, shuffling the cards around for a bit and then placing two in front of me and two in front of him. It was much more fun playing with a few more people, but we had business to settle, and I needed a quick win to get in the mood. The luck and cards were on my side tonight. I knew it.

After playing five cards upside down in the middle of the table, the familiar excitement filled my veins. My pulse spiked, and for some reason the cards were making me more receptive to my surroundings.

Zach checked his cards and then lifted his thick eyelashes at me. Drinking magical tequila had its advantages; after a couple of shots I was less receptive to human emotions, able to block all feeling and worries. This was supposed to be a fair game. My partner was a human, who most likely had no experience in playing poker. I needed to go easy on him.

"Hmm... I think you will tell me everything about you, Maxine, all your deepest secrets and sexual desires," he said, and sent me a flirtatious wink. I lifted my left eyebrow, tossing my long hair behind me. He could dream about me telling him anything at all.

We started with a pre-flop round. I put some cash on the table, so he knew that I was taking this game seriously. It was clear from the very beginning that Zach wasn't the amateur I assumed just a second ago. With that mad gleam in his eyes, he made a few moves. We both put the same amount on the table, and after betting and holding, the flop round had started. I kept topping up my glass, for some reason enjoying the company of the human that sat in front of me. It was much more fun not to know what he was feeling when his dark eyes were looking through me.

In a flop round, Zach bet more than I expected. Over two hundred pounds, and if I wanted to stay in the game, I needed to match it. The magical alcohol loosened me up, and the sudden rush of heat made my eyes heavy. Zach had of course noticed.

"You're flustered, Maxine," he pointed out. "So I assume this is what you like doing in your spare time. Playing poker and drinking?"

"Everyone has their hobbies, Detective," I sang, twisting a lock of my hair around my finger, as we moved to the turn round.

He kept his cards to himself. The warmth that surrounded me was welcome and comforting. Arthur didn't matter anymore; he was just a distant memory.

"True. Sex is an excellent hobby. I enjoy it tremendously," he chuckled as I placed one more community card on the table. I couldn't remember the last time I had fucked someone just for the sake of it. My relationships with men were complicated after my affair with Arthur, and I was too scared to mix pleasure with business again.

We both went with our turns. In this round my cards weren't that good, but I kept betting, hoping that might change in the final straw. When the last community card was placed on the table, I checked mine and raised the money. Zachary did exactly the same, watching me like a hawk.

He seemed confident that he won, throwing a few lousy compliments. I knew it was all a game to him.

"So I'm safe to assume that you're not seeing anyone at the moment?" he asked.

"Why? Because I spend most of my time in the pub, drinking and playing cards?"

"No, I think you're still hung up on Prince Charming," he pointed out. I narrowed my eyes at him.

"You know nothing about me. And what happened between me and the prince is none of your business," I snapped, angry that Arthur couldn't keep his mouth shut when we were standing in a room full of people.

Zach checked his cards again, but I couldn't read anything from his expression.

"How about we add something more to this deal? If I win this, then you agree to go out with me?"

That was it. We both needed to reveal our cards and I was certain that he was a sour loser, bluffing all the way till the end. He also had a nerve asking me out.

"No, I don't date. My work is my life. Besides, a deal is a deal. I don't recall there were any extras included," I said, suddenly wondering what he would look like naked, pressed over my body in my tiny flat. I hadn't gotten laid in a very long time, and the waves of energy reminded me that this was my first real opportunity to change that.

"We both could have some fun, Flower, and I could help you stop thinking about Prince Charming for a night," he whispered, leaning towards me. In that dim light, he seemed even hotter, and a violent bolt of warmth ripped through my system. My addiction was supposed to calm me down tonight, not push me into the arms of a human who wasn't looking for anything other than a night of fun.

My demonic side was completely shut down, but on the other hand, sex without expectations could help me forget about a crappy day like today.

"All right, fine. Let's play this game," I muttered, smiling flirtatiously. "But what will I get if I win?"

He looked down on his cards, then back to me, lowering his thick eyelashes to my cleavage. I wasn't very developed in that department, but Zach seemed hung up on that spot, more so than other men. Maybe he liked a woman with small tits.

"I'll tell you something about me, something that no one knows," he said—and then revealed his cards.

He had a full house, and I was kind of shocked staring down at his card sequence. I bit my lip, wondering if he liked playing poker on a regular basis or if it was just one off. He was obviously experienced, but right at that moment I wanted him to think that I had been bluffing, that he had me.

"Deal," I blurted out and then revealed my cards, presenting him a flush. His face dropped, his anger whisked through the air. He stared at my cards for several moments, like he couldn't believe that I won, that I had better cards.

"Well, cowboy, you better get ready to work with me, because I can tell you, I ain't going anywhere. And you'll be telling me all your dirty secrets." I chuckled, happy with the results.

Zachary muttered something under his breath, got up, and went to the bar. I bet he needed to have a very strong drink to numb the fact that a girl had just kicked his arse for the second time tonight. I started sweeping all the money to my side, feeling awesome. There was still half of a bottle of tequila left, and I was considering finishing it when someone sat in Zach's chair.

"Hey, Maxine. Fancy teaming up with the old crew. I see you have some money. Wanna double it?" Devlin asked, grinning at me. He was one of the regulars, the guy that lost me half of the down payment for a shabby loft apartment in London, if I ever considered getting on the property ladder. Behind him was Lea, a mongrel, and twins that were part of Mammon's faction. They must have sensed that I was in the mood for more.

"Yeah, why not? Let's do this," I said, not even considering going home. When the four of us were seated around the table, Zachary came and sat behind me, looking much calmer than before. He didn't say anything, just sat behind and kept watching the game.

I thought that I was in control, that this was finally my night, but by around two o'clock in the morning the magical bottle of tequila was empty and I was down at least a grand or more. I kind of lost count after the first couple of hundred. Nothing went how I planned; my good cards from my game with Zachary didn't follow through. The alcohol clouded my head and the strong vibrations of lust in my system became distracting.

The twins had won again, costing me my rent. Zachary hadn't moved. He kept going to the bar and drinking slowly, not taking his eyes off me.

Soon the whole place was empty, the last customer had settled the bill with Paul, and I was sitting in the same spot, completely wasted and pissed off with my own luck tonight.

"Max, that's it. I'm closing and you should go home," Paul said, taking the empty bottle of tequila.

He helped me get up and walked me to the door. I had no idea what happened to Zachary. He must have left too, pissed off that things didn't go to plan tonight. The world around me started spinning, and I needed to get to my bed. I was walking home slowly alone and once again I thought that someone was following me. The streets of Brixton were quiet, and when I turned around a few times I saw Zach keeping a fair amount of distance from me. I wasn't the kind of girl that needed to be rescued, but he kept following me all the way back to my street. Maybe he was worried that I wouldn't get home safely.

"Now, now, Flower, let's put you to bed. You won, so we're stuck together anyway," he whispered, helping me open the door when I failed miserably trying to remain in a standing position. When I nearly passed out in the corridor, he lifted me and carried me upstairs.

That night, even in my kind of state, I knew I was going to share my secrets with him.

Chapter Ten

"Midway upon the journey of our life, I found myself within a forest dark, for the straightforward pathway had been lost."
— Dante Alighieri, The Divine Comedy

"Cosy. I had no idea that you lived in such a shithole, Maxine. I thought that being the prince's mistress came with some advantages," Zachary mocked me, looking around my crappy flat. I lifted my hand, tapping my finger into my head as a reminder for tomorrow. I needed to call my landlady and ask her to fix the damn lights. Also the glass in the window was cracked. Some teenager from the council estate threw a stone when I told him to shut his dirty human mouth. Yes, my flat was a real rathole.

My head was spinning and I hated myself that I couldn't stop telling Paul to pour me more. All my rent money was gone. I was broke again.

"What the hell do you want? I'm fine now. You can leave. I don't … need a babysitter, mister," I slurred, stumbling on my feet and falling down on the sofa. My eyes wouldn't stay open. Zach sat beside me a moment later. He took my hand and touched my cheek with his cold finger.

"You do that often? Lose all your money in an obscure bar in a poker game?" he asked, forcing my chin up so I couldn't look away. He was composed, and very calm, almost not the same man that I met in the palace. I had the tendency of oversharing details of my life with strangers when I was drunk. That night when he was sitting next to me, I wanted to tell him all about the bad time in my life, about Arthur too. Tonight was one of those times when I needed a shoulder to cry on.

"I never used to do that, but getting wasted seems like a good idea lately," I told him. "Have you got a cigarette?"

He nodded, pulled the packet of Marlboro Lights from his jacket pocket, and gave me one. I had a lighter somewhere in the flat, but he used matches to light one for me. At this rate I was going to kill myself; even the magic wouldn't save me.

"What's on your mind, beautiful?" he asked, lighting one for himself.

"I want to tell you about that one night when everything changed," I said, wondering if this was really such a good idea. Zach didn't care, but he was still in the flat, sitting next to me. He obviously wanted to listen.

"Tell me."

"I had a close call a couple of years ago. I nearly died, so I decided to change everything. First it was the job and the fact that I had to rely on others to survive," I mumbled, sounding like one pathetic mongrel. I spent too many years keeping the truth away from everyone around me. My mother used to say that it was better to let all the worries out in the open. Now I had a man next to me that wanted to get to know me, so I needed to keep going. "I used to work as a waitress in an Italian restaurant in the city. That one night I was the last one out, closing the back doors, when some stranger attacked me. He came out of nowhere, took all the money and left me there to bleed to death."

Zachary was silent, staring down at me with a wary, slightly stunned expression on his face. I arched my head back, resting for a few long moments. The magic was rummaging through my system urging me to keep talking about the crappy past. The voices in my head were loud and nagging. Sometimes I had problems with shutting them down.

"I woke up in the hospital several days later, not remembering anything at all. I had a cracked skull, broken wrists, my kidneys were punctured. It took me weeks to recover, to actually want to keep on living. The police closed the investigation pretty quickly. They didn't have any leads or witnesses from that night. After that I didn't go back to that old life. I started hanging around in bars and nightclubs, playing cards for money. Some nice people taught me how to survive on the streets on my own. It was easier to act like I had nothing to lose. Soon I was making more money than I could ever imagine, so I took some self-defence classes, trained in martial arts too. People started to respect me, and I began getting some contract work in security. My life was suddenly good. I had friends, cash in my pocket and I was finally free. Every day I was making progress, making connections with the people in the business, and pushing myself during training. I started protecting wealthy clients, looking after rich kids, managing clubs and restaurants. Things were good and then the opportunity in Buckingham Palace came around. Nothing was ever the same after that.

I closed my eyes, dragging the nicotine from the cigarette deep into my lungs. I had never liked smoking. It was a nasty habit. Zach lifted himself off the sofa and went to the kitchen. I heard him pacing around the room for a bit. The night wasn't meant to end like this. He wasn't supposed to see me in such a state, telling him all about my shitty life.

"That's why you were brought in to this case, because of your previous connection to royal family?" he asked, staring at me from the other side of the room. The royals —that word was cut out of my vocabulary when I got fired and had to hide in the rabbit hole.

"Yes, mainly, but the truth is that a demon took Prince Georgie. You're a human, so you won't understand any of it," I said, forgetting who I was talking to. Zachary needed to hear the harsh truth. "Besides, I needed the cash to pay my overdue rent. I thought that tonight I would be responsible, that I could stay away from cards, but then you showed up."

He shook his head, and drew on a cigarette for longer than he supposed to. We were sitting in the darkness, but his eyes were focused on my face. I was too wasted to connect with his emotions, although I still wanted to know if he was ready to screw me.

"Are you blaming me for getting drunk, Flower, and losing your rent money?" he asked with that hard, accusing tone of voice. And that nickname—he knew it drove me mad, but he still kept using it.

"I'll blame you when I get evicted." I laughed. "Either way, I lost all the money tonight. Don't worry, it's not the first time and most certainly not the last."

It was time for me to go to sleep, to drift away from the problems of this fucked up world. Detective Zachary Quinton was a dream. All this time I was talking to myself, telling the other Maxine the real story.

"Sleep, Flower, because tomorrow is going to be a new day and I'll be there to mess with you all over again," the voice whispered in my ear, and I smiled falling asleep.

***

My eyes were stuck together when I woke up in the late morning the next day. I lifted my second pillow and pressed it over my face, hoping not to hear the emergency services just outside my window. I lived next to the busy street and it sounded like there was an accident outside. People were shouting and horns were going off. I felt like someone was hitting me with a hammer, as the blurry memories from last night slowly came back to me. After a few moments I realised that someone was banging at my door, loudly, too bloody loudly for such an early hour.

When I scrambled off my bed I was naked. My clothes were folded on the floor next to the chair, and the clock on the wall was showing eleven clock in the morning. I didn't remember undressing. What the hell happened here?

"Crap, I'm late again. Ricky is gonna kill me," I muttered to myself, throwing a T-shirt on and putting on clean underwear. I was surprised to find that I had any. I hadn't done the laundry for over a decade.

"I'm coming," I shouted as the person outside started banging harder. When I finally unlocked it, I saw that it was my landlady, Mrs. Patel. For a split second I wished that I had woken up somewhere else this morning, maybe even in someone else's body. She was here for the overdue rent and as far as I remember I had lost all my available cash last night.

"Maxine, sorry to knock on your door this morning, but you're three days late with your rent," she said, eyeing my naked thighs and most likely smelling the stale alcohol on my breath. I could mess with her head, make her forget that I actually owe her any money, but that was against my own rules. I hated tampering with human minds. Besides I couldn't get away with not paying my rent. This was morally wrong. "I can't wait any longer, and you should set up a standing order so I don't have to come to your door every month."

Mrs. Patel was a thirty-something Indian-born woman who was married to a property developer, Mr. Patel. Apparently they both started investing money in the housing market in the nineties, and these days they had quite a portfolio. I was forced to move in to this shitty flat a year ago, and Mrs. Patel was kind enough to wait for her security deposit.

"Mrs. Patel, can you give me a minute? I've had a horrendous night," I said, rubbing my eyes and stepping into the morning light outside, as it was dark in my hallway. I felt terrible, worse than normally and my head was hurting badly.

"My God, what happened to your face? Are you all right?" she asked, probably assuming that I was ill. I lifted my hand and touched my cheek. It bloody hurt, so I turned swiftly around and ran back to my apartment. I put the light on in the hallway and I looked at my own reflection in the mirror. My left cheek was swollen and I had a freaking black eye. Memories flooded my mind. I remembered fighting with Zach, and it looked like the bastard hit me.

Then, something else caught my attention: a white envelope that was placed on the dresser, next to my hairbrush. When I opened it I thought that I was dreaming. The envelope was full of cash.

I took eight hundred from the stash when you went to the toilet. You said that you were late with rent.

Now who should be your Prince Charming?

Z.

I re-read that damn note a few times, suddenly remembering everything from the night before. I was the last customer in The Broken Shoe, and Paul had sent me on my way. Zachary must have followed me back to my flat. I was completely wasted, and I couldn't remember why I let him in the first place.

"Maxine, are you all right?" I heard Mrs. Patel on the threshold. It was the exact amount that I needed for rent. Zachary must have taken some cash out that I won and kept it away, most likely predicting that I wasn't done blowing it all off after I outplayed him.

He couldn't have known that I would be that stupid, that I'd lose all my money and get so wasted I couldn't get home on my own. Well, it looked like I had misjudged him. I brushed my hair away from my face and headed back to Mrs. Patel, partly relieved and partly worried that I owed him a favour.

"Here you go. Everything should be inside," I said, handing her the cash. There was no one else I could have asked for a loan, so technically Zachary had saved my skin. That meant that I could stay in my shitty flat for another month.

Mrs. Patel counted the money, and after convincing herself that everything was okay, she smiled with relief. I couldn't remember when I told Zach that I hadn't paid my rent. I didn't know anything about him, but it seemed that from today onwards we were going to spend some time together.

"Good, I'm glad, but please set up a standing order as soon as possible. It will save us both a lot of hassle in the future," she told me. "And take care of yourself, Maxine. Maybe speak to someone. This shouldn't be happening to you, dear."

I forced out a smile. She needed to know that I wasn't a victim of domestic violence, that last night I simply had a playful fight with a hot cop.

"Thanks, Mrs. Patel, but this was just an unfortunate misunderstanding. I'm really fine," I mumbled, deciding to spare her that story. She gave me a faint smile, muttered something else and then she was on her way. I shut the door and locked it, hoping to get back to sleep.

On the other hand it would be a good idea to show up in the office on time for once and act like a responsible adult. Ricky must have extracted the potion from George's blood by now, possibly linking someone within a demonic faction to this whole kidnapping.

There was no point dwelling on last night. I got drunk, Zach saved my skin, and I had to thank him—that was the end of story.

Within a half hour, I put some clothes on, brushed my messy hair and left the flat, feeling tired, achy and very pissed off with myself. People were staring at me when I was in the tube station, possibly because I looked like someone had beat me up. On top of that I was very much hungover.

By the time I walked into the office, it was just after one o'clock.

"Maxine, I'm so glad that you're here. Ricky went out. He was called about another case."

Another case, what on earth was she talking about? Ricky didn't see any clients without me, but then maybe this had something to do with the evidence that we had found last night.

"Did he say anything else?" I asked, checking the mail.

"He said, well… he was kind of rude," she said shyly, looking at me with those big blue eyes.

"Just tell me. I can take it," I said. Humans, they appeared to be so fragile, always worried about other people.

"Oh my God! What happened to your face?" she asked, like she just noticed my black eye.

I placed my hands on her arms and said, "It's nothing, Emma, just focus. What did Ricky say?"

"For you not to fuck anything up before he came back. There's some information about a man in his drawer that he wanted you to look at," she rambled, looking anxiously at my black eye. Ricky must have worked really hard last night when I was getting wasted in the bar. There were some notes inside his cabinet, telling me that the demon that took George was part of Lucifer's faction.

"Maxine, can I ask you something?"

Emma followed me back to Ricky's room. She looked uncomfortable, like she wanted to tell me something, but was afraid to be rejected.

"What it is, Emma?" I asked, trying to be patient, trying to act like I was a good boss.

"Well, it's my daughter's birthday party this weekend and I was wondering if you would like to come. There will be mostly other mothers, but you have done so much for me already and I would love to have you there."

I glanced back at her, knowing that she was waiting for me to answer. Right at that moment, I was ready to forget I was running a business, that I was half demon and a weak soul. The pain inside my chest stung me hard, reminding me about the last twelve months, reminding me what exactly I had left behind.

"I didn't know you had a daughter," I pointed out, sounding odd, feeling vulnerable. Her face brightened instantly, like a bulb in a dark room, and my soul darkened. Some snippets of her memories were slowly coming back to me.

"Yes, she is five and she invited all her friends from school. We would love to have you there." She said beaming, clapping enthusiastically. I scratched my head, trying to push that deep, burning guilt away, knowing that I could have taken a different path a couple of months ago.

Emma looked happy, delighted, and I wanted to be like her, normal for once.

"All right, I'll come over. Leave the address and the time on my desk." I forced out the words before my brain could process what I agreed to. Emma jumped again and then hugged me. I was stiff like a wooden board. This was weird.

"Amaze balls, can't wait. This will be awesome."

Chapter Eleven

"In His will, our peace."
— **Dante Alighieri**

Ricky had left pretty good notes, and after triple-checking everything, I had a clear idea where I needed to head next. George could have been poisoned and smuggled out of the palace through the staff quarters. I still had no theory what exactly had happened that night, but I wanted to find the woman that Matt had spoken about. I needed to get back to the palace and question a couple of people that I had missed the day before.

Instead of taking the tube to the palace, I headed to the south side of the city. Zachary worked at the police station in Epsom and after our agreement I had to talk to him about my next course of action, without revealing too much. Part of me wanted to stay away from him, but the other part needed to thank him for saving my arse. My gut feeling told me that George was still in the city, but most likely not for very long. The royals were the key, but the problem was that all of them (apart from Arthur) hated my freaking guts.

Rubbing my achy thighs in the tube, I was listening to a mother that was telling off one of her twins for smearing chocolate over his brother's face. Deep down this woman wished that she could leave them in the tube. Yeah, everyone somehow had dark marks on their souls.

The crowds of people on the streets in early afternoon had put me off going out in the middle of the day, but at least it wasn't raining. This case was my priority, and I didn't want any unexpected visitors from hell looking into my background. Some mongrels with developed abilities like mine were summoned down below regardless of their role in society. Lucifer liked picking out half demons with exceptional abilities, and I had to stay away from hell as far as this was physically possible. The freedom in the underworld was limited; that's why many demons were willing to try a new life on the outside.

It took me a while to find the police station in Epsom. There was part of me that believed that Zach wanted to use me for something. He had his own dark secrets.

As soon as I entered the red brick building, I knew that I could never truly call myself human. Tequila emphasised the emotions that humans were broadcasting. I felt extreme anger, pain and resentment. There were many people in the building filled with troubled thoughts. Zachary was inside too. I had spent enough time last night with him to recognise his fiery attitude somewhere on the third floor. Sometimes I connected with strangers, still not understanding that odd side of my supernatural abilities. My father, whoever he was, must have been a very powerful demon.

I walked straight to the cop who sat at the front desk. Once I cleared my throat, he looked up and automatically frowned. He didn't like my colourful hair and the fact that I had a black eye. He believed that I could still be saved if I pray to God for forgiveness. Yeah, I was most definitely in the wrong side of the city.

"Hey, I'm looking Detective Quinton," I said, ignoring his judgmental look.

"Have you got an appointment?" he asked. "Are you from the press?"

Wow, paranoid much?

"We are on a case together and I need to speak to him urgently," I explained, not entirely happy that I had to have an appointment just to see Zach. Humans were awkward, and sometimes difficult for no apparent reason. I hated wasting my precious time and this guy obviously judged me from the start.

"Are you from another division?" he questioned.

"No, I run a private detective agency. Detective Quinton and I have been assigned to a new case. Can you just do me a favour and tell him that I need to speak to him pronto?" I pressed, more hostile, losing my patience. He didn't look amused or even impressed.

"He's busy. It might be a while," he replied, not even bothering to inform Zach that I was waiting downstairs.

I forced myself not to compel him to give me a pass upstairs. The hangover was hitting me hard this afternoon and I still had to head to Buckingham Palace. I didn't want to get drunk tonight again. I had no more available cash and Ricky would kill me, knowing that I was wasting time.

I waved my thanks and decided to wait for a bit, hoping that Zach would eventually show up. I found the bathroom after getting bored of waiting outside. There were a few female cops talking, some obviously in a hurry. I splashed some water over my face, wondering if I could sneak upstairs somehow and stop wasting time waiting around. I was just about to leave when I overheard a conversation between two police officers. One of them was inside the last cubical, and the other was washing her hands.

"Apparently Zach came in late today and had a massive argument with Dean," said the dark-haired one. I didn't want it to look obvious that I was eavesdropping, so I entered the free cubical next to the last one.

"Really? Zach is always in such a bad mood. The other day he nearly beat someone up on the street over some voodoo crap. I wonder why they haven't suspended him yet," pointed out the other woman, who was in the cubical next to mine. It seemed that Zach was well known at the station, obviously from his reputation as a stellar personality. All of a sudden I didn't want to leave. If I was going to work with this guy, I wanted to get to know him a little better.

"I don't know, but apparently the superintendent had his guts full of complaints. Zach believes in all sorts of supernatural rubbish. He is super hot, but too eccentric. Apparently he is trying to find something odd in every bloody case that he lays his hands on these days," said the woman who was now washing her hands in the sink.

Humans weren't aware of the other world, so it wasn't a surprise that both of these women believed Zach was simply odd. The Watchers had made sure that every human was protected from the real truth, but every mongrel out there knew that sometimes rules were made to be broken. There had been many unexplained cases on the streets of London that many cops didn't want to touch.

"He was normal before, you know… before this thing with his partner."

Okay, now I needed to know what "this thing" with his partner meant.

"I don't know, maybe. That's terrible what happened to Cora. She died at such a young age. Quinton had never believed in her suicide, you know," said the one that was right opposite me. Hell, Ricky had been right. And Paul.

Zachary was carrying a grudge over his dead partner. I should have let him win and solve this case on my own.

"Zach thinks that she didn't commit suicide, that some kind of dark forces were involved. He hasn't been the same since. I don't know, but the pathologist was convinced that it was a suicide, that no third party was involved."

There was a long moment of silence, as the woman in the cubical next to me was digesting all the information slowly. I had my answer now: Zach had lost his partner a while back. Of course I didn't know all the details, but it was safe to assume that he hadn't gotten over it yet.

"Right, you mean he thinks that there is some other world beyond this one," the other one laughed.

"Yes, something like that. He might have lost his mind," the one next to me added. A moment later I flushed the toilet and left like I was just some random girl done with her business.

Zachary believed in the other world, and there was possibly a good reason for it. Some demon had already tampered with his mind or he was simply just paranoid. I didn't quite believe in the second option. These days demons were unpredictable.

I left half an hour later, not getting anywhere with the cop at the front desk. Maybe last night was a mistake. I shouldn't have shared with Zach intimidate details about my past. He was obviously sensitive to things that weren't easily explained. His problems shouldn't really worry me, but I knew that in the near future I had to stop blabbing about my life to anyone who was willing to listen. Working alongside a human who believed in supernatural stuff could slow down the progression of the case. If the missing royal was kidnapped by another demon, then Lucifer's reputation would be in tatters.

I was hoping that the guy at the desk would tell Zach that I had been around, so I expected him to get in touch with me later on. It took me another hour to reach Buckingham Palace. I was pleased to see that security was tighter than normal and the guard at the front of desk made me wait for ages before I was eventually let through. Deep down I was hoping that Arthur was out gallivanting somewhere else with Natalie, so I didn't have to deal with him today.

"Ahh, Miss Brodeur, I presume that you have a reason to be here again?"

I turned around, not even making it a few steps into the main corridor. Rodriguez must have gotten the call that I was in the palace.

"My business partner has managed to extract an elixir from the samples found of George's blood. We are certain that the demon that took George belongs to a higher faction—Lucifer's," I said, getting straight to the point. I bet this wasn't what Rodriquez wanted to hear, but he needed to face the truth.

Rodriguez stroked his beard, grabbed me by the elbow and moved us aside, like he was afraid that someone was planning to listen in. Of course, the news was unexpected. That could only mean that someone within the faction was conspiring against Lucifer himself.

"A demon part of Lucifer's faction? Impossible. The prince never associates himself with any demons," Rodriquez snarled, looking alarmed. The royals were protected and, after me, no other demon apart from Rodriquez was allowed anywhere near them.

"Yes, sir, my business partner triple-checked everything. That's why I need full access to the prince's staff to assess if anything was missed the night in question. I also found out that the prince had been seen with redheaded, older woman outside the palace. Maybe this is nothing, but you would know who that might be?"

Rodriquez's eyes narrowed even further, and a vein in his neck began thumping faster. No one ever dared to rebel against the hierarchy in hell and now there was a demon on the loose—that had Prince George. This whole thing stunk like someone was looking to start an uprising.

"Of course, I will inform the guards to give you full access. Make sure you keep this to yourself. The Dark Lord wants this matter to be resolved as soon as possible. On top of that the Queen Mother is thinking about appealing to the press, and we can't afford the risk of panic in the nation," Rodriquez hissed, exhaling sharply.

He was right; things were tight and time wasn't on my side. I bet the other factions didn't know that the Queen's grandson was missing. There was only one master of the underworld, but I had heard rumours that some Watchers expected to see a change. Apparently not everyone was happy downstairs and, if there was going to be an uprising in hell, then mongrels like me were going to be used as a shield. Yeah, none of this was good.

"I shall, but right now I need to go," I said, letting him know that he was wasting my time.

"Use the back entrance. There is a meeting on the upper floor. I'll make all staff available to you should they need to be questioned again," Rodriquez said. "By the way, what happened to Detective Quinton?"

As soon as Rodriguez mentioned Zach's name, a fresh wave of heat shot over the nape of my neck. I didn't understand that new reaction. The guy was a still stranger to me.

"He's around. We made a deal last night to work together," I explained, faking a smile. "I'm planning to give him a full report later on."

"Good, I'm glad to hear it. Time is of the essence, Miss Brodeur, and I hope to hear good news soon," he said, turned around and then headed in the opposite direction.

My hangover reminded me that I had to get on with my task, so I used the back corridors to walk to the main kitchen. I still had friends amongst the staff. Not many of them were privy to what happened to me twelve months ago. Arthur was forced to cut whatever contact he had with me. I was relieved from my post within an hour. I never had a chance to say goodbye to anyone that I worked closely with, so I wasn't sure how some of the staff would react seeing me now. After all, I was an outsider now, asking them uncomfortable questions about their bosses.

It took me fifteen minutes to get from one wing to the other. Now and again, I had to stop as the heated memories blurred my vision, spiking my anxiety and increasing my heartbeat. Arthur was an impetuous man; he used to drag me to all of the secret rooms, away from guards, staff and other people, so we could be alone. I needed to keep the whole affair in the past, but right now I was reliving every second of it. My love for him burned deep inside me, and I couldn't get away, even after twelve months of hell.

"Hello, are you lost, little girl?"

An unfamiliar voice startled me when I walked through one of the back staff rooms. A woman appeared suddenly right in front of me. Her face was hidden in the shadow, and I couldn't read her emotions. I nearly tripped, but kept my balance. There was something odd about her ambiance. She was either a demon or something much worse.

Chapter Twelve

"Because your question searches for deep meaning,
I shall explain in simple words"
— Dante Alighieri, Inferno

Her long, silky hair was wavy, the colour of chestnut. She wore a long, fitted silky green dress. Whoever she was, she couldn't have been part of the royal staff. I wondered if I had ever met her before, but my mind was totally blank. As far as I knew, she was a stranger.

"No, I'm fine. I'm heading to the kitchen," I said, kind of wanting to tell her to stay out of my business. "And you are?"

She lifted her lips in a smile, but there was something disturbing in a way she expressed her joy. Her eyes were sharp and focused. My own energy danced across my neck, as I was trying to read into her emotions. Every human was unique, and everyone reacted differently when I was close, but I was always able to read humans, without exception.

"Alexis Frasier. I'm a close friend of Princess Layla," she stated with a sophisticated, icy tone of voice. "I don't think that Lord Chamberlain would appreciate seeing you running around their palace without proper identification."

I forced myself not to roll my eyes. She obviously wanted me to think that she was someone important, but I really didn't give a damn. Princess Layla had never mentioned her and as an ex-head of security I knew everyone in the palace.

"I'm working with Rodriguez, and I don't have time to chat, if you'll exc—"

"Oh, so you're the private investigator that is looking into the disappearance of young Prince George?" She cut me off, moving even closer. I was taken back by the way she changed her tune so suddenly. She had very green alluring eyes, and I kept thinking that I had seen her somewhere before. I had been drinking tequila for so long that I had problems with remembering certain people or events from the past. Maybe it was time to stop drinking this shit.

"Maybe I am, but right now I really have to go," I muttered, ready to leave, but she grabbed my elbow, and a spark of electricity shot down to my abdomen. I looked down at her hand, wondering what the hell her problem was. I didn't like to be touched.

"Wait, please excuse me, but I'm curious. Layla is my good friend and she's very worried. Have you got any leads? The prince had been difficult lately. His aunt did suspect drugs at first, but I thought that it was something completely different," she said, and released me. Good, because I was ready to slap her.

I sighed and relaxed slightly.

"Evidence has been found that suggested a possible link to drugs. Apparently the prince was seen with a much older woman, someone from outside the palace. I'm looking into this a bit further," I said. I felt like she almost forced this confession out of my mouth. This wasn't right. I normally wouldn't share information about a crime case. Maybe she was a demon after all and was concealing her true nature from me.

She arched her left eyebrow, smiling widely. I needed to shut my mouth fast. I don't know what was going on with me.

"And you must know this because you were close to the other prince, right?" she asked, innocently, like she didn't mean anything by it. A mad gleam started dancing in her eyes. She knew, she must have; otherwise, why would she bring something like that up? The bitch.

"I used to protect him, so there was no doubt that we were close," I replied, feeling suddenly uncomfortable. It was clear that this woman wanted to know juicy details of my encounter with Arthur.

"I believe that it was more than just protection. You were caught with him in one of the confer … oh, don't mind me. I know more than you think," she said, burning me with her intense gaze. Anger rippled through my system and I was ready to wipe that stupid smile off her face. Alexis had no business asking about my past. It looked like way too many people knew about me and Arthur.

"What the hell is your problem? Who are you?" I repeated, not able to bite my lip any longer.

"I have no problem, Maxine. I'm just a friend that wants to give you friendly advice. Continue with your investigation, but keep your claws away from the prince," she said, firmly and forcefully. An odd draft of cold air passed over my neck. I felt another person nearby, a demon, but I was too distracted to care. This woman obviously wanted something from me.

"Or what? Are you threatening me?" I asked, having enough of being pushed around. Friend of the princess or not, I didn't give a crap anymore.

"No, Maxine, it's something for you to remember. The prince has his future laid out for him and he's focused on his new fiancée. I gently suggest you to stay away from him; otherwise, the consequences might be severe. This is coming from the higher end," she told me, smoothing her long dress, creeping me even more with an aura that I didn't understand.

I was ready to snap, but the voice of reason told me to let it go. I quickly turned around and walked out of the room, heading towards the kitchen. My pulse was speeding, thoughts racing. Royals knew that Arthur was a player and we had always been discreet. There was something not quite right about Alexis Frasier, but I couldn't put my finger on what it was exactly. She appeared to be a human, not a demon, and if she was such a good friend of Layla's, then why was I only meeting her now?

Shaking with anger and trying to find the answers to some of my own questions, I bumped into the head chef, Laticia, in the kitchen. She threw herself at me and didn't let go. I held it together, pushing the discomfort from earlier on away. It felt almost nostalgic to stand in the kitchen. In the past I had spent quite a lot of time in here, chatting to Laticia about anything and everything. I missed the palace, and I never actually realised before now just how much.

Laticia and a couple of other members of the staff had never seen the prince with the redheaded woman. Apparently he had been acting up lately. He was angry and aggressive towards his whole family. Laticia confirmed that he hadn't been eating much, and a few times she had seen him with a bottle of odd liquid. This was some kind of progress, but I still had no idea with what kind of demon I was dealing.

Two hours later I was leaving the palace through the main courtyard, glad that I didn't stumble upon Arthur again. My heart was beating hard in my chest, and the softer part of me wanted to run to him and confess that I still loved him. I knew that it was impossible; that life wasn't meant to be. We were much too different, and our worlds clashed.

As I walked through the long path that would take me back to the main street, I looked back at the palace. A couple of stories up, probably on the third floor, I saw a face. Natalie, Arthur's fiancée was staring down at me from the window. My stomach tightened, and for a second I couldn't move. She kept staring down at me, probably wondering if I came back to steal her precious Arthur away. She couldn't have known about the kiss from yesterday. The guards were pretty discreet.

She was worried and jealous. I didn't need to be a demon to figure that out. I was with Arthur when they weren't together. He had mentioned a few times that they went out on dates, but I never thought it was anything serious. Natalie had always been nice to me, and I suddenly felt like yesterday I betrayed her.

The memory of everything that went wrong twelve months ago suddenly zoomed through me. I turned around and continued to walk back towards the gate, not knowing what the future held for me.

Everything was supposed to be good, tequila numbed me, but inside I was torn apart, hurt badly with no way of getting better. Arthur was long lost for me, quickly and without a warning. The only thing that remained was my guilt and the secret that I so desperately wanted to share with him. Maybe I needed to reconsider my decision from the past and give him a chance, see how he would react. Keeping the life-changing moment to myself was selfish and deep down I wasn't a selfish person. I wanted to protect him, protect us, but in the end I was only hurting us further. It was time to put his and my priorities in order.

***

I didn't go back to the office. When I called and spoke to Emma, Ricky wasn't back yet. I was starving, so I went back to The Broken Shoe. I felt slightly better when the sun disappeared behind the horizon. Paul served me his traditional fish and chips, and the hot meal eased away my hangover and exhaustion for a bit. I ate, thinking about Zachary Quinton.

Emma had brought her own laptop from home to set up a spreadsheet with all the cases that the agency dealt with in the past. She'd told me earlier on over the phone that the files were a complete mess (I knew that) and she wanted to sort everything out electronically. I told her that as long as she was confident enough to take on that kind of job, then I didn't mind. Ricky had mentioned a few times that we were going to have an audit, but nothing was set in stone just yet.

Lately we had a lot of cases, but the cash flow was still poor. We needed a boost. The case with the missing prince could bring a lot of revenue, but I had to bring young George back, safe and sound.

"Empty tonight, Paul," I pointed out to the retired Watcher when he came in to remove my plate once I finished. It was still early, but there were only two demons at the back, drinking Guinness and talking in hushed voices.

"It will get busy later. I'm glad that you're all right and that human didn't kill you," Paul said. "I should have called Ricky. You drank way too much the other night."

"I was fine. Besides, Zach acted like a gentlemen. I woke up without my clothes though."

"I told you that he wanted to get into your pants."

Paul looked tired tonight, like he hadn't had much sleep last night, but he was right. There was definitely a spark between me and Zach.

"I think he's one of those humans that believes in supernatural stuff, in another world. I went to the police station to talk to him. Apparently his old partner committed suicide."

Paul was looking at me with that vacant expression on his face, probably thinking that I was sticking my nose into something that I shouldn't. After years of knowing Paul, I knew that he preferred to keep his own affairs to himself.

We never truly spoke about his time as a Watcher and I had a feeling that he wasn't allowed to say much. At times, Paul could read humans much better than I ever had. Most of his abilities were lost, but he was still able to connect to his demonic soul and use it to his own advantage.

"You need to be careful with him. That kind of exposure might cost you more than you are prepared to give, Maxine," Paul mumbled and strolled back to the kitchen with my dirty plate.

I wanted to play tonight, but I couldn't be hungover tomorrow. Besides I was skint. This investigation was moving along slowly and Ricky was going to be on my case. My mobile was back in the office. I didn't like taking it with me all the time.

Several moments later, as I contemplated asking Paul for some tequila, two scruffy-looking female mongrels barged through the front door. They were both blond, flustered and excited about something.

"The body was found down by the canals," whispered one of them, giggling like this was the most exciting thing that she heard in a very long time. I automatically rose back on my feet and moved closer. "It's one of us apparently."

"Yeah, it's a big deal. Apparently the head of Leviathan faction is down there. It's one of his girls," said the other one.

Paul stopped polishing the glasses and looked at me.

"Maxine, you have to go there now. The dead demon has something to do with your case," he stated.

I opened my mouth to ask him what he meant, but then I changed my mind. Paul didn't need to tell me twice; he just knew, like the other Watchers and demons in the city. I had known him long enough to trust him. The two female demons looked at me then to Paul, but I didn't have time to explain anything to them.

Outside it was raining again. Harsh cold drops of rain beat over my leather jacket as I ran to the tube station. I spent a good forty minutes getting from Brixton to King's Cross. No one had to tell me where the police had found the body; the torn emotions, the sadness were sending me all the way to the canals. There was a gate to the underworld somewhere in that area, but only certain demons were able to use it. Sometimes my kind just knew. If a demon or mongrel died, everyone around the area felt it instantly. This didn't happened often.

By the time I found the crime scene, the edge of the canals was filled with police, and a crowd of people stood behind the yellow tape, probably trying to get a glimpse of the dead body or blood. There were reporters there too, so the word must have gotten out quickly.

I walked up to the older officer that stood on the other side of the yellow tape.

"Let me in. I'm on the case here with Detective Zachary Quinton," I said, hoping that somehow that could guarantee me a pass. He narrowed his eyes at me, and checked me out pretty much from my head to toe.

"Let her through, Gordon. She might be helpful," the voice behind me stated, sending chills down my spine. I turned around and abruptly faced Zach, who managed to sneak behind me undetected. That could only mean one thing: I was connecting to his emotions too comfortably.

Chapter Thirteen

"I wept not, so to stone within I grew."

— **Dante Alighieri**

Someone took my picture when I was passing through the yellow tape. There was a couple more camera flashes as I started walking along a canal with Zach. He was calm, but slightly apprehensive that I showed up without a warning. The body was lying several meters down, just by the cycling path. The forensic technicians were using black lights and ethanol to check the space for DNA. Most of the time demons died in hell, and I was surprised that Watchers hadn't found this poor demon first.

"How did you know to come here tonight, Flower?" Zach asked, when we stopped on the edge and he turned to look at me.

"Some women came into the bar blabbing about it, and I had a feeling that I had to be here … you know, kind of like a sixth sense," I told him, forcing out a smile. The man next to me was aware of my Achilles heel—tequila and Prince bloody Charming. Last night was a blast, and I had way too much fun with him. It was time to get on with my task.

He grabbed my arm and stopped me from going down to see the corpse. Her energy was circulating around the place, shooting goose pimples alongside my neck. There were a lot of other cops walking around. I spotted two guys I guessed were runners, judging by their outfits, by the police car, probably giving their statements. The mist began drifting around the space, as I blocked the fear, the anger and sadness. The crowds weakened my abilities, and I didn't want to be here when the Watchers showed up.

"I don't believe that you came here because you heard about it in the pub," he snapped back as the heat shot down between my breasts, heading south. "I heard that you were looking for me today?"

I held his dark gaze, trying to convince myself of the fact that his touch being comforting to me meant nothing at all. My breath caught in my throat as lust increased my breathing rate, tingling the places that were supposed to be immune to any attention. Maybe he was right. I shouldn't have come. I would've saved myself a lot of hassle.

"Well, I needed to speak to you about last night, but the guy at the front desk at the station wasn't very helpful."

His grip tightened and his eyes narrowed.

"How did you do that last night?" he asked.

"Do what?"

"Outplay me only to lose all your cash. I never lose, Maxine, and I think you cheated just so you could stay on this case with me," he told me, pulling me closer to him. Crap, what was with this guy and him enjoying manhandling me like this? I kicked his arse once, and I was ready to do it again.

"Stop being such a sore loser, Zachary, and get the hell away from me," I hissed, angry that I was suddenly feeling all these strange and wonderful sensations. "I can easily embarrass you in front of all your colleagues, and trust me, you don't want that."

He smirked and looked down admiring the other revealed parts of my body. Okay this was wrong, but he made me a little wetter in certain departments.

"I care about my reputation, Maxine, and I don't want to hurt you. Now let's get on with business," he said, finally letting go of me.

The body was partly covered, washed all the way up on the edge. As we got closer I sensed demons nearby. I had seen many dead people in my short life, but never a real corpse of a demon. I had heard stories that our bodies simply burned when our time came. The female demon was possibly in her late forties. Her pale almost white face was bruised, left eyebrow cut. Her wide blue eyes were parted, and most of her clothes were in pieces. She must have been in the water for several hours, as the corpse appeared to be in a well-preserved condition. It wasn't something that I wanted to see ever again; down here the corpse looked more like a human than any other supernatural creature.

She also had long red hair. Yep, it was that one small significant detail that mattered right in that moment.

"May I?" I asked, hoping to examine her closely. Zach wanted to say no, but he took something from his pocket and handed it to me.

"Fine, but use gloves. I want to make sure that forensics has a chance to scrub everything off her later on," he said. I put on the white latex gloves and started brushing her hair off her face. I noticed deep, purple bruises all over her arms and cleavage. She must have been beaten badly before she was killed. This didn't make much sense. As a demon she could have used her power to defend herself or at least attempt to.

After I made sure that I hadn't missed any other unusual signs. I started checking the pockets, thinking that Zach or the other cops must have already emptied them out earlier on. I didn't find anything in her jacket or jeans, but when I lifted her sweater there was a small bag with hair attached to the other side of her cardigan.

"Wow, that's unusual," I said, and got up waving the bag in front of Zach's face. He grabbed it, frowning.

"It's a bunch of hair," Zach stated, looking at it like it contained some kind of bomb.

"Hair, it's red hair, and I bet you it belongs to Prince George," I said, before I could stop myself. I took a breath and released the absorbed emotions and energy from the gathering crowd around the crime scene. An electric shiver passed over my spine, and I inhaled deeply, aware of the crackling energy that was dissipating from the space, getting it out of my system.

Zach grabbed my hand then, and when our eyes met his pupils dilated. My inner self connected with the dead demon, and sometimes when it happened, my eyes would shimmer. I was so pumped with my new discovery that for a split second I forgot that I wasn't around my own kind.

"How do you know who the hair belongs to?" he demanded, staring at me intensely, like he was certain that he saw something in my eyes. I meant to keep my mouth shut, but my assumption was correct. As soon as I touched the bag, I knew that the hair inside belonged to the missing prince. Zachary was supposed to be unaware of my abilities, but he was much more sensitive of our world than anyone else around here. I suppose I could blame the tequila for making me a little sloppy, and I was still paying the price for messing around with a royal.

"I'll tell you, but stop squeezing my arm. People are staring," I hissed, narrowing my eyes. I was in so much trouble already. If the prince was dead, then I was going to be called down to hell, and now Zachary was hypersensitive to my abilities, aware that I was hiding stuff from him. None of this was good for my business.

"I don't care, Flower. I want to know how you know that this hair belongs to the missing prince," he repeated, forcefully.

"Is everything all right, Zach?" asked a slightly overweight cop that stood closer to the edge of the crime scene, looking down at us. Zach didn't let go of my arm, until we both felt the heat brewing between us. Our attraction was transparent, and I could deny it till the cows came home, but I couldn't stop myself imagining what if.

"Fine," he replied, releasing me. "We need to send this to the lab ASAP. Apparently the hair inside the bag belongs to Prince George."

The cop didn't ask any questions. He took the evidence off my hands and began climbing back up the embankment.

"I questioned someone last night, a guard from the palace. The prince had been seen with a red-haired woman, an older woman. They were quite intimate," I explained, using a compulsion to wave off his fears of the unknown. This was against my personal rules, but he had a right know and I needed to make him believe that everything was perfectly normal. His overactive imagination could cause problems with The Watchers. Sometimes they took on the identity of humans, so they could access crime scenes and take care of the problem. Right now the dead demon was a problem.

Zach was forced to leave me alone five minutes later, when he was called by another female cop.

"Stay here and don't touch anything. I'll be right back," he told me.

I had to get my shit together. I had never lost control like that before. The hair was filled with charms used for rituals, to summon other creatures from the underworld. As soon as I brushed my hands over it, I got shot with a strong source of demonic current. The prince was too valuable, and whoever had him wouldn't simply kill him just yet. The dead demon was somehow connected to my case, and I still had no idea how or why.

After a few minutes, Zach came back. He was pissed off and reluctant to share anything at all. I knew that I shouldn't have said anything last night, but tequila made my lips flap. I just didn't know when to shut up.

"I just had a phone call from one of my sources. Apparently the dead woman was a well-paid high-class escort. Her friend showed up at the station ten minutes ago. We need to go and question her," Zachary said.

"I'm not a cop," I muttered. Maybe I should have let him beat me in poker. Then we wouldn't have to be stuck working together. I wasn't his dead partner; maybe he thought that I could somehow replace her.

"We made a bet last night. You yourself agreed to be part of this investigation, Flower, and I'm not done with you yet. There are some things that we need to discuss," he said. "I don't think you want to miss something like that."

He was right; I had no other leads, and maybe the woman at the station had seen the prince with the victim. A few mongrels and a demon blended in the crowd of people behind the yellow tape. I felt them watching me, trying to break through my protective wards. I was tired of being on the other side, fed up that others were ready to tear apart my mind to satisfy their burning curiosity.

Zachary was tormented, his emotions unsettling. There was unexplained tension between us. I was nervous getting to the car, thinking that maybe I was taking this too far. Rodriguez asked me to work with this guy, and I was never planning to be friends with him.

"Hey, Detective Quinton, a quick word please?" shouted someone behind us.

"Fuck, what now?" Zach muttered under his breath, turning around. A very attractive tall blonde human ran towards us. She wore a long, brown trench coat and high heels. Her thoughts were burning with curiosity, looking for answers. I didn't have to jump into her soul to figure that out.

"What do you want, Lori? You know that I'm seeing someone else. Find yourself a decent guy without any psychopathic tendencies," Zachary said hoarsely, but there was a playful tone in his voice. The woman tossed her long shiny hair behind her and glanced at me, well, mainly at my old jeans and leather jacket.

"Oh, Zach, you're such a joker. We always had a good time. Don't forget that," she laughed. "Any comment about that murder in the canal? There are rumours going around that young Prince George hasn't been seen in public for quite some time."

Zach didn't move, didn't even appear to be caught off guard, but I nearly unleashed my power, as panic soared right through me. This was bad, a human reporter knew about the prince and the fact that we just linked the dead woman to his disappearance? How? The royals couldn't have leaked this. Everything about this case was classified and I had always been so careful.

"Young Prince George? As far as I know he's still partying in Cannes," Zach said, and the vein on his neck bulged. He was getting impatient, and he wanted to get the hell out of here. Yep, I couldn't block anything that he was feeling at this point. "And the dead woman is just a hooker. Nothing exciting about that."

Lori wasn't buying his lie. She had a very reliable source and wasn't planning to let this go.

"Cut the crap, Zach, the body down the canal is linked to the missing royal. I'm running this story tomorrow unless you give me what I want. The woman is dead, and she was the last one seen with the prince," Lori insisted, moving so close to Zach that their foreheads were nearly touching.

"Don't push me, Lori. I don't know who is feeding you this nonsense. You don't want to have an enemy in me."

"All right, lady," I said, pushing Zach to the side and grabbing blondie's hand. "Listen to me carefully. There is no story here. The dead body down by the canal is just some unknown hooker. She was raped and abandoned there. Walk away, go back to your boss and report to him everything that I just told you." I was going to pay for compelling my power later on, but we couldn't afford any leaks just yet.

As the energy surged down my body, connecting with Lori's, Zach didn't take his eyes off me. My demonic soul produced enough charms to make Lori believe what I said. I hated doing this to anyone, stripping them of their memories, interfering. Sometimes I hated that I had been born this way, detested that my mother hooked up with a demon and created someone like me. A person that never belonged anywhere, that had to fight to survive in the cruel world where, no matter what, she would never find acceptance.

"Of course, the hooker was murdered, that's the story that we are going to run tomorrow," she mumbled with a detached, blank expression on her face. I let go of her, ceasing the energy transference, and felt slightly on edge. I just had to pray that no one had witnessed this.

"You owe me a lot of answers, Flower, and I'm going to get them even if I have to drag your sexy arse to the station," Zach said, watching as the beautiful blonde walked back through the crowd.

Chapter Fourteen

"Thence we came forth to rebehold the stars."
— Dante Alighieri, Inferno

The woman ambled away and I ignored Zach's comment, walking ahead, towards his car. The tension inside me escalated, as I tried to ease my anxiety. Zach was silent and that could only mean one thing: he was thinking about that night when he found his dead partner. I exposed myself and now he was suspicious. Fuck, if it wasn't one thing it was another. It's true what they say: the road to hell is paved with good intentions.

Demons had first escaped the underworld centuries ago, breaking the rules set in hell, wanting to taste the life on the outside, amongst humans. When things started getting out of control, Lucifer established a faction system to keep order and a better control of the population. Things had started going wrong downstairs a long time ago, before the Watchers tasted life on earth. No one kept a tab on things upstairs. It was in a demon's nature to break rules, to taste the freedom.

Soon mongrels were being born that would never be accepted in the underworld. Half humans gifted with demonic abilities. Later on, the decision was made to send them all to orphanages, where they could mix with other humans and possibly end up having a good life here on earth. Lucifer wasn't too happy with the fact that demons enjoyed copulating with humans, so new rules were put in place and any sexual contact with any human was strictly controlled downstairs from then on. That rule didn't quite apply for mongrels.

My own mother died because she wanted to protect me. Most of the time if a human woman gave birth to a half demon, her instinct told her to abandon the newborn. That was the new price that every demon had to pay. I didn't remember much from the time I spent with her. She cared for me for some time, then after her death I was sent to live with nuns in a monastery. It took me years to figure out that I wasn't like any of the other kids in the orphanage, that I had gifts and could use them to my advantage. Being able to use my gifts early in life stood me in good stead as I had control much earlier than other demons. I made my mistakes and learnt early that there was always a price for magic.

"I came to the station earlier to thank you," I blurted out, wanting to break the uncomfortable silence that settled between us. He shifted in his seat, as he took a sharp turn, driving into the main road.

"You don't need to thank me. I'm the enemy," he responded. "I looked into your background. I couldn't find much; no records of your birth parents. Why is that?"

I exhaled sharply, knowing that my records were tightly sealed. I should have predicted that he was planning to run a background check on me. He wanted to make sure that I was clean. His last partner ended up dead, so his checks were more than fair.

"I don't know why that is so surprising. I grew up with nuns, without parents and I don't like talking about it. I'm just a girl that keeps on living her own life," I said, sighing loudly.

"You might have grown up in an orphanage, but I know that you're hiding secrets, Flower," he added, harshly.

"Roland. Who is he and why does his name keep popping up in your records?"

The colour drained from my face, as I tried to appear unfazed. Zachary wasn't supposed to hear about Roland. This part of my past was insignificant and I wasn't prepared to explain anything.

"I think you're trying to make something out of nothing, Zachary," I told him. Zach was digging for information, and I knew that this wasn't about his own curiosity. Someone must have told him stuff about me, a foe not a friend. The only person that I was ever close to was Ricky. Friends came with responsibilities and I didn't need that hassle.

"I don't think so, Flower. You're hiding your true self away from me, and I'm the kind of guy that wants all or nothing, and now it's all," he added with a flirtatious wink. At that moment his phone rang and he had to stop the car on the side road. I was so grateful that this conversation was over for now. The bottom line was that I was fiercely protective of my privacy. Ten minutes later he was back and he didn't press me with further questions.

We arrived at the police station in Hackney forty minutes later. Zach headed straight to the guy at the desk, probably because he was outside his designated district.

"Where is the hooker that was brought in earlier on?" he asked, without any introductions. The guy had a superiority complex and no manners.

"Hold on a minute. I'll check with the dispatcher," said the officer at the desk. He disappeared for a good ten minutes. After that we were taken through the wide door, inside the building. The policeman that led us was short and fat. He was worried about the payment for his new car, and the fact that he hadn't gotten laid in years. I was wearing quite a revealing top today, and he kept staring down at my boobs. It was a boy school error, but I had no idea that I would be hanging around horny cops all night long. We stopped in front of what looked like an office door.

"Her name is Natasha. She reported her friend missing five minutes after we had a phone call about the body in the canals," the cop said.

"Okay, thanks. We will take it from there," Zach said. The cop unlocked the door and let us inside the interrogation room, but it was empty.

"I don't understand. She was here. Hold on. Maybe someone moved her to another room," the guy said, looking around, like he was expecting that the girl was hidden under the table. Zach exhaled sharply and I instantly felt sick. A demon was here not long ago. I smelled arsenic and blood. The girl was taken against her will; we had gotten here too late.

He vanished for about five minutes, but when he came back, his whole face was red, his hair was tangled.

"She's gone, but that's not possible. I locked the door and I wasn't out for any more than five minutes," he said.

Zachary was staring at me. He probably noticed that I'd gone slightly pale all of a sudden. Sweat ran down my temple and the sudden rush of energy was pushing my lunch up my throat. I didn't like how I was feeling, and I was certain that the hooker had disappeared because the police had found the body of her friend down by the canals. The Watchers were on their way. I felt their presence outside.

"Show me her statement," Zach demanded. "And her fingerprints. You did take her fingerprints, right?"

The guy started stuttering, saying that he was going to do it, but then he'd forgotten about it. Zach was fuming and he wanted to see all the CCTV footage from around the station. I couldn't wait, hanging around humans when Watchers were sweeping the area. My past was complicated, and I had a lot that I needed to keep away from the whole demonic community. The demon had taken the girl, and the humans could look through that footage as long as they wanted, but they weren't going to find anything there. She was most likely dead already.

I was hoping to head straight to Ricky's to discuss what I found out so far. We also needed to go through previous evidence again. Zachary was busy, so I sneaked away half an hour later through the back entrance. I didn't get very far, well, not unnoticed.

"Where are you going, Flower? We are not done here yet. Our witness is missing," he shouted after me.

"I'm going home, Detective. It's late and I need a strong drink," I said.

"So you were just planning to leave without saying a proper goodbye?" Zach asked, catching up with me.

"I didn't think you would miss me that much. I'm tired and tomorrow is a new day," I complained, turning around to face him. Zachary was a man with his own set of priorities and it would be easier if I stayed away from him. Our worlds were poles apart.

"Oh yes, I would... very much so. Come on, I have a good bottle of tequila at home. Besides, you need a lift. You ain't walking home alone in this shitty weather," he said, winking at me.

I appreciated the fact that he was looking after me, but right now I didn't need the company.

"The offer is tempting, but I can take care of myself," I told him, then turned around and started walking towards the tube station. I took a couple of steps when I was lifted off the ground. Zach threw me over his shoulder and started carrying me through the car park.

"What the fuck? Put me down, caveman, or I swear to God I'll kick your arse," I shouted. He held me tightly and when I attempted to wiggle away, he slapped my arse hard.

"Shut up, Flower, you wanna drink, so let's have a drink together," he said hoarsely. For a moment I forgot that I was supposed to be a tough and independent kick-ass demon. Instead I felt kind of cared for, special, normal for once. It was stupid. Zach was acting like a total alpha male, but surprisingly I liked the fact that he wanted to take care of me. No one had ever done that for me, not even Arthur. We were together, but our relationship was initially based on sex. Later on it turned into love.

Several moments later we were back in his car and I was sitting in the passenger seat, feeling torn between what was right and wrong. The trouble was that I knew that Zach was looking for answers, and I was trying to hide them away. We could never be truly honest with each other.

He smiled at me and switched on the engine. When it started raining I was glad that I didn't have to walk home. He drove for what felt like hours, before he parked the car in a private housing estate on the north side of the city.

"This is where you live?" I asked, stretching my arms above my head.

"Yes, Flower, it's not what you were probably expecting, but it's home," he smirked. "Plenty of women before you left satisfied."

"Well, it's a good thing I'm not like other women," I told him and then got out of the car. I followed him to his front door, asking myself if this was a good idea after all. Arthur had always managed to trick me into going away with him. At first I'd pretend that I didn't see it, that he was simply polite and genuinely liked spending time with me. There was that instant connection between us, a spark that quickly turned into something more. After he made a move, I couldn't stay away from him. Now I was in control of the situation with Zach, and I needed to remember that he wasn't my prince, just some random human.

He unlocked the door to his semidetached house and gestured for me to come inside. When the lights came on, I was a little taken back by the natural decor and ordinary furniture. Maybe I was expecting something completely different from a man of his character.

"Make yourself at home, Flower," he said, taking off his jacket. I walked into the small living room. I wasn't used to normality. My dates with Arthur were crazy, and intense.

"Zach, I think I should go. This isn't a very good idea," I said, glancing around, hoping to find some picture of his family, something that could indicate that I wasn't suited for his lifestyle, for him. He brought out the bottle of tequila and a shot glass.

"Why? Are you scared of me?" he asked, pouring some yellow liquid down.

"No, I'm not, but I know for a fact that I shouldn't be here," I mumbled, losing my cool. He pulled the bottle away from me when I tried to grab it.

"Not so fast. First I want some answers," he said, suddenly sounding completely serious. "I have seen enough weird shit in my life, so tell me—what kind of crap are you into?"

Suddenly he was broadcasting a lot of anger and frustration. I finally realised that he enticed me here for an interrogation, not because he wanted to seduce me. I should have known. After all, I had lost my grip on my usual control down at the canals. Why wouldn't I have totally misread this situation?

"I don't know what you're talking about," I said with a nervous chuckle, trying to relax.

"Your eyes glowed when you were leaning over that dead hooker, and you did something to Lori. She doesn't listen to anyone and doesn't just let go of a story, so tell me before I stop being a gentleman," he snapped, moving closer.

Crap, so he had noticed my glowing eyes amongst other things. I didn't think I had gone too far earlier on knowing that Zach was sensitive to my world. I had to turn this around somehow, but I didn't want to use my abilities to make him believe that nothing happened and that I was a normal human.

"This has something to do with the death of your partner, right? You want to believe that it wasn't a suicide?" I asked. His eyes were roaming over my face like two bright spotlights searching for the truth.

"According to the official reports she took her own life, but that's a lie," he said. "I knew her, and she had no reason to kill herself. Someone made it look like a suicide. She told me that someone had been following her for weeks, that she was in danger."

I was trying to put my thoughts back together, send calming vibes to his erratic emotions.

"I don't know anything about that case, Zach, and I can't help you," I explained. "I thought this was going to be a friendly conversation. You don't have to tell me anything about what happened. Let's just have a drink."

He shook his head, but his eyes were wary, like he was waiting for me to do something out of the ordinary. It wasn't like I was going to pull a bouquet out of my ass—David Copperfield I was not.

"You can take your clothes off, then we can get to know each other a little better," he suggested. "But this ain't going to happen until you tell me what you are."

I knew then that someone else had used charms to keep him away from the truth. He showed the classic symptoms of paranoia. He was right: I was hiding stuff away from him, but he wasn't ready to hear the truth, to know that his world wasn't what it seemed.

"What am I?" I repeated, laughing. "I'm Maxine, the girl with a complicated past, but very simple future."

I got up so I was standing close. A second later I smiled and stole his precious bottle of tequila, crossing the room. He was playing some kind of game with me and I needed to ease his anger somehow. The lust I had for him brewed deep inside me, as he approached me a moment later, still unsure if he could trust me.

"I have been working the street long enough to know that normality doesn't exist. It's just a shame that our path hadn't crossed sooner. The missing prince, we both know that he is still in the city, that your kind has taken him."

And then it hit me. I finally began to understand why Zach was behaving in such a way, why he wanted me away from this case. Someone must have been filling him with doubts, messing around with his thoughts. I still had no idea what exactly had happened to his partner, but I suspected that another demon was using him against me to steer me away from George. Zachary was used from very beginning.

"There isn't such thing as 'my kind' Zachary," I explained, furious with myself that I hadn't figured this out sooner. The demon that took George must have known that I had an affair with Arthur and that was why Zachary was brought in to assist in the first place.

Then, before I could put all this back together and work out what was really going on here, Zachary did something that I truly wasn't expecting. He pushed me against the wall and kissed me with a fierce passion. This whole thing happened so quickly that I completely forgot about the fact that I wasn't supposed to trust him.

Chapter Fifteen

"I did not die, and yet I lost life's breath"
— **Dante Alighieri, The Divine Comedy**

My knees threatened to give out, as he pushed his hard body closer. His mouth captured mine in a hard, demanding kiss. Over the past twelve months, I swore not to let this happen to me again, to endanger my life like this, but in that moment the heat sizzled my blood before my mind could grasp what I was doing. Zachary pushed his hips towards me, and I moaned, aware of the hard bulge pressing over the spot between my legs.

I was losing my fucking mind. This human was obnoxious, paranoid and was a complete alpha, but whatever he was doing to me restarted my heart, bringing it thudding back to life. His hand reached out, smoothing down the lines of my hips, as his kiss grew harder, clouding my judgment. He slid his arms around me and grabbed my butt cheeks, lifting me up and carrying me across the room and pushing me down on the table.

My demonic soul unleashed sparks, my skin grew hotter, blood boiled as he began to thrust his body against mine, the delicious friction giving us a taste of what was to come, both of us breathing hard.

My hands busied themselves diving into his curls, tangling his hair as he covered my neck with his lips. His kisses pushed me further, consuming my mind with unexpected passion. I shut my eyes, as liquid heat filled every nook of my oversensitive weak body. Finally there were no flashbacks, no bad memories—in that one sweet moment there was just me, enjoying making out with this glorious male specimen.

He sucked on my bottom lip, moving his hand underneath my T-shirt, circling his rough fingers around my hardened nipple. The pressure between my legs grew with every passing moment. I wanted him to tear my clothes apart, to fuck me hard in his home, on this table. The consequences didn't matter anymore. Our attraction was explosive and we needed to become one.

Then we both heard the loud knock and a second later the vase on the table crashed to the floor. Zachary pulled away; his eyes bored into mine intensely as he tried to catch his breath. It took me couple of seconds to pull myself back together, to actually remember that I was supposed to keep breathing. I held the heat from his lips that was now boiling in my veins, burning like hot coals on the soles of my feet. I couldn't remember when I ever lost control like that before. Zachary brushed his finger over my cheek and then winked at me.

"Stay here, I'll be right back," he said, his voice hoarse.

My T-shirt was lifted, revealing my bare stomach, and my hair was a tangled mess when I jumped off the table and glanced at the mirror. A second ago, I thought that he was ready to kill me, and then the sudden anger transformed into passion, stealing away the arguments and his unexplained frustration. No, I couldn't keep doing this to myself. I had failed myself once, and now I was pushing something that could never work.

"Hello, handsome. I know I meant to call, but I was in the area and I thought that I would just pop in." I heard the feminine, seductive voice coming from the threshold.

My heart hadn't stopped pounding yet, and my oversensitive abilities alerted me that there were more than two horny people inside Zach's house now.

A second later a very human woman entered the living room. She had bleached blond hair cut nicely in a trend bob, her beautiful face was made up immaculately, and she wore a very short skirt that barely covered her thighs. She raised her left eyebrow, eyeing me up and down from the short distance. Zachary was right behind her, his eyes still filled with brewing fire.

There was a slight pause as she opened her mouth then closed it. My tangled clothes gave away the fact that just a moment ago, I was lost in the swirl of a passionate embrace with the man of the house. It was easy to read that it wasn't the first time the woman had been here. She was Zach's regular.

"Oh sorry, darling, I had no idea that you had company," she sang with a very annoying high-pitched tone of voice. At that point I was lucid enough to get the fuck out of there. I needed to regroup as soon as I could.

"No worries, I was just leaving actually," I said.

"Maxine, wait—"

"It was nice meeting you," I cut him off, and rushed out before things got more awkward. Whatever he wanted to say, it didn't matter. It was a spur of a moment lapse in judgment. We both lost control of our bodies. I flew through the door, aware that the woman in his living room was his usual fuck buddy. Her vibes were crystal clear and I didn't want to stamp into that territory.

I had been played, possibly by someone that wanted to see me down or possibly by Rodriguez himself. Whoever was working against me knew about my affair with the prince. Rumours at the palace had circulated, as no one could explain why I left my post so suddenly.

Zach and his demons weren't my problem. Missing Prince George was and I couldn't afford to get distracted. I had broken the rules once, and I paid the price and suffered until this day. The factions were designed to keep demons under control so that would help to keep order on earth, and I had to protect my wounded past. My future was at stake, and the future of others.

I couldn't afford to make another mistake like that, especially with another human, and especially with a man like Zachary Quinton. I headed through the dark estate, ready to get lost and never face another day like this again.

***

The next two days passed in a haze, and it seemed like I was stuck in my flat for a long seventy-two hours. My phone kept ringing, but I didn't answer any calls. When I got home the night I made out with Zach, I sent Ricky a quick text message, telling him that I wasn't going to be in the office on Saturday. At times we had an understanding. I mentioned that I was planning to work on our case on my own, that I needed some time alone.

I didn't hear back from Zach and maybe that was for the best. He took away my focus. After the episode with the royal family things became complicated and I kept reminding myself that I had been happy before. Paul came to visit me and he even brought bottles filled with the magic elixir that was supposed to keep me sane for a while. When the sun went down and I was intoxicated enough, I wandered off, searching for new clues, talking to old contacts, hoping to find something that could lead me to the elusive missing Prince George. It was a productive weekend in terms of drinking and working, but no one was willing to talk. I didn't play poker that weekend and it was a first for me.

I woke up much more sober than usual on Sunday morning. It felt strange to open my eyes with a clear head. Normally during these drunken phases I was able to block out my toxic thoughts, but that morning everything came back. When I checked my phone, there was a text message from Emma. Ricky must have given her my number. Her daughter's birthday party was today and she just texted me her home address with millions of smiley emoticons.

Yet again, I had forgotten that I made a promise to be there. Now this didn't seem like a very good idea, but I couldn't disappoint another person. She made an effort, probably slaved over decorations and food, so this was the least I could do.

After a quick shower, I pulled my tangled hair into a messy bun, put some clean clothes on and headed out. The first stop was to the toy shop. I had no idea what a little girl Emma's daughter's age needed, so I bought Barbie dolls, three in case she didn't like what I had chosen for her. My chest was tight when I was paying for it. Luckily the stash of a very small emergency fund allowed me not to look like a complete dick in front of other guests.

Emma lived in Greenwich, and I had to walk half a mile from the tube station to get to her place. All the way I kept telling myself that I should turn around, that this wasn't a good idea. My previous experience taught me that I wasn't quite myself when I was around other mothers. My anxiety shot up when I stood in front of an old terrace house an hour later, fighting with my thoughts, trying to act like this wasn't an issue for me. After a couple of deep breaths I forced myself to knock. I was late, but I was much more sober than I usually would be for this time of day. Maybe that was part of the problem, showing up and expecting to be treated like someone that fit in. Several moments later Ricky opened the door, holding a glass of champagne in his right hand.

"Maxine, what a treat. I wasn't expecting to see you here today," he said, looking good in his blue sweater and black trousers. I shoved the present into his chest.

"I was invited, but what are you doing here yourself?"

He gave me his mischievous smile.

"I was invited too. The little girl is quite adorable. Besides there are at least a dozen mothers out in the living room, very yummy mummies, if you know what I'm saying." He winked at me. I rolled my eyes as he shut the door. A few seconds later Emma strolled through the corridor, wearing a lemon dress, a red birthday hat on her head.

"Max, oh, I'm so glad to see you. I hope you didn't have to walk far. Come … come meet Suzi and the others. OMG, I'm so excited. I hired a proper magician, and everyone is dying to meet you. They love Ricky …"

She was still talking, dragging me through the house filled with balloons, cards and some other decorative crap. Emma's place was decent enough. It was an old Victorian terrace house filled with a lot of clutter, funky furniture and sparkly clothes. For a split second I imagined myself in her skin, living this ordinary life and waking up happy. This whole life was tempting, but I wasn't cut out for a life like that. I wasn't the type of woman that needed any semblance of normality.

In the light, spacious living room a dozen pairs of human eyes landed on me as Emma began introducing me around. The kids were running up and down, screaming and giggling. All the mothers were typical homemakers, ordinary, not the high-end class like I was expecting, which was a good thing.

"So you and that handsome partner of yours are running the detective agency, right?" asked a guest called Lucy. The woman was in her mid-thirties with a bad perm and overdrawn dark eyebrows. She was on her second glass of wine and she was worried that her husband would scream about the fact that she had one too many.

"Yeah, Doomed Cases. We have run it for a few years, but only recently has the business picked up," I explained, grabbing a glass of champagne. My head was fuzzy, and the temperature of my body was shooting up. Something else burned the back of my mind, the dooming guilt.

"Wow, that's a very spooky name. It sounds like you're dealing with magical stuff," she whispered, giggling. I gave her a weak smile.

"Some of my clients can be spooky," I admitted, hoping that she would drop the subject.

"Suzi, this is Aunt Maxine from work. She brought you Barbie dolls for your birthday," Emma jumped in, beaming with pride. I looked down at the small blond creature that was looking at me with her huge brown eyes, holding the dolls in her tiny hands. The wave of emotions suddenly made me sick as memories flooded my head.

"I like your hair. I want to have colours like that when I'm older," the child said, swinging her body from right to the left, staring up at my hair in amazement.

I swallowed hard, pushing myself to get a fucking grip. This wasn't supposed to make me teary at all.

"I prefer yours. The blond curls are super awesome, like your Barbie's hair," I replied, most likely sounding like an idiot, but at that point I didn't care anymore. I needed my tequila or a shotgun.

The girl grinned, mumbled something else about playing with her later, and then ran away. Emma squeezed my shoulder. She was so happy, so relaxed about everything, standing next to the person that was so damaged that she couldn't even have a proper conversation with a five-year-old child.

"Oh, Maxine, she loves them. Thank you again for coming. All the mums love Ricky. I bet you can't wait to have your own kids?"

I then proceeded to choke on the champagne so hard that Ricky had to come to my rescue. By that time one of the children dropped something in the kitchen and all Emma's attention was luckily diverted away from me.

"Come on, let's go to the garden. You need some fresh air, sugar plum," Ricky muttered, using his own powers to stop me from getting choked up. I grabbed a few more glasses of the bubbly and drank them all in one go. The human alcohol was too weak to numb the turmoil in my heart, but at least it smoothed my crappy mood.

"Just say it; I know you want to," I said to him once we were away from the crowd, standing under a wide tree.

Ricky rubbed his clean-shaven jaw, and drank some more. "I won't. I know that you're picking yourself up at your own pace," he said. "I went to The Broken Shoe a couple of nights ago. Paul said that on Wednesday night you went home with a certain individual. The troublemaker?"

Fucking Paul and his big mouth. Why on earth did he have to say anything to Ricky?

"Yeah, I couldn't get rid of him after I beat him in poker," I said. "Don't worry, he behaved and we are a team now."

Ricky then touched my cheek and turned my face, so I couldn't avoid looking at him.

"Maxine, are you all right with this? Being here? You should have told Emma that you were sick. You didn't have to come," he said. Yeah, Ricky had read me and he was simply asking me if I could handle being the other Maxine, the one with a heavy load on her shoulders.

Chapter Sixteen

"The experience of this sweet life."
— **Dante Alighieri**

I stared at the empty space ahead, trying to put my answer together. Two days ago I had lost my head, and today I was standing around other people, acting like my addiction wasn't real. Ricky wanted to make sure that I could cope. He pushed me to keep going, to keep solving cases, to live. He was supportive and I was lucky to have him; however, that didn't stop me thinking about the moment when everything changed.

"Your Highness, I don't think it's a good idea. You're vulnerable. It's an open space and we both know that we shouldn't be here without at least two more guards," I said, wondering if this was the day when I was going to lose my well-paid job. Arthur was getting on

my nerves, driving through narrow country roads. He woke me up early in the morning and a told me that he had to be somewhere very important. I had my own responsibilities for the day, and he had his personal driver.

It'd been a couple of weeks since I shook hands with him on the corridor in Buckingham Palace. The roller coaster ride started when he asked me to accompany him to an underground party in one of the clubs in the city several days later, when I was still trying to learn the whole protocol. I was slowly getting used to the fact that Arthur wasn't one of the most responsible royals in the palace.

He was going on a tour to Afghanistan in a couple of months, and I had a feeling that he was hoping to have some fun before his freedom was taken away from him. Either way I was responsible for his safety and quite frankly fed up with being put in these kinds of situations. I kept ignoring the spark that sizzled between us over the past few weeks. I kept dismissing the fact that he flirted with me on any given occasion, that I enjoyed his charisma, laugh, and his impulsive character.

"Stop with the 'Your Highness' stuff, Max. Just call me Arthur or I swear to God, I'll leave you here in the middle of nowhere," he said, driving his four-by-four like a maniac.

I smiled to myself, feeling the familiar butterflies in my stomach. This was completely absurd; I had never developed a sweet spot for a client. Men, especially human men, were foreign to me. Arthur was different; he made me laugh and calmed my demonic soul; he made me forget that I was only a pathetic mongrel.

"Okay, Arthur, just turn around. We're breaking protocol and if something happens, I'll be in trouble," I pressed, gently letting him know that I was in charge. This new life forced me to see things from another perspective. Maxine Brodeur was now part of the Royal Court. That other darker life was pushed aside. Now other people came first.

Arthur turned to look at me, his blue eyes drifting over my face, down my body, suddenly making my heart beat wildly in my chest. The cook and other staff in the palace kept saying that one of his second cousins, Natalie, was going to be his wife. The Queen Mother wanted to keep the bloodlines pure by keeping it in the family.

He laughed, stopped the car abruptly a moment, and placed his hand on my thigh.

"Come on, let's go for a run, hottie. See if you can keep up with my amazing stamina," he whispered leaning closer. His earthy cologne paralysed me for a moment. Arthur got out of the car and vanished behind the trees while I sat there in the same spot thinking about the way he touched me.

This was a very bad idea and I couldn't predict if he was playing with my conscience or really going out for a run. His touch melted my insides, and I shouldn't feel this way about him. This was so wrong.

I started running, using my demonic abilities to track him down, worried that we might bump into someone who would recognise him. He was pumped with excitement, ready to have a real race with me. The flirting and small gifts and trips away, it was just a game, nothing else. Arthur wasn't planning to seduce me. We were getting on and had similar interests, but that didn't mean anything. Any scandal was unnecessary and I was enjoying myself too much to get fired after I started to adjust to my new life. On top of that, the faction kept an eye on royals, and I didn't need to get in trouble with them too.

"Arthur, this isn't funny. I'll kick your arse if I catch you," I shouted, feeling him nearby, sensing his wild excitement.

He laughed, then sped past me several meters away. He was thinking about his trip abroad in a couple of months' time; he knew he had to pick up his training, that he wasn't quite ready yet. I shouldn't have been in his head, knowing that he was hard thinking about my sexy arse and toned body.

God, I really had to start blocking his emotions away. I needed to stop to regroup my energy, to tell myself that I had read him wrong. He couldn't have been thinking about me in any sexual manner. I was no one, just his security guard.

"Gotchya!"

A split second later, the strong body knocked me down and we both fell on the ground. I was lying flat with the future king of the United Kingdom on top of me and, oh boy, my whole soul lightened instantly.

Indeed, he was hard and I was aware of every single part of his body pressed over mine. His eyes met mine and I was lost quickly with the lust that pushed me to the edge, igniting a fire deep in the pit of my stomach.

"How are you, Flower? You should be glad that I'm not making you run further. I know that you're quite fit as it is," he said, with that husky, seductive voice. Heat blossomed across my cheeks, stirring around me, making tiny beads of sweat break out across my skin.

"I'm fine," I breathed out, trying to keep still.

"Ask me anything, Maxine. This is your chance," he added, touching my cheek.

"I don't need to know anything. I'm here to make sure that you're safe."

He laughed.

"That's why I like you, because you're always honest, don't play any games. The other guys were always so bloody fake," he muttered.

I waited then, not able to take my eyes off his fully kissable lips. I shook my head dispelling those hopeless thoughts and desires. The tiny voice inside urged me to stay away, tell him no. This was going to get me into so much trouble.

"Deep down, I just want to be a normal guy that can walk around the park without getting harassed by paps. The guy that wants to live his own life without other people telling him what to do," he said, leaning over and whispering his confession in my ear. "I want to

269

have a family, kids. A wife that won't have to worry about getting stalked every step of the way, happy children that won't have a mad life because of who they are."

I liked listening to his smooth voice, his dreams. For the first time someone other than a demon had noticed me. It was never simple to build relationships with other humans, especially men. When I was with Arthur these barriers didn't exist. He treated me as an equal.

"That's not unreasonable. Everyone wants to feel normal," I whispered back, not able to get my heart under control.

"And if I could have that life and choose my own wife, then I'd choose you," he said lowering his eyes, his lashes fanning his cheeks.

His lips brushed the corner of mine. The kiss was tentative at first, but it grew hotter. I wanted to break it before this whole thing went too far, but I was lost, indulged with something beyond amazing.

Arthur's kisses were spontaneous, warm and gentle. We were lying on the ground, tangled in each other's arms and legs. My body stopped listening to my stupid head. Arthur cradled my face then, intensifying the pressure of his lips, and my energy sparkled to life. Within a few moments I'd forgotten about my responsibilities and continued making out with him.

The kiss ended, and when I opened my eyes, my chest kept rising and falling rapidly. Arthur's eyes were gleaming with heat, and he wasn't thinking about his family anymore. I could read in his thoughts that he wanted to rip my clothes off and have sex with me. He kept *telling himself that it wasn't just a playful game, that he really wanted me.*

"Let's run away together, Flower," he suggested, keeping my chin in place so I couldn't stop looking at him.

"Maxine, hey, are you even listening to me?" Ricky's stern voice brought me back to the real world. Suddenly I was aware that I wasn't in the forest anymore, but back in gloomy reality. What was the point remembering that I was happy before? The future could be bright if I could just stop dwelling on what I had lost.

I rubbed my face, staring as the children ran around in the circle. The garden needed some landscaping, but the kids didn't seem to care. They were so excited and happy. Suzi was in the middle of the circle, bouncing and screaming.

"I'll be fine, Ricky," I said, clearing my throat. "You worry about me too much."

The mums were chatting amongst themselves, watching their kids playing. Ricky didn't need to know that my stomach was in knots, that my T-shirt was stuck to my back underneath my leather jacket. My stupid head couldn't let go of its heavy emotional burden. I was glad when Emma called everyone for a cake. I could handle being around such a happy human for some time, but I wanted to go to the bar later, ease the pain with some tequila.

"Great, cake time, that means I can go home soon," I said, walking over to the house with Ricky. He grabbed my elbow suddenly, stopping me from running away. His own energy was at ease, connecting with mine, trying to push all my fear away. He either got laid last night or he was excited about something else.

"Max, just don't do anything stupid. Detective Zachary is a troubled man; you don't need that kind of burden on your shoulders right now," he warned me, like he knew exactly what happened between me and the detective a couple nights ago. "You have to stay focused on this case and move forward."

Ricky must have sensed that I was slipping down, losing focus again. He was like family to me and he wanted to protect me. I needed to remember that Zachary was being influenced by another demon that wanted me to lose my focus in George's case.

"I'll be at work tomorrow, so don't stress. I have it all under control," I assured him, walking back to the kitchen.

Emma gave me a piece of birthday cake, telling me about her daughter's upcoming school trip. I stayed for another half hour, making a real effort to look like I was enjoying myself, then left.

Other mums watched when Suzi hugged me, thanking me for her presents. I patted her gently on the back, pushing my discomfort away.

I didn't know how, but I managed to lose several hours of that day, although I recalled enjoying my time with little Suzi. Later on I remembered walking through the streets of London for some time after the party until I stopped at small bistro for food. There were days when I didn't eat much at all, especially after a heavy drinking session. That evening I was moving through a fog unable to shake off the gloomy darkness that kept drifting over me.

Around eight o'clock I ended up in the bar, sitting at my usual seat having a chat with good old Paul. It was a busy night and I needed to drown in tequila to shut down the loud voices in my head.

"Ricky told me that you mustn't play tonight," Paul stated, reluctantly giving me the whole bottle of the precious liquid. Ricky knew that I wasn't in the best of moods, but we had an agreement. I didn't interfere with the way he ran our business and he didn't interfere in my addiction.

"Ricky knows shit. I'm going to win. I have that feeling in my gut," I said, grabbing the bottle and heading to the room at the back. Two Watchers, a warlock, and some demons were just getting ready to shuffle the cards. This was my doom; I had only a couple hundred on me, but my head needed to be straightened out.

"Right, boys, I'm in. Let's get this party started," I called out, taking a seat next to Devlin, who thought it was his lucky day, that he could outplay me again. Soon the poker rounds began rolling in and I drank. The pain was vanishing, the thoughts weren't bothering me anymore. I started winning small sums at first, then gambled more, pushing my luck. It was all perfect until I saw Arthur standing on the other side of the bar watching me. Then everything went to shit.

Chapter Seventeen

"Here pity only lives when it is dead - Virgil"
— **Dante Alighieri, Inferno**

I didn't want to believe that Arthur was in The Broken Shoe. I had drunk the whole bottle of tequila throughout the poker game with Devlin, and now I was finishing the second one. I suspected that my brain was playing tricks on me, that Arthur was just a mirage, someone my twisted mind had created for me. However when I walked up to him, touching his hard chest, his arms, and that handsome face, I was certain that this wasn't any kind of demonic trick. He was truly standing in front of me, looking completely relaxed.

"What are you doing here?" I asked, swaying from one side to the other.

"Waiting for you, beautiful. I've been watching you for a while. It's impressive. How long have you been playing poker?"

I burped loudly and nearly lost my balance, but he caught me quickly. I had gone overboard with magical tequila tonight, but the yellow liquid quieted my demonic soul, the burdening thoughts. Paul was swamped at the bar; it looked like a group of mongrels didn't know what to do with themselves and they were looking for trouble. Arthur had no idea what kind of scandal he was just about to start if any of these people recognised him.

"You know exactly how long I've been playing poker. Now, let's get out of here before anyone sees you," I said, and popped a shot of vodka down my throat just so I could stand straight. It burned, but human alcohol gave me the courage to actually talk to him.

"What? Are you afraid to be seen with me?" he whispered.

"I might be, but we both know that you shouldn't be here, that this isn't the place for you," I said, and started dragging him towards the back exit. Once we stepped outside I had to stand for a minute as the dark gloomy streets of Brixton were spinning in front of my eyes. My body trembled with cold. Arthur was staring back at me. He seemed amused and curious. I had lost more money than I thought was possible tonight and drunk twice as much as I usually did. I had no idea how I was still standing.

There was no way that Arthur came all the way to this part of the city to find me. Where were his guards? His Natalie?

"Let's go to your place; it's freezing out here," he was saying.

"You have never been in my place," I pointed out.

"There's always a first time." He chuckled and wrapped his arm around my waist. When he was holding me so close, I felt like the past didn't matter, that I was still protecting him. Arthur whispered sweet complements to my ear as we walked home. Tequila had muddled my mind, magic made me see wonderful things, sealing off my demonic soul. Reality and illusion blended together, and we reached my street half an hour later, singing and laughing. I was in a great mood, telling him all about the time when I realised that I had a crush on him.

I was ashamed standing in front of my building, knowing he would see that my tiny hole wasn't up his usual standard.

"I want to have you in my arms; it doesn't matter where," he whispered, helping me out with unlocking the doors. I closed my eyes, enjoying the blissful moment when he trailed kisses down my neck. The heat between us boiled the blood in my veins, or maybe it was tequila working its magic, leading me down a path of destruction. Either way I was swept off my feet by Prince Charming and carried upstairs.

His strong arms embraced me as raw and unmasked desire zoomed through the room, enchanting our lost souls. Nothing was making sense anymore, but I needed more, wanted him to take away the sorrows. His body vibrated with need, and my own limbs shook when he touched my naked flesh. My powers were suddenly awake, rippling through our bodies roughly, and electricity flickered over the room, scorching my neck. I loved him before, I had to give up my life for him, and now we were back together.

He lifted me and carried me to the bedroom, smiling in the darkness. I touched his face gently with my palm and whispered in his ear.

"I love you, Arthur."

He looked almost puzzled, somehow disturbed, but I no longer cared. The three magic words were the reason that he was with me tonight. After he laid me down on the bed, I let him devour me with his mouth, I let him remove all my clothes and make sweet, forbidden love to me. His smooth hands showered me with electricity that zoomed over my body. I was lost that night, as my head sizzled, filled with magical liquid that made me numb, that supposedly made me forget about everything. His mouth claimed mine gently but firmly. My heart raced as the liquid heat poured from my core.

I was in the skylight, drifting away, touching the moon and stars. As he made love to me that night I made a decision that in the morning I would tell him everything, the whole truth. I had nothing else to lose, because he finally had chosen me.

***

Somewhere in the room the alarm was going off, but I refused to move, to open my eyes. The beeping sound eventually forced me to lift my lids, but my chest heaved when the pain shot violently through my body. I twisted on the bed, trying to swallow, but my mouth was dry as the Sahara Desert. I moaned loudly, cursing magical tequila yet again, not remembering much of what happened last night.

My room was dark, but tiny beams of light from outside got through the curtains. I inhaled, trying to deal with the fact that my head felt like it was cracked open and millions of tiny humans were drilling holes inside it. I smelled someone else close, a male human, but that was impossible.

I turned around abruptly when I felt movement on the bed. Pushing through the pain and confusion, I tried to focus. In the darkness of the room I saw a naked man, sleeping peacefully next to me. Raw and unbridled panic clawed up my throat as I tried to figure out what the hell happened several hours before. He was tall, lean and completely naked.

My mouth was so dry, my soul drenched with overactive energy as the throbbing in my head intensified. The human was alive, and he was breathing normally. It took me several long moments to gather that we had sex last night. I didn't remember even getting home, let alone bringing home a one-night stand, but I was certain that this guy had sex with me.

Parts of my brain attempted to piece together everything that happened. Snippets of conversation were slowly coming back, and I began to realise that no one had pushed me into this, that it was my own stupid choice. After getting wasted, I somehow convinced myself that Arthur was at the bar.

I held my face in my palms, breathing hard, feeling the blood draining. I had fucked around after I got fired from my post at Buckingham Palace. It was a dark time in my life. I partied a lot, slept with random strangers, mongrels and other demons just to ease the longing for Arthur, but last night I had completely lost it.

There was something wrong with me. Maybe it was time to get help, to learn how to pull through without magic or tequila.

"Hmm, hon, come here. I want to feel your warm body pressed against mine," the voice next to me murmured. I needed to take a shower and then sign myself into a rehab programme. There was no way I was going to be able to stop drinking on my own.

I pushed the guy to his back and with my inhuman speed I climbed on top of him. He was instantly turned on, but I wasn't planning to take advantage of him again. He opened his eyes and stared at me for a moment, shocked but open for any kind of possibility. He was good looking, with broad cheeks, light blond hair and cute hazel eyes.

"Hey, listen to me. You're going to get up now, put your clothes on and disappear. From this moment, you won't remember me, you won't even remember how you got into my apartment," I said, loud and clear, ignoring the looming headache.

It was easy to compel him to do what I needed. The tiny voice in my head reminded me that I had no right to tamper with his mind, his memories. Every part of me hated that I had gotten myself into this situation.

A minute later I was sitting on my bed that stunk of sex and booze. The handsome human was putting his clothes back on. He kept glancing at me, like he wanted an explanation, but he was too confused to ask anything. His name was Adam and he was only looking for some fun last night.

I was so relieved when I heard the door of my apartment shut a moment later. I sat in the darkness and then started crying over what I did. Yep, for the first time in my life I pushed aside the fact that I was supposed to be strong and I let the tears fall. I could no longer deal with the fact that I kept making wrong decisions.

Arthur was unreachable and we were never going to be together. He was rich and there was royal blood in his veins. How could I ever think that we were going to be more than just lovers? How could I let him fool me like that?

I was a half demon, a woman without a real father, a real background.

As all these thoughts kept floating in my head, I got up and walked around the room for a bit.

Some time after I had a shower I stopped feeling sorry for myself. I couldn't stay in my shitty flat and dwell on what happened, on what kind of pathetic mongrel I turned into. The prince was missing and I had to look beyond my own problems. It was a mistake, an error that taught me that it was time to pull my shit together and get sober.

I left my flat around one, erasing everything that happened last night from my memory. I was very much hungover, disappointed in myself and angry that my self-control was in pieces again. The human last night could have killed me, and no one would have known.

I used the tube and headed over to one of the places that in the past made me feel stronger.

I hadn't visited the children's ward since my disappearance from London twelve months ago. Deep inside I knew that this could only trip me over the edge, but I had to at least try to push myself through that gloomy depressing mood. The roads outside the hospital were busy and there was a lot of traffic. My stomach revolted when I entered the familiar building, the place I used to love sharing with the man that loved me. Arthur's pictures were all over the ground floor. He let anyone take his picture and children used to love being the centre of attention with him.

I took the lift to the first floor, knowing that this would either cure me or push me further in despair. I was wearing my usual clothes, and when the lift reached my floor, I stood inside unable to move.

"Are you all right?" asked the woman behind me, when I stood frozen looking ahead. We were the only two people in the lift. I cleared my throat and nodded, finally stepping out of the lift. I was hit with a strong antiseptic smell, and a wave of excitement mixed with incredible sadness.

Everything looked exactly like I remembered, colourful walls, toys stacked around the corridors and medical staff rushing around. I headed over to the other side of the building, knowing that this time around I wanted to change my routine, to see if I could handle seeing a newborn child.

My heart was longing for some affection. I remembered the way Arthur interacted with children, the way he naturally bonded with them, making them laugh. Deep down I knew that he would have been a great father. That thought left me shaky; my legs trembled but I continued to walk.

After some time I found the delivery corridor and situated myself behind a few women that were staring down at crying newborns. I took a few deep breaths and lifted my head to look at the tiny humans. It was surreal and crushing at the same time. The past had changed me, and suddenly I felt like my own loneliness was slowly choking me, wrapping its fingers around my throat.

All these orphaned children reminded me of myself when I was taken to the nuns for the first time in my life, after my mother was gone and there wasn't anyone who could take care of me. I was so scared and tired. I didn't remember how old I could have been then, maybe four or five. My whole world shattered and suddenly I had to stay away from home with strangers, surrounded by other kids, sleep in a bed that wasn't mine. My powers hadn't started to develop yet, but I was aware of the sadness and sorrow behind the walls of the monastery orphanage. Everything was so fresh in my memory.

I wiped the sweat off my forehead, staring at those tiny humans that couldn't be more than a few hours old, wiggling their hands and feet. That's why I had to keep going, so I could turn my past around, change everything.

Getting drunk and gambling couldn't last forever, tequila wouldn't numb me forever. I had to face reality—and maybe even consider telling Arthur the truth.

We had something special going on, and twelve months ago I had given him exactly what he wanted.

I couldn't afford to slip back into old ways. I had dealt with my past the best I could, and the choices that I made then weren't necessarily right. Maybe everything could still be fixed.

I left the hospital, feeling less wounded, somehow refreshed. But I still had a long way to go. In the tube station I told myself that this was it—I had to change, push through. No one was going to hold my hand. It was time to grow up.

I reached the office some time before two. On the threshold I heard Emma's laugh. Inside I found her with Detective Zachary Quinton, who sat in a chair near the desk, probably waiting for me. My heart made a flip, reminding me that it'd been three days since I spoke to him, since we made out. Ricky was standing by the window, looking like he was ready to strangle someone.

"Hey, Ricky … and Zach," I said. "And Emma."

Zach zoomed his deep dark eyes over my face and smiled. My stomach reminded me that I needed to fuel it with some food. Ricky could probably smell magical tequila from the other side of the room, but I pretended that I could work, that my hangover wasn't a problem today. We needed to have a chat about our other pending cases, but I could see Ricky wanted me to get rid of Zach first. I sensed that he didn't like him very much or maybe he just didn't trust him yet.

"How are you, Maxine? Missed me much?" Zach asked, standing up.

"Not particularly. What are you doing here?" I asked.

"He's here to talk to you," Ricky responded for him, not looking too happy that Zach was hogging our space. Sometimes he liked marking his territory way too obsessively. Both Zach and Emma seemed to sense his magic circulating in the air. I could only hope that Zach was immune to Ricky's tricks.

"We had an agreement, Max, and you're lucky enough that I'm sticking to it. I should be in the field, solving this case, searching for leads. Instead I'm here, waiting for you to show up," Zach pointed out, checking his watch.

Then the phone rang and Emma answered it. I narrowed my eyes on Zach, trying to figure out if he was here because he was forced to it by a demonic influence or if he made his choice. Part of me knew that he came back because we were working on the case together. Prince George was still out there, hopefully still alive.

"There's someone on the phone for you, Max. A woman, and she is saying that it's important," Emma said, covering the phone with her palm. Zach shook his head, and nodded to me to take the call.

"Hello, Maxine speaking," I said, taking the phone from Emma and flopping my sorry arse on her desk. It was going to be long day today.

"Max? The one that is looking for a missing prince?" asked the nervous-sounding voice on the other side of the phone. It was a female, but the line was crackling. I clicked my fingers in front of Zach's face to get his attention.

"Yes, that's me, who are you?"

"Natasha. My friend Jessica was with the prince a couple of nights ago. She said that he wasn't himself," the woman was saying. "I called because I heard that you can help me. I'm in trouble because of her."

Zachary and Ricky were staring at me in confusion.

"She was with the prince? Where? When?" I questioned her. The hot detective walked around Emma's desk and leaned over, trying to listen in. His presence was suddenly distracting. I smelled his sexy cologne and my hormones suddenly went berserk. Magic from last night still circulated through my system.

"In the club Zander in North London. We both waitress there. The prince looked ill. No one recognised him apart from me. Then he went out with Jessica. She called me last night, saying that he bit her and she had to go to the hospital," the woman said, while Zachary was breathing close to my cheek.

"Where are you right now?" I asked.

"It doesn't matter. I don't want to see anyone. I'm just worried about Jess. Please can you go and check on her? She hasn't come in to work today and that's not like her. What if the prince has done something to her?"

The human woman on the line couldn't have known the prince was missing. Rodriguez made sure that there was a block on the story, but we finally had a lead. Someone was with Prince George last night, a human.

"How did you know who to call?" I asked.

"Someone in the club gave me your number. He said that you deal with unexplained cases, that you look for missing people," she explained. "My friend lives in St. Richards Avenue in Hackney, Apartment twenty-four. Headlands Court. Please, someone has to check if she is all right."

Zach's body brushed over mine and my nipples got hard. I wanted to ask her a few more questions, but she hung up. I slammed the phone down and cleared my throat, ready to leave.

"Get your coat. We need to go now. We may have something," I said, and walked off, not waiting for him to follow me.

Chapter Eighteen

"In each fire there is a spirit; Each one is wrapped in what is burning him."
— **Dante Alighieri**

I kept thinking about my drunken mistake, and my gut filled with guilt whilst I walked downstairs with Zach. Our drive was going to be filled with an awkward and uncomfortable silence. It was time to think about other means of transport. Maybe I should buy a motorbike to avoid situations like this in the future.

The woman on the phone was vague and I wasn't sure if it was wise to believe anything that she said. The bottom line was that the prince was missing and there was no reason for him to be around some hooker. This just didn't make any sense, but we didn't have anything else, any other leads.

Zach was hard to read today, and I struggled to focus through the rushing tide of heat that blossomed through my system. I couldn't deny that there was something about his domineering personality that appealed to me. I guess it's some weird human trait harking back to cavemen, some me-man-you-woman type thing. Today he wore black jeans and a white shirt with stripes. His gun was strapped around his back, and even after my eventful night I was still kind of turned on.

On the other hand, even though what happened between Zach and me back in his house was a mistake, I bloody loved every second of it. Maybe we had gotten off on the wrong foot, but that sizzling attraction between us was still stirring the air, tempting me to make a move.

"Are you all right? You seem quiet," Zach said after some time. The car stopped at a traffic light, and his eyes shifted over to my face.

"I'm fine, had a rough night last night," I said, wondering how the hell I could believe that Arthur would show up in an obscure bar in the middle of the night, just so he could talk to me.

I was stupid and emotionally vulnerable. It was time to go on a detox; I finally hit the rock bottom of my miserable life.

"We should go out, Flower, after this whole case is solved and the young prince is back to his aunt's nest," he said, with that playful tone of voice. I exhaled sharply and looked at him, realising that he just asked me out on a date.

"Go out? As in, on a date with you?" I repeated, just to make sure that we were on the same page.

He smirked casting one of his hot looks in my direction. The truth was that I didn't really know him, but I believed that some other demon had tampered with his mind. After all, he was able to sense that I was different, not completely human. Our last conversation worried me, and I needed to be careful with charms when he was around.

"We both know that you want me, Flower. A couple of nights ago you humped me dry and who knows what would've happened if we weren't interrupted." He chuckled, smoothing the steering wheel. "My mother has been telling me for years that I should settle down; maybe that's me and you. I mean we have chemistry."

I was shocked that he was so forward with me. Three nights ago, he was ready to kill me in his own home and now he wanted to date me. I just couldn't get my head around it.

"Want you?" I questioned him, laughing, suddenly aware of the warmth building in my chest. "You were the one dry humping me, Detective. Besides, who said that I would want to go out with you in the first place?"

"I can make you forget about your prince. Once I jump your bones, you won't go anywhere else, Maxine," he said darkly, with that tone of voice that had my insides turning to a mush.

"Gee, can you be any more arrogant?"

"I'm just speaking the truth, suggesting something that is obvious. We're attracted to each other, don't deny it, and I promise you, you'll never think of another man again," he said, his eyes on me studying my reaction.

I hated the fact that he was bringing Arthur into this awkward conversation. He had no idea what I gave up, what happened between us in the past. Things were still complicated and I didn't want to jump into yet another doomed relationship.

"Stop calling me Flower, arsehole. You won't get to go out with me if you keep talking about the wrong prince. Besides, I'm not looking for anything, and I won't go on a date just because your mother is expecting you to settle down."

"It's not a lifetime commitment and I'm not doing this because of my mother. You're hot and something tells me that we could enjoy each other's company on a whole new level."

Really, he was delusional, but the images of us together kept moving in front of my eyes. Zachary was a human and sleeping with him was too risky. I made one big mistake last night. The streets were monitored by Watchers and I bet that my name was back on their radar.

"I'm sure we would, but I don't think it's a good idea, Detective. I have too much shit on my plate and I don't want to complicate things between us," I muttered, knowing that a one-night stand could get me into a lot of trouble. Demons liked spreading rumours, and I was running a business, trying to keep away from hell's affairs.

"Sex would make you forget, Maxine, and I'm good with making women forget. Stop denying yourself a basic need that I can help you with," he purred.

He stopped the car several moments later. Zachary Quinton just proposed to fuck my brains out and I said no. After all, sex changed things between people and I had a tendency to hang on to people that were giving me attention.

It amazed me how quickly he could forget about the pending investigation and talk about sex like this as if it was perfectly normal. Humans honesty amazed me at times.

"Don't worry, we can discuss this later, when you're less tense, Maxine."

I rolled my eyes and looked around the housing estate that stretched in front of us. It was cold, and dry freezing wind blew through the streets. I wouldn't want to get stuck in this part of the city if I were the missing royal. George wasn't one of the most responsible people that I knew, but he wouldn't just get involved with a hooker. He liked partying and, as far as I knew, he could pick and choose the ladies interested in him.

We walked for five minutes, until we found the right apartment block. Mr. Detective, who claimed to be the leader, managed to convince some old lady on the fifth floor to let us into the building. We called the lift and Zach pressed floor nine. Demonic energy began coursing through my veins as we moved higher. I suspected that the effects of magical tequila were still colliding inside my bloodstream, confusing my sharp senses. I was pretty much still hungover, suffering after my drunken party at the bar. This neighbourhood was very human, but we had to be ready for anything.

We found Jessica's apartment several minutes later. I inhaled the strong smell of sandalwood and other rare herbs. It seemed that there might be an illegal production of potions going on behind the closed door. The woman that we were looking for was a hooker, and a human, so that just didn't add up.

After a few minutes of banging at the door, I figured out that the apartment was empty and the girl was either already dead or missing. I tried the doors; they were unlocked so I walked inside.

"We need a warrant. We can't just walk into her apartment like that," Zach told me.

"Then go ahead and get one. I'm going in," I said and carried on. We were running out of time and this wasn't the time to follow his police rules.

The apartment was small and dark. The fumes from the brewing elixirs drifted in the air. A human couldn't have known about stuff like that. I suspected that a demon had been here, running the whole show. His energy was strong, and I recognised the scent. It belonged to someone that I'd met in the past, but couldn't remember where and when.

"Jessica!" I called out, just to be sure the apartment was empty. The curtains in the living room were drawn. There was an old sofa in the corner that smelled of sex and sweat. Zach obviously couldn't stay away, and he strolled in after me, looking around.

"Blood, still fresh. We might have just missed them," Zachary pointed out, touching the soaked carpet with his fingers. My mind was racing all of a sudden, as I tried to pinpoint if George had been kept here as a temporary measure, considering all the crazy possibilities.

The table in the living room was filled with flasks, dried herbs and blood. There were some pots placed on a gas heater. The liquid inside smelled of lavender, but when I dipped a spoon in it, the metal melted instantly. The consistency, the light smell and the strength told me that someone was trying to create Second Chance Potion, but couldn't quite make it right. The elixir of life, the one that gave energy to the broken soul. Royal blood was part of this complicated recipe and I had a feeling that a significant amount of George's blood was already brewing inside the pot. I had studied a couple of books in the past, and I knew that this kind of thing was supposed to give strength and power to the half demon, someone like me.

"What the hell is this crap? Did the woman on the phone mention that her friend was into some satanic rituals?" Zach asked, lifting a dead snake off the floor that I only noticed as he pointed it out. This wasn't good. Humans were oblivious to our world, and Zach wasn't even supposed to be aware of the strong magic in the apartment.

"I don't know, but this doesn't look good," I said, smelling the other flasks. Some of them were filled with mongrel's blood that was more than likely obtained illegally. Jessica was in a right mess, but I suspected that she wasn't part of it anymore. A demon that had George was using her apartment as a lab.

Zach went to look around, leaving me alone with my racing mind. Whatever George was part of wasn't good. Now it was quite clear why Lucifer wanted to find him so urgently.

"I might have something here," Zach shouted from the kitchen. I wiped the sweat off my forehead and headed to see him. He was looking at a calendar that was tacked to the wall. Today's date was circled with dried blood and there was a note next to it.

"Cemetery, 4 p.m., don't forget girl," I read it aloud, leaning over Zachary. A second later, he was typing something into his phone. I didn't understand why all the humans were so obsessed with technology these days. I hated having my phone on me all the time.

"There is a cemetery close by, at least a mile away," Zachary stated, looking at what seemed a map on his phone. I checked the time. It was half past three. I didn't want to leave such dangerous potions near humans, but we had to get down to the cemetery to check the next lead. Maybe Jessica was meeting someone there, maybe she was still alive.

"All right," I agreed, thinking that this was a bad idea. If that demon was planning something at the cemetery then I had to make sure that Zach was out of sight. His mind had already been pushed to it limits, thanks to his mystery demon tampering with him, and I couldn't risk exposing him to anything that couldn't be physically explained. Sometimes demons used the human energy that remained in corpses to find an alternative way down to hell. Mongrels weren't allowed downstairs because they were classified as second-class citizens. Watchers were responsible for taking care of order on earth, and at times if any mongrel pushed their luck and did something that exposed the demonic world, the Watchers stepped in and dragged them down to hell for interrogation. They had their ways of punishment, and no one really knew what waited for mongrels down in hell.

Zach took some photos with his fancy phone, probably for the evidence. The police were going to swab the place. I suspected that eventually Watchers would show up. They were also responsible for keeping humans from knowing about the other world, from any supernatural exposure.

The blood on the floor belonged to Prince George too, but I didn't need to tell Zach. My head was hurting, as my overactive energy rolled down my spine. There was a possibility that I could be called down to underworld to provide a full report of what I had discovered. This wasn't something that I wanted, but Zach was pumped. He wanted to check the cemetery.

We left the apartment several minutes later. Zach called for backup; his team of officers were going to sweep the place for evidence. He seemed positive that the prince was close by.

It was already getting dark and the temperature was quickly dropping. The housing estate seemed deserted, immersed in a gloomy silence. It seemed like the humans were sealed in their cosy houses, compelled to stay in tonight. Those familiar bad feelings kept stirring my guts. Normally I wouldn't pay attention to these odd sensations, but Zach was agitated too. The homemade lab led me to believe that we were dealing with someone very powerful, someone that had nothing to lose.

It had gone completely dark by the time we reached the cemetery, after walking for what seemed hours. The gate was open and an absolute silence had descended over the area, sending chills through my body.

"Where to?" Zach asked.

"Let's look around; if she is still alive she must be here somewhere," I said, concentrating on the emotions nearby. I sensed at least two people further up, between the graves. Zach and I spread out, crossing the pass and the creepy graves. I was never a big fan of being around dead people. I still remember staring down at my mother's sullen dead face in the church, trying to grasp the reality that she was long gone.

The air buzzed with electricity, and my breath became laboured. A moment later I felt a wet patch on the back of my neck. The small drizzle quickly turned into a heavy rain. I got soaked within seconds, shaking with cold and unexplained exhaustion. Thunder and lightning lit up the sky and the tiny sparks of power somehow alerted me to the presence of a demon.

Then I felt it. Someone was high on magical charms, filled with advanced elixirs. It was a male human; his circulation was poor and his mind completely confused. A second later I saw a figure beyond the steep hill several meters away, standing by a tomb. It took me a moment to recognise a human woman. She was staring down at someone else. That other person was below, like he was in a hole or an open grave, and it looked like he was digging something in the ground.

The rain was pouring down heavily and I had to keep wiping the water off my face see more clearly. Zach joined me when I lowered myself down, hiding behind an old tombstone filled with unlit candles.

"There is someone down there, possibly two people," he said, narrowing his eyes and pushing away his wet curls. It was difficult to see exactly what was going on in front of us, even with my excellent vision. The rain blurred out most of the view and I was hoping to sense a demon, someone that was tampering with the two humans by the tomb.

"We should move closer, but we don't want to scare them," I said gathering the energy inside me. Zachary took out his gun and readied it.

"The woman out there is probably the girl from the apartment," he said quietly His agitation grew, and suddenly it shifted into red hot anger. Pure fury hit me hard, turning my stomach upside down.

"You two turn around now. Slowly or I'm going to blow your heads off," shouted the stranger's voice behind us.

Slowly Zach and I did what we were told. With heavy rain obscuring my vision, I could still see that we were surrounded by three human men, all of them high on drugs. That's who I sensed just a second ago, but I was still filled with magical tequila that dulled down my abilities. One of them was holding a gun, and he looked like he wouldn't hesitate to fire. A second later, the woman further down had spotted us. I turned my head just in time to see the young human climbing out of the hole with a shovel in his hand, noticing all of us for the first time. There was no doubt that it was the missing Prince George.

Chapter Nineteen

"If you follow your natural bent; you will definitely go to heaven"
— **Dante Alighieri**

Zachary cursed under his breath but didn't drop his gun. I had to make a split second decision, either to use my powers to get these morons out of my way and keep chasing after the prince or let him disappear. I didn't think that these men were in any way linked to the missing royal. Their thoughts would give them away otherwise. Questions kept rushing through my mind. There was no way that my excellent vision could have misled me. Prince George was at the cemetery, most likely under the influence of the human woman from the apartment.

"I'm a cop, you fucktards, so I suggest you drop that gun and walk away," Zachary shouted. Yeah, he wasn't really helping the situation. That insult only made the guy that was holding a gun even crazier. On top of that, I saw he just said in his thoughts that he hated cops.

I glanced back, seeing that Jessica (well, I was certain that Jessica was somewhere in the body of a demon that was likely controlling her) was shouting and pointing at the prince to move. I chewed on my bottom lip, concentrating on the strong current of my demonic power, calculating the risk of using it against humans. The burst of energy made the tiny hairs on my body rise.

The man with a black moustache and long untidy hair, the one holding the gun replied to Zach, "I don't believe you, arsehole. My sister's grave was vandalised. We caught you and now we're going to deal with you accordingly."

My skin was itching to hit them with a strong bolt of energy, but I couldn't let myself be exposed. This whole situation was beyond comical. The rain kept pouring down, and I couldn't see well through the streams of water. There was another demon in the vicinity. I felt him or her leading the prince away from the cemetery.

Zach's anger escalated and he gripped his gun tighter. He was ready to shoot these idiots and I couldn't let him do that. His career would be on the line and I still wanted to live.

"You fucking arseholes, you will be rotting in prison for obstruction of justice. We are on a case here," he shouted furiously. Then too many things happened all at once. First someone—and I had no idea who—fired a gun. Then a loud terrifying scream spread over the whole cemetery. I struggled to remain on my feet, suddenly showered with waves of my own light energy. I was able to gather it from earth, from every living being, from water that ran underneath the grounds, from leaves and plants. I felt it surging through me, igniting my demonic soul to action.

I brought my hands together, making time pause in its natural moment. Now I had more than enough time to destroy the flying bullet and deal with the human, but bending destiny like that was going to cost me big in the long run.

Everything stopped—the small dots of rainwater had been suspended, the air shifted and all the humans around me became frozen statues. It took me a second to realise that the bullet was heading straight in my direction. I was going to die here, in this wet cemetery. I had never truly experienced using my abilities to this extent. The demon nearby was watching, sensing the fact that I was breaking all of Lucifer's rules, just to save myself and possibly Prince George.

I knocked Zachary off his feet, moving at least a meter away from the speeding bullet. Those couple of seconds gave me enough time to reboot time again. I screamed at the top of my lungs landing on top of Zach, reaching for the energy of the storm. The light pulsated, became more of a living entity as waves crossed over, feeding me with bits of nature's power. Lightning slashed its angry light through the sky and then I summoned it. My fingertips were red as they throbbed, and tiny wisps of smoke began drifting away from my arms. The lightning hit the human man that fired the gun, but the impact knocked the others off their feet.

My eyes started to glow, as I shot back on my feet, feeling the enormous power of my energy begin tearing my flesh apart and joining itself with my demonic soul. Two humans that landed on the soaked ground were screaming their heads off.

I didn't even realise that Zachary was fully conscious now, staring at me with his eyes wide open. The pain eased off as the power slowly faded away. Mist began covering the entire space, drifting through the graves. I had brought it in, so whoever was watching couldn't see what I was planning to do next. A second later, the bullet hit the grave behind me, missing my hair by about an inch.

"Your eyes, Maxine, your eyes are glowing," Zach shouted. He shot back on his feet and lifted his gun. We didn't have time to play this game right now. The prince was already out of sight, somewhere behind the cemetery walls, and Zach was ready to shoot me on the spot.

My head was banging loudly, and for the first time since I came back, a human had witnessed the real me. This whole thing was supposed to turn out differently. Zach was meant to be knocked out when I landed on him, so I could deal with the rest of the guys.

"Zach, put the gun down. We have to go after the prince!" I shouted back, wondering if he was really ready to kill me. His mind was confused, convinced that I was the cause of his partner's death.

"You were one of them this entire time. I knew there was something wrong with you," he shouted. The other two guys stopped moving and that wasn't good. Zach was ready to blow my head off. He believed that I was evil, that he was finally seeing the real me.

"I'm Maxine. You know me. Just put the gun down, so we can talk about it," I said firmly. A haunted look crept into his eyes right before he averted his gaze down to my hands that were most likely still sparkling. His dark eyes turned into the furious shade of liquid tar, as his mind filled with dark images of his partner that spread over the bed, her wrists were sliced, sheets soaked with blood…. The prince didn't matter anymore.

"Witch, you're a witch, like the rest of them. The government is twisting our minds, but I finally know the truth," he kept mumbling, shaking the gun right in front of my face. More humans were on their way and I couldn't let him ruin us both.

I concentrated and froze the bullet in his gun with the magic that was still alive in my sore fingertips. He pressed the trigger convinced that he was doing the right thing, and I covered my face with my palms, ready for the worst. The gun didn't fire, so I took this opportunity to jump and deliver a roundhouse kick that would knock the stuffing out of him and leave him disorientated.

He was lying on the ground, touching his face. I reached out and grabbed his hand. A second later my wet palms connected with his cheeks, and the words started floating out of me before my mind could process what was happening.

"You made a mistake; I didn't do anything extraordinary. The thunderstorm hit the tree nearby, distracting the guy that held the gun and he fired it accidentally. The bullet nearly hit me, but now everything is fine."

His pupils were dilated, and his eyes darkened as he ran his thumb along my face. I was in his head again easing the anger slowly until I saw that one covered-up memory from the past that someone replaced with the image of his dead partner.

"Hey, Cora, I brought your favourite chocolate cake, the one that makes you extremely horny," I shouted through the threshold, knowing how much that kind of thing wound her up. This whole thing between

us was very new, but somehow exciting. We started sleeping together over the past few weeks, after I made a move on her in the car.

First I thought she would slap me, but she kissed me back instead. This wasn't something that I planned; it was a spur of the moment thing.

My mother kept nagging me, saying that I would end up alone, never marry and never settle. There was some truth in that, because I'd been enjoying myself a bit too much, partying most of the time and sleeping around. Women liked the fact that I had a badge, that I wasn't looking for anything stable.

I walked into the living room, smelling the odd burning scent, suspecting that she most likely ruined our dinner for tonight. Being in the kitchen wasn't one of her strong suits. There were masses of paper lying on the floor, the sofa was turned upside down.

Something was wrong. I took out my gun moving forward. There was an intruder in the house. This area wasn't one of the safest.

I started climbing upstairs, quietly, listening in. A few days on the run Cora had been acting strange. She seemed convinced that someone was after her, telling me that she had been followed home a few times. I kept telling her that she was working herself to death. Sometimes we spent over sixteen hours on a case, driving around the city and checking all the leads. She was drained and needed some time out.

"Please, no. I didn't do anything wrong. You can't take me, you can't," I heard her talking to someone. I stopped halfway up the stairs, wondering what the hell was going on inside her main bedroom. There was someone there with her. I swallowed hard forcing myself to move.

Another voice spoke. "You broke the rules of your faction. Leviathan needs you in the underworld. There is a new army being formed. You cannot say no; this is your duty." The man, whoever he was, wasn't from around here, and he had an unrecognisable accent. The lights from candles flickered, and an odd terrifying sensation rippled through my spine. My grandmother had told me that there were things in this world that couldn't be explained. Somehow she fucking sold me her sixth sense.

"But I paid off my duty. Leviathan cursed me out a long time ago. You can't just expect me to go back. I have a life here on the outside."

"That's true, but you have broken the rules, bedded with a human. Lucifer sends others to pits; he punishes them severely. He doesn't want to see any more mongrels being brought into this world," the strong voice stated.

I shook my head and barged into her bedroom, holding the gun in my hand. My own voice died when I saw Cora naked on the bed with the older, bare-chested guy. There was something wrong with his eyes —they were white, without any pupils. He jerked back with a hiss.

"So he is the one that services you with earthly pleasures?" the man questioned her, standing up. He was taller than me, wide through the shoulders, and his chest shined with sweat.

"Zach, leave, please. You don't want to get involved. There is always a price and I have discarded the rules. I thought that no one would care," Cora said in a sad tone of voice. She was radiant, her hair sleek, eyes gleaming in the dim light of the room. There was something wrong with the way she was staring at me, with that overwhelming sadness. That crazy-eyed guy most likely had done something to her. This was beyond normal.

"Get up, you son of a bitch. I don't know what the hell is going on here, but you have two seconds to get the fuck out of here!"

Then I felt the pain in my head, gut-wrenching pain that spread to every part of my body. My gun slipped from my fingers and I fell to my knees, screaming in agony. Suddenly the man was standing beside me, and bright yellow light filled the room, but I couldn't see anything. I was holding my head, wanting to bang it against the floor just so the pain would ease.

"I'm taking her with me, human. She's going back to the underworld where she belongs. You will grieve her here, but you will never know what happened," the voice in my head said.

The pain faded as quickly as it came. I woke up on the floor in Cora's bedroom. Then I saw her. She was spread on the bed; the sheets were covered with blood; her wrists were slit.

When I got to her, I knew she was dead, and my thoughts went racing. I didn't even remember how I got upstairs, why I was in her house. Everything was blurry, until a quiet sob escaped me.

I pulled away from Zach, breathing hard, trying to gain some oxygen into my lungs. Suddenly everything was clear. His partner, the woman that he'd worked and slept with, was a demon cast out of hell. That night when Zach arrived at her house, a Watcher was there, ready to claim her back. All this time I suspected that Zach was under someone else's influence, but I was wrong. He'd simply witnessed something that he wasn't supposed to see.

Cora used him as an escape and he fell in love with her. She lied to him. She knew about the rules from the very beginning. The Watcher couldn't leave himself exposed, so he killed her and made it looked like a suicide. He made a choice to end her life there.

Now I was sitting on the cold grave filling Zach's head with images that were far from the truth. When we were surrounded, I exposed my true self, not caring for the consequences. The violence could have been avoided, but that human had fired a gun. I had to react, and not thinking things through I merely acted on instinct.

"Max, are you all right?" Zach asked, looking around, disoriented and confused. His gun was lying on the grass, a few meters away. The prince was gone. I couldn't sense him anywhere. The fried humans were alive, barely, but they were going to make it.

"I'm fine. The prince was here, with Jessica. Her friend was right, she had him," I said, falling to the ground exhausted and shivering with cold. I had lost my focus, my strength, and all because I was high on magical tequila. Nothing else mattered because I failed to recognise the danger, failed to see beyond my own stupid ego.

Zach got up, wiping the excess water from his face. Then the stranger's voice echoed in my head.

"Maxine Brodeur, surrender yourself to the temporary hearing outside the dark gates. You have broken the rules and exposed our world to humans. You have until midnight to show; otherwise you will be brought down to the underworld by a Fallen."

I tangled my hair, knowing that this was it. I had finally crossed the line, exposed my own abilities. The head of my faction was summoning me down to the gates. My death was upon me.

Chapter Twenty

"The poets leave hell and again behold the stars."
— **Dante Alighieri, Inferno**

Zach and I heard the police sirens nearby. I suspected that some human alerted the authorities. There was a lot of lightning in the sky and that unexplained mist that now drifted away. The guy that tried to shoot me was hit with lightning; he was unconscious, and the other two were moaning on the ground. They were going to be just fine, but I had to clear their minds too, just in case. My hands were trembling, my knees felt like paper. If I hadn't gotten completely wasted a night before, maybe this would never have happened. Now I had to answer to the Lucifer faction and a tiny voice in my head kept whispering that this was possibly my last night on earth.

I couldn't cry over spilt milk. What was done was done. I had exposed my abilities and the world below to humans. The rules were put in place to protect all the demons that lived on the outside, and my sloppy energy nearly killed an innocent man. Whoever witnessed my theatrics knew that I was powerful. That kind of magic was limited to a demon. My human mother had told me many times that I was different, that one day someone would come for me and explain everything. Now I was getting what she meant, now it all finally made sense. The demon that knocked her up must have revealed our world to her, must have mentioned that I was going to be much stronger than other mongrels.

"Stay with him. I will look around," I told Zach, who was back on his feet checking the guy I accidentally fried earlier on. His mind was in despair, but at least he wasn't questioning his own sanity. I felt really guilty, knowing that I could never tell him the truth about his partner, that I could never truly explain that the world around him was doomed.

"We have to question these two and search for the prince. He can't be far," Zach said, standing up. "That guy there is alive, barely, but he will make it."

"I'm not a cop, Zach, it's your job. I'm just helping out. I have somewhere that I need to be," I stated, rubbing my neck and wondering if I was going to be sent down to the underworld tonight. The faction couldn't be that cruel, but it was a possibility.

I didn't wait for him to stop me. Besides, the cemetery started filling up with other cops. I backed away, seeing flashlights moving quickly towards us. Uncomfortable questions would follow and I didn't have time to fill out any statements or talk to the human shrink. I had messed with enough minds tonight. Maybe Ricky could pull some strings and get me out of this mess. The only problem was that Ricky had pissed off a few people down below too, and his hands were tied.

On my way back home I felt much worse, shaking all over and being sick everywhere on the street. When I got inside I threw myself on my bed and lay there for a good half hour, telling my stupid self that this was the last time I drank more than I could handle. Paul must have put more magic than he intended in one of my bottles. It wasn't his fault that I was an addict. I forced some food through my mouth later on, knowing that I had to fuel my body with new energy. After my stomach was full, I felt slightly better.

The Watchers were most likely around. I saved Emma a couple of weeks ago and I managed to get away with that kind of outburst of power, but thunder and lightning down at the cemetery pushed its limits. My days were numbered. Most of the time demons downstairs didn't care to listen to explanations. They needed to punish mongrels like me.

I must have fallen asleep for an hour or two, because a car horn outside woke me up. The clock on the wall was showing half past ten. I was an hour and a half away from my judgment hearing. Part of me wanted to call Ricky to warn him that he might never see me again, but I didn't want to worry him. I had a small advantage: the missing royal and my case. If I could just get in touch with Rodriguez somehow, maybe he could stop the hearing and let others know that I was only trying to do my job.

The voice of reason reminded me that it was too late for that now.

I swallowed the tears down when I stepped outside in the cold. Arthur had showered me with attention and I suspected that maybe my involvement with him triggered new attention back, but this time from hell. Only certain members of the royal family knew what happened between us, but word may have spread. Demons in hell only knew black or white. They didn't believe in love and desire. These emotions were foreign to them.

I headed to Payne's Wharf. It was a wasteland, a deserted part of London near the River Thames. Most of the time humans avoided it. Lately there had been reports that a couple of females had been raped in that area. The police advised everyone to stay away.

I believed that it was just hell's propaganda, to keep humans away from the only official entrance to the underworld. The Gates of Hell were guarded by the Watchers so that no one could enter without their say-so. I never had the courage to actually check this theory out, but I knew that many mongrels had, ending up lost down below.

The night was windy; a new storm was approaching from the west. I walked through the streets, passing humans that had no idea that a world below actually existed and that some of them would end up there at some point in their lives. I took the tube down, and my anxiety rose, filling my stomach with heavy bricks.

I reached my destination just before midnight, pushing the fear away, telling myself this was the price that I needed to pay. I could only blame myself for what happened.

In the distance the tall facade of Payne's Wharf spread in front of my eyes, and my stomach blossomed with a fresh dose of rippling trepidation. Fear drifted behind me in tiny tendrils, stinging me with its sharp claws. This was it, my time had come. I didn't have any regrets. I made my choices, and I couldn't do anything about the fact that the rules of hell weren't fair.

A demon crossed my path several moments later. I stopped, inhaling the raw musty smell of stagnant water close by. Maybe after the incident at the cemetery I was immune to other supernatural beings. My normally sharp senses didn't register any danger, not just yet.

"Are you the one that everyone is waiting for?" a female demon with nice long blonde hair asked.

"Presumably," I responded. She smiled, like she was genuinely excited.

"Come, she is waiting for you."

We walked through the wasteland for the next few minutes in silence. Behind the pillar of another ruined construction I spotted at least five demons, all from the same faction. Lucifer's presence around here seemed profound, and it surprised me that everyone was so calm. The woman who stood on the large piece of concrete looked familiar. I stopped in my tracks, feeling fooled and betrayed. She'd called herself Alexis at the palace, but this couldn't be her real name down here. She warned me to stay away from Arthur, selling some crap about being connected to the Princess Layla. This was some kind of a joke. She couldn't be the judge.

"You don't have any authority to summon me here. I don't answer to you!" I shouted, getting really tired of being a pushover. I had demonic blood in me, but that didn't mean that I had to obey anyone.

She smiled, and a strong wind ruffled her chestnut hair. She waved her hand, like she was making some kind of gesture, bowing in front of me. Then I felt the ground beneath my feet shaking and a cold shiver crawl over my back, stirring the waves of warning vibes in my stomach. I felt like something was in the ground, pulsing with energy and trying to get out.

Everyone around me sensed the shift in the air, the rising electricity. Then the ground began shaking, moving, and the strong wind whipped through, almost knocking me off my feet.

And then the ground began descending, creating a large hole; rocks started falling into it, an invisible power trying to suck in every nearby living being. The heat exploded, stinging my skin, and I felt myself being pulled too. Melted lava appeared on the edges. I had a fifty-fifty chance of staying up on my feet or being pulled inside the fiery pits. The smell of burning ozone filled the air. My lungs contracted and I found it hard to breathe.

My skin was itching with roaring power, as invisible voices whispered that I wanted to discover what was down in the underworld, what other secrets demons were keeping from mongrels. The itch of curiosity began brewing inside my stomach, pulling me closer to hell and further away from this world. The craving burned my throat, as I launched back away from the hole, taking long pulls of air.

Alexis was staring down at me, smiling. Her eyes were penetrating, her energy invading my mind. The bitch was bulldogging her way in, hoping to untangle my wards. I ground my teeth together, fighting back the heat and her unbearable pressure inside my skull.

I didn't know what was happening when a wave of heat suddenly threw me to the ground, and I slammed down on my back. Everything stopped, the hole in the ground, the entrance to the underworld had vanished as quickly as it appeared, sucking the bits and pieces of stones around, like an invisible whirlpool in the middle of the ocean. The craving had gone away, but the bitter taste in my mouth remained.

I was breathing hard and quickly repairing my wards. The bitch was strong and she knew my sloppy spectacle of powers at the cemetery weakened me.

"You're accused of conspiring against Lucifer's faction, revealing all the secrets to the human and failing to comply with the rules," Alexis shouted, pointing at me. A couple of demons that gathered around to look cheered, agreeing with her. Her fingers were black, covered with thick liquid, what looked like blood. My stomach tightened and I forced myself to look when she started licking them, closing her eyes with an expression of euphoria.

I had no doubt that it was human blood, as the smell of burning flesh wafted in the air. I wanted to gag. Some of the demons were known for consuming human flesh, but I could never figure out why. My stomach revolted at the thought. I didn't understand how she had been put in charge, her authority was limited, but at the same time she summoned the gates. I wasn't planning to leave earth just yet, and she couldn't send me over there, unless she was a Watcher.

The other demons stared at me, looking excited, rubbing their hands together.

Alexis was slowly breaking through my wards that protected my memories, my deepest secrets. I was reading her well, and she was thinking that I wasn't just an ordinary mongrel, a half demon. I couldn't let her see the past, discover what I was forced to hide in order to survive.

"I had to stop those humans; it was in self-defence and I had no other choice but to use my powers!" I shouted, angry that I wasn't even getting a proper hearing. Sweat ran down my face when I watched her coming down. Her mouth was smeared with blood, eyes shimmering with rippling power. "I demand to speak to a Watcher. This is a joke; you have no right judging me!"

"The missing prince has been taken down to hell, so you must cease your investigation. The Mammon faction is going to take care of this from now on. His soul had been taken, and you failed to bring him back," she said, circling around me.

She was beautiful—her skin radiated with small crystals, her long brown hair shined in the night fire that suddenly started burning next to me, but her eyes were the most mesmerising.

"I have seen him on earth; he hasn't been taken down to the underworld yet. You're wrong and I have been give —"

"That task is no longer relevant. Lucifer sent me here to condemn your investigation. Another demon confirmed that you used your abilities tonight in front of others, that you nearly exposed us. This is a strict violation of underworld code."

She was close, standing no more than a meter away from me, fighting her way through my energy. I gathered my strength and somehow I tore myself away from her influence. No one could have predicted that I would scramble back on my feet and throw myself at her.

She didn't have time to back away, so I grabbed her shins with both my hands, hoping to use her own energy against her. We connected, and I cleaved my way in, passing her wards, tearing my way through. The demon inside her was weak and fading.

Our eyes met and a silent scream filled my throat when I saw through her. Her powerful demon in front of me was fading away, dark, consuming shadows eating bits, parts of her fully intact demonic soul. From the outside, she was just a human and that was why I couldn't fully understand who she was in the palace.

I was suddenly affected by her pain, her suffering. Rivers of blood filled my eyes. I parted my mouth, wanting to scream as her lack of power continued to get worse. She was losing hours, days, and years. Her demonic soul was dying slowly and that had something to do with the fact that she had been on the outside world for too long. The threats were coming together in slow burning marks.

She roared at the top of her lungs, and I felt the hot burning sensation on the back of my scull. The fire inside my chest soared. I couldn't let her drag me back to hell, just because I discovered her secret.

Darkness covered me completely and the next thing I knew I was falling down. I saw my mother's face, heard her weak voice whispering to me, saying that no one could touch me because I was protected.

A second later I must have passed out from heat, landing down in hell. Literally.

Chapter Twenty-One

"Justice does not descend from its own pinnacle."
— **Dante Alighieri, Purgatorio**

I woke up in pain, completely disoriented, on a much softer surface than I expected, next to the body of a man. Panic shot through me as I tried to gather myself, but the pain in my skull escalated yet again. My eyes were hurting too when I tried to see where I ended up this time. A wave of familiar cologne permeated the air. Part of me wondered if hell really existed or maybe it was just one big fat lie.

This wasn't how I imagined the pits would look. And when I felt movement next to me, I exhaled with relief, knowing that I wasn't in the feared underworld. My senses registered a sexy alpha male next to me. Whatever Alexis did…worked. She obviously didn't like the fact that I had learnt about her disability, and she somehow transported me back to the other person that I was trying to stay away from.

Zach.

I was in his bed, in his house.

"Son of a bitch," I said loudly and then slammed my hand over my mouth. Zach snored and turned to face me, at the same time using his arm to bring me closer to him. He stunk of whiskey, spice and male, and like he had been outdoors somewhere. Suddenly heat rushed up my spine, creating a pool of heat between my legs. I could get turned on in the worst circumstances.

He was so close to me that I could count the hairs on his dark beard. Warmth swept through my veins and I felt dizzy with a headache. I had no idea what kind of mess I was in now, but the clock on Zachary's dresser registered three a.m.

Time had been paused, like in the cemetery. One moment I was standing in the middle of the wasteland, and in the next I was in Zach's bed. Alexis was a demon, a dying demon, and involuntarily had transported me back to the human world. She must have panicked, used her last bits of power to get rid of me.

Slowly and as quietly as I could, I pushed Zach's arm off me and got out of the bed. He was out, lost in his own dreams. Sometime between the incident at the cemetery and my hearing, he managed to get drunk. I left the room and then ran downstairs, pushing my conflicted emotions away. I thought about his strong arms, and those lips that I'd tasted. I could go back upstairs and wake him. In a moment, Arthur, my problems could have been a distant memory.

Instead I listened to the voice of reason and used the back door to disappear. Part of me wished that things were different, that I could just vanish from this world and start somewhere else. I began walking home, disoriented, cold and worried that I just made a new enemy. There was always a price for magic, but tonight I was still free. George couldn't have been lost; his soul was in the city. Alexis was wrong.

It was late when I finally reached my flat, sometime after five a.m. My whole body was shattered, head banging. The truth was that I could have taken a taxi home, but I was skint and it would cost me a fortune to get from one side of the city to the other. There was also the possibility that Ricky could have picked me up, but then I would have to tell him what happened and why I was stranded in the middle of North London with half of my energy missing.

As soon as my head hit the pillow, I was out, and nothing was going to wake me up then.

***

I stirred myself awake and shot up on my feet, waking from the nightmare. Sweat rolled over my cheek. I recognised my own messy bedroom and the clock on the wall indicated that it was quarter past nine. Bile rose in my throat, and I ran to the bathroom. Before I knew, I was throwing up. My stomach revolted, as memories from the night before rolled in front of my eyes. My body's temperature was up and my hands were trembling. When I was done with emptying my stomach, I rolled over to the cold tiles, breathing hard, hoping to rest a little. There was something wrong with me. My heart rate was up, pounding loudly in my chest. The effects of magical tequila were wearing off, and I hadn't drunk anything in the past forty-eight hours. Maybe my body was trying to tell me that it was time to refuel.

Fortunately for me, the symptoms had gone an hour later, and the headache eased off. In the shower I started analysing all my mistakes and that eventful hearing in the wasteland. The prince was gone. He was so hooked on advanced charms that he wasn't lucid any longer. The lab in Jessica's apartment confirmed that a demon, possibly within Lucifer's faction, was rebelling against hell's rules. Someone was planning to use the prince's blood to create Second Chance potion—an illegal substance that brought power and strength beyond the norm. And if the rumours were to be believed, it made a mongrel a full demon. I wasn't getting four when I was adding two and two, and I needed to figure out if Rodriguez was part of the scam. Something just wasn't right about him.

I hadn't had much sleep at all, and I looked pale. Too bad, I needed to get to the office and talk to Ricky. There was a lot that happened in the past few days, and I needed to figure out what was important. It was cold this morning, so I tucked my jacket tighter, walking fast through the crowded streets of grey London.

Inside the building where our Doomed Cases office was, I sensed three demons upstairs. Two more than I expected. So I sped up, wanting to see what was going on.

"Identify yourself, mongrel," barked the demon that guarded the entrance to my floor. I didn't know what was happening to me, but I was ready to explode, anger blurred my vision. This was my fucking business and the faction had no authority to tell me what to do. The craving for tequila burned my throat. The energy built in me again, and I was ready to kick some arse.

Emma was anxious and scared. Demons behind these doors should have known that a human being was with them, but they didn't bother to ease her fears. Someone was going to pay, and today I was too pumped with adrenaline to think rationally.

"I'm the owner of Doomed Cases; who the hell are you?" I asked, raising my voice. The demon from Mammon's faction was bigger, scarier and much more important than me. He lifted his hand, probably to use his power against me, but I wasn't having any of it. Well, the dude didn't stand a chance. I grabbed his elbow twisted it and smashed his face into the wall, pushing my whole body weight into his back. He moaned—yeah, the dude actually moaned—and my head only began pounding more rapidly.

"Fucking mongrel, you have two seconds to let me go or I'm going to report you to Mammon himself!" the big, stupid idiot shouted. Then the door of my office opened up abruptly and I turned around to see who I needed to deal with this time around.

The demon that stood in the door looked like a samurai from fifteenth century Japan. I was completely startled by his attire. He was dressed in a yukata, which is a less decorative version of a kimono, and had what looked like a katana, a short Japanese sword, hanging over his left hip. I could guess he had Japanese heritage, but with cosplay who can tell. He had very dark short hair and startling brown eyes that most likely seduced women with one wink. Badass, that's the first thing that came to my mind when I lay my eyes on him.

"Dominic, can you be anymore pathetic? I told you to keep an eye on the door and instead you're getting beat up by a woman—no offence, Max," the Asian dude said, with some sort of twisted amusement in his eyes. He had a very clear London accent, almost perfect. If I'd heard him on the radio, I would never say that he wasn't British.

"None taken," I muttered.

I frowned but didn't let go of the other demon that was now trying to conjure his power against me. He was all about the muscles, not brain.

"This fucking mongrel wanted to get inside. She should be locked up. Psycho!" he shouted, trying to get away from my grip, but I was having too much fun humiliating him in front of his boss.

"Language, Dominic. There are other humans inside this building, and we don't have time to play with their minds too," the Asian dude stated, keeping his sharp gaze on me. I kicked the disruptive demon between his legs and then let go. He slid down the wall, cursing me out.

"Am I allowed to go inside my own office now? Or is that too much to ask?"

"We were actually hoping that you would show. Mammon's faction has questions for you and it's going to be easier if you come inside. Dominic, stay here and try to act like a human for a change," the Asian man barked.

I nodded to the Asian dude and walked inside, passing the useless demon who was glaring at me with pure hatred. Inside, Ricky was going through some paperwork. Files were scattered all over his desk. His face was red and he looked genuinely pissed off. Emma was on her laptop, typing furiously. The Asian dude must have done something to calm her down, because she seemed much more like herself now than a moment ago.

"So can you tell me what the hell is going on and why Mammon is suddenly so interested in my business?" I asked, placing my hands on my hips, thinking that this had to have something to do with last night and that bitch Alexis.

"My name is Cyril. I'm the senior investigator for all factions in this district. I had a phone call last night. Someone warned me that you're using this office to conspire against Lucifer and his order. Apparently your staff is encouraging other mongrels to start an uprising. We were bound to investigate," Cyril explained, in a stoic voice, like this whole thing was perfectly normal.

"What? That's absurd," I said, not believing that this was really happening.

"Apparently you're using this agency as a cover, to gather resources and reach out for more people," Cyril added, stroking his sword. Emma seemed completely oblivious to this conversation. Cyril must have filled her system with a certain charm so she could only hear what appeared to be a normal conversation about taxes or something.

Ricky snorted from his office, but didn't say a word. He knew that these accusations were ridiculous.

"Listen to yourself, mate. Do you really believe that I have something against the system or Lucifer? Demons and mongrels come to me because no one else cares. The police won't help them and I have no interest in Lucifer and his business on earth whatsoever. Check all the files. You can go through every single case that I ever worked on," I said, angry and frustrated at that point.

"Personally I don't think that there is anything like that going on here, but your recent case brought some concerns. I was bound to investigate, to make sure that you follow the protocol like every other mongrel born on earth," he said, still staring at me intensely, like he wasn't fully convinced that I wasn't hiding anything.

Royals, of course. My reputation had preceded me. There was only one Maxine Brodeur in London that screwed the future king. People downstairs must have found this hilarious.

"Well, carry on. I have work to do," I said, and walked off, heading to my office.

As it turned out, Cyril had a few other idiots with him to go through all our files. Emma was very keen to show them around, so that kept him busy for the next several hours. Finally when the whole party was moved to the storage on the next floor up, Ricky exhaled with relief, flopping on the chair in front of me. There were so many things that I needed to discuss, but I had no idea where I was supposed to start. Alexis wanted me to back off this case, claiming that she had direct orders from Lucifer and now we were accused of conspiring against the underworld.

"Strange rumours are going around the streets, very concerning," Ricky said, rubbing his forehead. I meant to talk to him about the case that he had taken on recently, but things got in the way.

"What's going on now?" I asked, thinking about my next step. There was no way I was going to drop looking for the prince, just because a demon told me so.

"Demons are saying that the prince is in hell and that Lucifer has lost control," he whispered, leaning over. "And this whole investigation. Someone wants to bury us. And the case."

I swallowed hard, seeing fear in Ricky's eyes. I knew that he was right. Too many things had happened and now we had some investigator going through our files, telling us that we were conspiring against the master of the underworld. We were running out of time and I no longer knew who to trust. Ricky was right—someone was working very hard against me, hoping that I would drop the case and forget about missing Prince George. And I was ready to do just that.

Chapter Twenty Two

"Fate's arrow, when expected, travels slow."
— Dante Alighieri, Paradiso

"I saw the prince with Zach last night at the cemetery. He was with the missing hooker. These rumours aren't right, Rick. George is still in London and whoever is spreading this story is hoping that we give up and forget about the case," I pointed out, looking at the door. "We went to that hooker's apartment and someone had set up a lab there. She couldn't have known how to brew the Second Chance potion. The prince is the key to all that."

Ricky was worried about our future. He didn't want to leave his life in London behind and start over somewhere else. We were both in the same boat.

Normally Watchers dished out the punishment before they asked any questions. I was obligated to answer to

Rodriguez, who wanted me to find George quietly, but I still didn't trust him. Lucifer couldn't afford to lose control over his own demons. There were most likely many that wanted things to change. Maybe that's why the prince went missing in the first place, so he would be used as a bargaining tool in the upcoming election in hell.

"What happened after that?"

"Nothing. Things went tits up, and he disappeared," I admitted and then stood up. "I need to shut myself in the office and make a few phone calls before Zach gets here."

"So you didn't play poker last night?" Ricky asked.

"Poker? No, I was working for a change, trying to get the faction off our backs," I told him, thinking that it'd been long enough since I tasted tequila. Maybe tonight if I made any progress, but Ricky didn't need to know that.

I didn't want him to leave Cyril alone for too long. He was still nosing around our cases on the other side of the building. I knew that my partner was anxious about our missing prince, his future, and the fact that I wasn't stable enough to carry on with this work on my own. He wanted to keep his life away from faction business.

My only other lead was the waitress that called the office yesterday, and I needed to track her down. She would most likely lead me to her friend and then to the prince. There was a reason that prince was in the cemetery last night. He was digging the grave, searching for someone that must have died recently, but why? I had a feeling that I was working against a very powerful and power hungry demon that had nothing to lose but a lot to gain.

I went back to my own room and collected a protection elixir that I used sometimes when I was challenged by unknown powers, then locked the door.

Months ago, when my mind wasn't so screwed I brewed a few useful potions. Some of them were good for a fight, some were useful in situations like today's, but I was running low on stock.

It was time to start getting in touch with people that owed me favours. Zach was probably curing his own hangover today, just like I had been yesterday, so I had some time to figure out my next step.

Eventually Cyril packed his stuff and left with his people. He slipped his card down on my desk and told me that he might be in touch again. Around five I had a phone call back from Rob. He lost quite a lot of money in a poker game with me a couple of months back and then tried to do a runner. He didn't get far, and after a long night of bargaining, I eventually let him go. We started working together after that. I said that I could forget about his debt if he helped me out sometimes tracking people down that didn't want to be found. My knowledge of technology was limited, and Rob was a computer hacker during the night.

Rob checked Jessica's background and told me she lived alone and she didn't have any family. He managed to get me the address of a hotel in Shoreditch. Apparently that was where the waitress had called from the last time I spoke to her.

When I left the office later on in the evening, the guilt settled in. Zach had gone through a lot and he was still searching for the truth. There was no doubt that he was guided by his own beliefs. We could never be in a relationship (not like I was counting on it) because of who I was, someone between a human and a demon.

I took the tube to Shoreditch High Street station and then walked for about ten minutes to the hotel. My feet were sore from yesterday, but my head was clearer. Zach could have died in the cemetery. I exposed my world and risked a lot more than just my skin.

The girl that asked me to check on her friend had called from a five-star hotel. The building went through an extensive renovation six months ago and now the new hotel attracted people from all over the world. Natasha was hiding, and she wouldn't be stupid enough to go back to her home address. This was the only other place where she could have been staying, probably with someone that was covering her expenses.

Inside the entire lobby was covered with white tiles, tall black desks and pretty receptionists. There was a fireplace along the wall that created an electric flame effect. All the staff were wearing matching uniforms. There was a large bar at the back, so I headed there first. It was still early, so many people were sitting alongside the window, reading their papers. There was nothing out of the ordinary going on, and these humans as usual were oblivious to the noise and busy road outside.

I sat at the corner of the bar and looked around. Rob had given me the address of the club where she was last registered for work. Natasha hadn't shown up for her shift for a good few days and her boss was ready to fire her. I got what I needed from him, which was her most recent photo. The trip across the city was eventful, and without Zach breathing down my neck everything was going more smoothly than usual.

"Hey, handsome, can I ask you a question?" I asked the barman when he came to take my order. He was very young, possibly only nineteen or twenty. He was thinking about the older lady that flirted with him yesterday in the afternoon. I had to shut down my demonic abilities and concentrate on my tasks. The girl was somewhere in this hotel and she was the only other person that could lead me to missing Prince George.

A blond with nice blue eyes smiled at me, glancing over my colourful highlights. I didn't fit into the shiny surroundings, wearing my second-hand brown leather jacket that kind of made me look like a badass.

"That's depends on the question," he said, leaning over. I took the picture of the girl from my side pocket and put it on the bar, itching to order tequila. My taste buds could already imagine the sharp, woody taste moving down my throat, spreading over my system. God, there was really something wrong with me. I had made too many bad decisions whilst drunk. Maybe I had to stay away from the yellow liquid until this evening.

"Have you seen this girl? I know that she is in this hotel, but I'm more interested in knowing who she is hanging around these days?" I asked, touching his hand and sending snips of electric power over the surface of his skin. The small dose of energy could make him talk more than usual, and I needed to know everything before I headed upstairs.

Brandon (he had a name tag) stared at the picture for a long while with a frown. His thoughts started racing all of a sudden, and he scratched his head like he wasn't sure if he had seen the girl here. I glanced around, thinking that someone was watching us, but all the humans were minding their own business. After a long moment, his face brightened up.

"Yes, I have seen her around here. She is very pretty. Comes in late in the evening and orders a cocktail," Brandon blurted out.

"What room number? And was she alone?" I pressed.

"She was in the company of a woman and an older man. They were staying in the penthouse suite on the top floor, in the most expensive part. Prince George stayed there once a couple of months back," he continued with a wink. I only encouraged him to talk, but it seemed that his tongue was already loose.

"Thanks, handsome, you were helpful," I said, smiling and leaving a five-pound tip on the bar. I wanted to order the damn shot, but a strong voice of reason shut the temptation down pretty quickly. The craving was loosening up my focus.

Brandon was convinced that George had been here before, staying in the penthouse, and that was a good sign. On my way to the elevator I felt my phone buzz. Zachary was trying to get hold of me. He already left a couple voicemails on my mobile. The doors closed and I pressed the top floor, but the light indicated that I needed to insert a special key card. Right, so there was a problem; that floor was restricted and only accessible for the guests.

I pressed floor sixteen and decided to improvise, possibly use the stairs. My demonic energy rose as I was moving up. The temperature of my body shot up as anticipation settled in. When the door finally opened, I realised why. Royal guards were scattered around the sixteenth floor. I recognised their matching suits and a couple of familiar faces. A bulky man that was part of hotel security stood in front of the main door that most likely led to a conference room.

Someone from the royal family was staying on this floor, and I didn't need this right now, renewing the old contacts. I turned to the left and started walking in the opposite direction, thinking about my options.

"Max, hey, Max," someone shouted after me. I cursed under my breath and stopped. A moment later Jonathan Blackwell caught up with me. He was personally responsible for the security of Prince George when I still worked in the palace. I had no idea what he was doing in a place like this.

"Hi, Jon, how is it going?" I asked, pretending that this meeting was one huge coincidence.

"I'm good, everything is fine. There is some sort of meeting going on here," he said, looking relaxed. I exhaled with relief, knowing that the guards were here for completely ordinary reasons. I needed to stop worrying. "But what the heck are you doing here?"

"Well … I need to investigate something on the top floor, but I can't get—"

"Jon, what's going on?"

I didn't have to look up to see who was walking towards me a moment later. My senses registered him before I had a chance to even face him. I had no idea what the hell happened to my abilities. How could I have missed the fact that Arthur was staying in the hotel? We were connected and I was always able to tell if he was close. This wasn't the time or a place for a friendly chat.

"Maxine, what a pleasant surprise." He beamed when he saw me. Jonathan didn't know about our history, so he nodded and started backing away. Crap, seeing Arthur right now wasn't on my list of priorities.

"Hey, Arthur. It's good to see you," I greeted him. "I'm actually heading somewhere."

His whole entourage stared at us from the other side of the corridor. I needed to do something, either use my abilities to make him forget that I was here or knock him out for a bit. Both options were reasonable enough.

"Well, let me go with you. I'm on my break. We aren't due to come back to the room for another half an hour. We need to have a proper catch up," he said and heat flared up my neck. Last night I had my first sober night in a while, so my mind was clear enough to know that I needed to leave. Arthur looked bloody handsome wearing a black most likely designer suit. When he stared at me like this I lost my breath and all sense of time.

"I have to go. I'm on a case," I said, quickly breaking our eye contact and turning around. My heart turned in my chest as I continued pushing my legs forward. He had his morning planned out, and I was hoping that this time he wouldn't follow me around. The end of corridor was blocked off; the doors were only accessible with the special key card. I couldn't use my abilities; there were too many humans on this floor, all aware that I wasn't supposed to be here.

"Flower, I can help you with access to the top floor," the voice behind me stated. Arthur leaned against the wall, holding a sliding key in his hand.

"Then let me in. There is a girl upstairs that might know where George is," I snapped at him.

"Your wish is my command," he whispered and slid the card in. The doors were unlocked and I went in heading upstairs. The only problem was that Arthur was right behind me, and his whole entourage followed through.

Chapter Twenty-Three

"If the present world go astray, the cause is in you, in you it is to be sought."
— **Dante Alighieri, The Divine Comedy**

I turned around to tell him to get lost when we reached the top floor, but Arthur had something entirely different in mind. The doors to the room opposite were wide open and he pushed me inside, shutting them behind us with his left leg. A fresh dose of anger boiled my blood, but at the same time his presence was like an antidote for all my pains.

"Two seconds," he told me and then cracked the door open slightly. "Jon, make sure that no one enters or passes through this door. Am I making myself clear?"

"Yes, Your Highness," said Jonathan, and then Arthur shut the door in front of his face. I glanced around the room and scratched my head, slightly taken back by its size. This must have been one of the private suites. A four-poster wooden bed stood in the middle, there were a couple of leathers sofas by the window, a huge TV with other high-end gadgets.

"Arthur, I really haven't got time for this. We have nothing to talk about," I said, placing my hands on my hips. Secretly I wished that I had the ability to change the past. I could have saved myself a lot of hassle if I had never accepted that job in Buckingham Palace. He clasped his hands together and approached me.

"We are going to talk, here and now," he said, sounding completely serious.

"No, you're not forcing me to talk. I have shit that I have to get on with, Your Highness," I snapped, emphasising his royal title. He dragged his hand through his hair and started moving closer, so I took a couple of steps back until I hit the wall. I could easily wave my hand and stop this whole nonsense, but the line between doing what was right and wrong was thinning with every passing second.

He lifted my arms above my head and pressed himself closer, deeper. God, I was losing complete control of myself so quickly.

"You know how much it turns me on when you call me that, Flower," he said, shifting his voice to that husky tone. My body pulsated with the rhythm of my heartbeat, and the energy started to circulate, this wild anticipation that was suddenly building deep inside me, a promise that this could go somewhere. "I looked for you everywhere after you disappeared, Maxine. Someone in the palace had discovered the truth and went to Queen Mother. All my choices were taken away from me twelve months ago. The guards were following me around almost twenty-four-seven nonstop. I felt suffocated."

Our last kiss nearly broke me to pieces, but right then I didn't care about the rules. My heart beat loudly in my chest, telling me that things were different now and he needed me back. Warmth danced in my belly, reminding me about the euphoric times in his private study.

A tiny voice in my head shut down these conflicted emotions and roared *no* and *stop*. I pushed him away. It hurt, it fucking tore apart my stupid heart, but I couldn't let him cloud my judgment.

"No, you have no right to me," I snarled, and lifted his right hand, so he couldn't deny anything. "You gave Natalie a ring and you're going to marry her. There is nothing more between us. It ended when the Queen discovered the truth, when everything fell—"

"Flower, I nearly lost it then. It fucking hurt so badly when you vanished. I wandered off to the wildest places in the city, hoping to find you. I drank and lost control. Everyone tried to lead me back to the straight and narrow, but I still loved you. Listen to my heart … listen, Maxine, it beats for you."

I wanted to laugh from his claims, but a messy lump formed in my chest. My throat was raw with emotions as I stared at this man that transformed my life for the better, then the worst. It was now or never. I needed to tell him, but after that there was no way out. He would hate me for the rest of my life.

"She fired me. Your precious grandmother pushed me out as soon as I stepped into her quarters. I had five minutes to pick up my things and leave, Arthur," I shouted, remembering the humiliation. He was pale and his hands were clenched into fists. The undying love that beamed from him was crushing. I remembered that day when I was thrown out of the palace with no way of coming back, like a pleb, someone that needed to rot in hell.

"After I'd gotten myself into yet another fight, I was called to the base and within days I was being deployed to a combat mission. I searched for you, but Ricky didn't want to tell me anything. When I beat him up, he called the palace, sold me out. I was sent to Iraq, Maxine, and got stuck there for months without any way of getting out."

I didn't have to listen to that. I knew the truth, but he had no reason to lie to me. Frustration boiled through me. There were two broken hearts in this room, and I never thought, not in a million years believed that this whole affair would cause so much drama. I should have stopped myself when there was still a chance, when we were only playing with each other.

When I came back to London, Prince Arthur was already engaged to Duchess Natalie Morgan. Somehow Ricky had convinced me that I needed to regain my focus and keep myself busy, so I went back to work. I was fully aware that Arthur had forgotten about me, about what we had.

"What?" he yelled hoarsely when someone knocked at the door again. We'd both ignored it the first time.

"Your Highness, a few other people are asking for you. The meeting is just about to start," said Jonathan, who was standing outside the door. I needed to remember the reasons I was here, and even if Arthur was telling me the truth, nothing changed the fact that he was already taken.

"They have to wait. I'm not finished here," Arthur snapped back. I shook my head, wondering what the hell I was still doing here. He was determined to keep me here as long as necessary.

"The past is no longer relevant. I'm putting my life back together and you have Natalie, your fiancée. The Queen Mother won't let you break the engagement and the royals can't afford another scandal," I explained. We both knew that his future was set, and his family stood firmly with the Queen Mother's decisions. He was in his early thirties, and he was expected to settle down, to start a family. This was something that he'd always dreamed of. "I'm no one, Arthur, just a woman that used to work for you, that grew up in an orphanage run by nuns. Come on, let's get out of here. You have a meeting and people are waiting for you."

He was furious with the fact that I was right, that he had lost me a long time ago. There were too many people that wanted to keep us apart, too many responsibilities to make it all go away. Besides, he knew that I returned to London six months after we got separated and still he didn't come to see me. I had no right to expect anything from him, but deep down I had hoped that he still cared.

"No, Maxine, we are going to sort this out now, here. I'm not marrying her. When I came back from Iraq, I was lost and she was there, but I never loved her the way I used to love you. Please believe me, please let me make this right."

He was begging me now. The future king of Britain was begging me to take him back. The pain inside me felt too real, and I couldn't imagine that it would ever ease. We couldn't have that second chance; no member of his family would ever accept the fact that we were in love. Besides, Lucifer kept an eye on royals and the faction would make sure that we stayed separated.

The knock persisted and I moved towards the door, passing Arthur on the way. I tried to open it, but he shut it with his body and then grabbed my wrists.

"Go away, Jon, or I swear to God I will fire you," he shouted and wrapped his arms around my waist. I considered fighting him off, but his fingers were touching my skin. The caress sent jolts of electricity through me, and the stream of power followed all the way to the tips of my toes. He pushed me down to the large bed and had me pinned underneath him within a heartbeat. Around him, I wasn't even myself, my abilities shifted. It was easier to wait until he was done with me, than fight him.

His hair fell sexily on his forehead and the warmth that travelled down between my legs was melting my biting anger into submission. Arthur was the only man in the world that had this kind of power over me. I could beat the shit out of other demons, creatures of the underworld, but when he pinned me down with his hard lean body I felt hopelessly lost to him.

Thoughts about Zach entered my mind. I felt more in control around him, but my emotions around him were running wild. Arthur was a man that craved more and expected all. I shivered, hopelessly drawn into his pale eyes.

"What are you trying to achieve, Arthur? This won't change my mind. I'm moving on, leading a new life away from you. Nothing that you say will change things. Just let me go," I whispered, pleading and thinking that we'd had our chance, that he was only hurting himself.

When he didn't answer and leaned down to kiss me, I moved my head to the side. His lips started tracing the skin on my neck, zipping away the hesitation, the determination of staying immune to his tortures. I moaned, suddenly aware how ready he was for me, parting my legs with his.

The knock gave me a chance to flip him over onto his back and stop this nonsense. One kiss a couple of weeks back had nearly killed me, and I wasn't going to sleep with him. Too many things went wrong the last time.

"Your Highness, everyone is waiting for you." Jonathan kept talking through the door. Arthur was holding my wrists, but now I was sitting on top of him, aware that he was hard, and he was stripping me with his eyes.

"You're going to marry Natalie and live happy ever after. Don't worry about me. I'm going to be fine. I'll find George and then disappear—"

"No, Flower," he growled, fighting with me.

"Yes, Your Highness, I'm not worth it to be chased, not worth it to lose, because I'm not even—"

I couldn't finish the sentence and risk the life of other demons. I also knew what happened to humans that found out about our world. Sometimes their twisted minds couldn't be repaired.

"What, Maxine? You're not what?" he asked with anger and resentment, but then the door opened and Jonathan barged inside. He took in the scene in the bed and muttered "fuck" under his breath.

Behind him was a guy in a suit, a human that I hadn't seen before.

"Blackwell, you're out of line and I'm going to fire your arse. I didn't give you permission to enter," Arthur shouted, looking like he was going to lose it and batter Jon to death. The guy behind Jon was a demon too. I scrambled away from him, gathering the energy that slipped inside the room. All of a sudden I was lucid and alert. Another member of my kind just saw me on the bed with the prince. This wasn't going to end well.

"Your Highness, Miss Morgan is downstairs. There was —"

"I have to go," I said, as the coldness settled in my chest. Natalie was on the way upstairs and she couldn't see me here, especially like this. On top of that I had to find Natasha. She was somewhere on this floor.

"Maxine, we are not done. I can tell her now."

"Your Highness, your fiancée. There is no time," Jonathan said, more forcefully, staring at me, looking uncomfortable. He knew that Natalie could enter this floor at any time, and he wanted to spare us both embarrassment.

"Arthur, your guard is only doing his job, so listen to him for once. Get it together. I'm leaving," I snapped, and then left the room. My legs pushed forward even as my brain screamed at me to stop. I glanced back a few times, but only saw more guards. Arthur didn't follow this time, so I exhaled with relief.

I had lost my head, and it was a huge tactical error. We could have been caught again, and this time I didn't think I could last on earth longer than a day.

As I walked through the long corridor, I realised that there were only a couple of rooms on this floor. Around the corner I nearly bombed into two Chinese men that were talking rapidly in their native tongue. My skin still burned, demanding Arthur's touch, asking for more of what I considered distraction. Zach was different, rougher and more demanding. Maybe I was deluding myself. None of them were ever going to be suitable for me. They were both humans with many flaws and they weren't part of my world.

I stopped in my tracks in front of Room 106. My heart kicked me in the ribcage as I sensed the painful struggle inside.

My intuition had never let me down, even when it came to tracking down someone who didn't want to be found. I cleared my throat and knocked, after I made sure that there was no one watching. The two Chinese men had left, and there was only silence—except for the heartbeat of the woman inside the room. It was pounding in my ears. There was something wrong. I hesitated, then entered the dark room.

After I closed the doors behind me, I knew that it wasn't a human anymore that I was facing, but a creature that came straight from hell.

Chapter Twenty -Four

"This mountain is so formed that it is always wearisome when one begins the ascent, but becomes easier the higher one climbs."
— **Dante Alighieri, Purgatorio**

The silence of the room was broken by long raspy breaths. Someone was standing by the bed, watching me through the gloomy darkness. The large windows were shaded with thick red curtains, and it'd been an hour since the sun hid itself behind the horizon. The creature in this room most likely had taken Natasha's body; I felt her human heart still beating wildly in her chest. Her face was hidden by the hood, somehow deformed, twisted at a strange angle. A wave of frigid air blasted me when I shut the door behind me. The creature that possessed this human's body was desperate to tap into my demonic energy. I wondered how it escaped from the underworld. In theory the Watchers were meant to keep an eye on unofficial entrances to earth, but that didn't quite work in practice.

Suddenly her appearance shifted, and she turned into a pretty woman with long curly blond hair, a perfect small nose and long bare legs. The ugly hood disappeared, and was replaced by a silky pink dressing gown. The creature that now stood in front of me was an A'rea, a mythological being, a female demon of curses. Centuries ago these creatures were worshipped by Lucifer.

They used to be in charge of dying humans, but things got out of control quickly enough. The A'reas had suddenly possessed too much freedom and began using their powers to feed on the human's souls, playing with curses, and placing them randomly on innocent beings just because they could. They were doomed years later and sent to the pits when Lucifer discovered their insubordination. The funny thing was that I never believed that A'reas were real, well, not until now, which was ironic when you think most people don't think I exist either.

"I was waiting for you, hoping that you would take me to the boy," said the A'rea, using Natasha's body to communicate with me. I had a slim chance of saving her, but still a chance. The A'rea was feeding on Natasha's soul, but her life essence was slowly fading. I should have gotten here quicker. Then things would have been different, if only I hadn't been waylaid by Arthur.

Bits of her flesh were damaged, and I could see the parts of her cells breaking down, in some places revealing bare bones. This creature must have been hiding here for days, using Natasha's body to walk around London, to spy on humans. The Watchers must have been aware that there was an A'rea on the loose; they couldn't miss her energy signature. They would already be tracking her down; at least I was hoping that this was the case.

"Where is Prince George? Your human knows his location. Come on, we both know that you have no chance of escaping the pits again, but I can still save her," I said, calmly, pushing any distractions away and mentally preparing to attack. I'd never fought a creature like an A'rea. They were the stuff of legend and I had no idea what to expect. They were strong and had been in residence of the pits for as long as I remembered.

She picked up a cigarette from the table and lit it, lifting her lips in a creepy deformed smile. Now I could clearly see bits of the skin hanging all over her face. I needed to use an elixir to trap her; my strength would work too, but I didn't want anything to go wrong. I had a feeling that I might lose this fight without magic.

"My assignment was supposed to be simple. We both wanted the special boy... such a shame that he was gone long before I got here," the A'rea whispered, and then shifted into her true form. I didn't have time to reach out for my elixir hidden in my back pocket. Sudden pain exploded in my stomach, shooting through my limbs. I lost my balance, slamming my back to the floor, completely paralysed. I didn't even feel any weird sensation or shiver that would tell me to react. The creature from the underworld was on me, and for a split second I was convinced that this was the end, especially when I saw her long, deformed claws in front of my face. One struck me, tearing the skin on my cheek and forehead to pieces as if my skin were nothing more than a sheet of a paper. The fresh raw pain tore through me. Once I let out a sharp gasp, my instincts of a fighter kicked in and I grabbed her arms, throwing her across the room. Blood oozed from the wound on my face and blinded me for a second.

She slammed into the wall so hard that the vibration caused some bits of the ceiling to come down. She let go of a howling scream, releasing some of her curses. I bit down on my lips, as my pain escalated. Her deadly curses were sliding inside me quickly, damaging my nervous system, and draining some of my remaining energy. I felt like my head was going to explode, my ears popping with pressure. If I could just reach my elixir, this could be over already.

I collapsed to my knees and saw her coming towards me. Her claw morphed into fists, and the bone in my jaw cracked when she punched me. I landed on my back, and hot pain started at my scalp and scorched down to my toes. Oxygen wasn't getting into my lungs. The A'rea was standing over me laughing and licking her fingers that were covered with my blood.

The pressure inside my skull was building, and I was struggling to see through the blinding pain. Chances were that I was going to die in this room. Every breath felt like I was inhaling fire, and my own power was lost, gone.

"This human was a fighter. She is still fighting now, but she won't win," her demonic voice rang in my ears. "And I have eaten enough mongrels in my lifetime. You won't take my freedom away from me."

I screamed, at least I attempted to, but the pain exploded, and tears of anger started dropping down my cheeks. Now I understood how it felt to be prisoner of my own body. The A'rea used her curse to turn my own abilities against me.

She leaned over my face. The skin of the human girl smelled so bad, rotting so quickly, decomposing, it was unbearable. Natasha must have been dead for hours now, but I heard her beating heart; surely this was impossible. I wanted to close my eyes and just wait for it to be over, but then I remembered the elixir. Hearing her wheezing breath I reached out, using my left hand. The powder made from olive tree, cow tail, sand and pure gold spilled onto the floor when I pierced the bag with my nail. The homemade mixture injected some new energy into me, turning my heart in my chest. I absorbed it with my energy, inhaling the strong smell of each ingredient. I roared at the top of my lungs and used my right leg to kick the A'rea, hopefully cracking her skull.

She landed on a chest of drawers, smashing it to pieces. For a moment she wasn't moving, and I secretly hoped that the fight was over. I shot back to my feet, inhaling the air that burned my chest. The A'rea moved, wiped the blood from her face, but that moment of distraction gave me an advantage. I was on her, pounding my fists into her face, breaking through the charms. It was as if some evil force possessed me. I couldn't stop even when my knuckles were bleeding.

When she lay motionless on the floor, I poured the rest of the elixir all over her body. Her muffled screams began to fade, and the shadow of the creature that centuries ago was beautiful was drifting away from the body of dead Natasha. A shadow hovered over the room, and I clasped my hands over my ears, trying to block the howling screams. The window had opened itself, the curtains flapped wildly as the wind began sucking the shadow towards the world outside. I reached out and spread more dust, hoping to chain her up to the body for a bit longer, but her shadow was already fading into the darkness. The strong wind knocked me down on my knees, and the A'rea vanished, sucking all the air out of the room. A split second later the door slammed open and Zachary barged inside holding a gun.

"Hands up and stay where you are," he shouted. There were other humans outside and possibly half of the floor had heard the screams and banging.

"It's me, Zach, Max," I snapped, attempting to lift my hands up, but my muscles refused to obey me. The last bits of my strength left me and I collapsed, losing consciousness.

"Max? What the fuck is going on here?"

I must have passed out for only a split second, because a moment later Zach was leaning over my face. Every part of my body burned, the pain spreading everywhere. I had never felt weaker. A fight normally kicked my libido into action from all the excess adrenaline; it gave me strength, but I was drained of all my powers. I lay slumped on the floor, next to the rotten corpse of Natasha. Her face was barely recognisable and the smell was making me nauseous.

Zachary was panicking; he was mumbling to get me help. People were pouring into the room. The sudden stream of human emotions scorched through me, waking me up with their excess energy. Now I began to understand why no one ever fought with A'reas. They were cold-blooded killers.

"She attacked me, she wanted me dead, and I had to defend myself," I blurted out, closing my eyes for a second. Natasha was dead because of me. If only I had gotten to the room earlier, maybe I could have prevented her from experiencing death in such a barbaric way.

"Someone get the medic here now. This woman is injured!" Zach shouted. His own pulse was frantic. He squatted next to me and pressed something cold to my torn cheek. "God, Max, what the hell happened here? I've been trying to get hold of you all morning."

"Help me get to the bathroom. I should be fine in a sec," I told him, trying to lift myself up, but he pushed me down. I needed to swallow some charms. The skin on my cheek was in pieces, bits were hanging off and I would probably need stitches. My jaw was aching like hell, and I knew that the real pain would come later.

"Hold your horses, Flower, you're barely breathing. The paramedics will be here at any second," he told me, holding me on the floor. I didn't want to turn my head and look at the corpse that lay a meter away from me. A woman lost her life, because I refused to say no to a man that used to love me. Two Watchers were already in the building, and they were looking for some sort of explanation.

I grabbed Zachary's hand and squeezed it hard.

"Help me to the bathroom for fuck's sake and don't argue," I snapped, feeling even shittier now as the adrenaline was fading away from my body. I hated the fact that my arse was nearly kicked and now I had to rely on a human.

"Stubborn. Why do you always have to be so stubborn, Maxine?" he muttered when he helped me to get to the bathroom.

Once the doors were locked the world around me started to spin. My demonic soul was defeated and I needed red elixir to gain my strength, to walk again. It was going to take me a few days of recovery, but at least I was still alive. Natasha was dead, and now I couldn't question her about the prince. My main lead was lost. Someone was working really hard to cover all their tracks. I reached into my leather jacket back pocket and took a small bottle filled with red liquid.

The elixir numbed the pain around my cheek and started to replenish some of my lost energy. I finally took a long deep breath. The torn skin needed to be stitched up and I most probably was going to have a scar. This wasn't the usual magical injury so I knew that I wouldn't heal on my own. I looked terrible—there was dry blood and skin in my hair, and my pupils were purple, and no one could miss the intensity of the colour.

I managed to walk, so that was slight progress. Zachary was waiting for me outside the door; the forensics probably from his unit were already examining the body.

"Wow that's a nasty wound. Let me take care of that for you," said one of the paramedics that pushed Zach away and dragged me to the bed.

I let him take care of the bits of my skin since I was the only patient, after all. Natasha was lying dead on the floor and the A'rea had escaped. Suddenly the hotel suite was filled with people, mostly cops that were zooming around the crime scene. Once Zach was done with examining the body he stood by Rodney, the paramedic who was patching me up.

"There are some flasks in the other part of the room, someone's hair and nails," Zach said, looking at me intensely. "What exactly happened here, Max?"

Hair and nails were used in potions and elixirs. I was too busy trying not to die, so I didn't have a chance to look at the odd stuff that Zach was talking about.

I felt their presence even before they entered the room. Two Watchers showed some kind of identification to the policeman that was guarding the door and walked right passed him. I had always been wary of them, mainly because they had the authority to drag anyone they wanted to the underworld. These two looked like lawyers; both were slim, dressed in sharp black suits. The humans noticed that the atmosphere had shifted, that those two people inside were somehow important.

The one with blue eyes stopped by the bed, eyeing me with interest.

"Evidence, we need all of it," he said, looking at me, but directing his request to Zach.

"The table in the other room. Everything is there," Zach replied, with a hazy look on his face. The humans just stared while the two Watchers scooped everything off the table, but no one dared to say anything. I could, but I didn't want to risk being dragged down for interrogation. Once they were done, everything went back to normal and everyone continued to do whatever they had to as if no one had ever showed up.

The Watchers always got what they wanted.

Chapter Twenty-Five

"Soon you will be where your own eyes will see the source and cause and give you their own answer to the mystery."
— **Dante Alighieri, Inferno**

"I have never seen a body in such a terrible state. She looked like she had been dead for weeks," Zachary said when he was taking me to the Accident and Emergency Unit. Will, the second paramedic, had done what he could, but my face needed to be seen by a plastic surgeon to limit the scarring. I refused to go to the hospital in the ambulance. I couldn't afford to lie in bed when there was an A'rea on the loose, and I still had her scent all over my skin. Besides, I had a few other useful elixirs at home, and getting doped on human medicine didn't particularly appeal to me.

My whole body was like one open giant wound, and I needed some time alone in my dark flat to recover. Ricky had already been on the phone; apparently two Watchers had paid him a visit at Doomed Cases. The cold chills crawled over my spine when I thought about meeting them alone in the dark alley. Apparently they passed the evidence from the hotel room to him and asked him to assess it. Someone must have spilled the beans about us, and now our business was on their radar. My name had been linked to the missing royal. I didn't mind getting free exposure, but Ricky and I liked keeping out of hell's business as much as we could. It was bad enough that Cyril had gone through our files and now we were being investigated for conspiring against Lucifer.

"Yeah, she was pretty messed up when I got there. It all happened so fast," I explained, sinking back to my seat. I didn't know what to say. Zach didn't want to believe that the girl was alive when I got to her hotel room.

Arthur had been scheduled to be in the meeting probably way before I got there, and I hated the fact we'd bumped into each other yet again. Fate was a stone cold bitch and hated my guts for some reason. I stayed with him and listened to his story, but I didn't want to believe in it. The tiny voice in my head kept whispering that he was telling the truth. The Queen Mother was capable of sending him away, destroying our happiness. He did look for me, but I wasn't in London, and I didn't tell anyone where I spent the last six months before I came back. That transition was necessary and I had to get away from the mess that I created.

Zach scratched his head. I could see he was wondering why he didn't insist that I stay in ambulance. My cheek was covered in bandages and the throbbing pain was slowly coming back.

Zachary was swearing at the driver in front of us. We were stuck in traffic for about half an hour. The roads were busy and I wanted to lock myself between four walls and just sleep forever. I hadn't ever had that kind of beating before. Surely it wouldn't be the last time either.

"What were you doing up there alone anyway? Weren't we supposed to be working together on this case?" he questioned me. He was pissed off too. That was standard for him, but this time it was more with himself than with me. He was at the station when he got a call about a disturbance in the Shoreditch, dealing with some pointless robbery, and he was blaming himself for arriving too late. I was exhausted, too tired and my throat was burning. Tonight I wanted to hit the bottle hard, but I was reluctant to get wasted, especially after what happened with Natasha.

"I managed to track Natasha down through a spurious source, and I didn't think that you would approve. Anyway I thought that I could just talk to her, but things kind of got out of control pretty quickly. She attacked me with the knife," I explained, hoping that he would believe me.

"Did she say anything about Prince George? Give you any further leads?" Zachary asked. I arched my head back, breathing calmly. This wasn't a very good time to analyse my failed relationship with Arthur or the steadily growing attraction towards Zach. When the car finally moved, he looked at me, waiting for my answer. We were working together, and I was lying to him. How could this ever work?

"No, she was screaming most of the time, like she was in pain. We have nothing to go on," I said, looking away. I needed to put all the previous leads together and figure out where to head next. It seemed to me that hell was panicking, and Lucifer was determined to get to the bottom of who was conspiring against him. If that theory was even true.

For about twenty minutes after that, Zach didn't ask any more questions. I could barely walk when we arrived at the Accident and Emergency room. My elixir was fading and I was losing strength. After filling in countless forms, I waited an hour to get my face sorted. The young human doctor applied some anaesthetic and got on with putting my cheek back together. My abilities were slowly recovering, but my energy level was low, and my body wasn't coping with the injuries that I sustained. Ricky kept calling. He was concerned about my health and the unexpected visit from the Watchers.

"I'm going to take you home, Flower. You had a tough night. We can pick up this whole mess tomorrow," Zachary said when several hours passed and I had taken at least four tramadol. Yeah, I couldn't stand the pain, and after getting loaded on some painkillers my good mood came back. Zach seemed calmer and I wanted to tell him that I was willing to give him a chance. Maybe he could help me forget about the prince. I couldn't keep going, pretending that I was in control of my life.

"I need a drink, but I'm going straight to bed after that," I told him, feeling guilty even saying that.

He narrowed his eyes at me, scratched his sexy beard and said, "You're not supposed to drink when you're high on painkillers."

I waved my hand dismissively. "Maybe, but I don't think I can stay sane without one."

"I want to take you out this weekend and, before you say anything, yes, it's a date," he said unexpectedly once we were heading back to the car. Warmth rippled over my face, heading down between my breasts and then further and further. I stopped for a second, thinking that he must have read my mind earlier on.

"Right, so let me get this straight. You want to go out with me, and am I supposed to just say yes?" I asked, just to make sure that I wasn't hearing things. The human painkillers made me feel good, and the pain was muted. My life was fucked up, but that didn't really matter—I had a date.

He turned around, staring at me with those dark eyes, like he wanted to kiss me. My demonic soul sparked when he was around, and when he ran his fingers over my face my future looked brighter. This sudden intimate moment between us pumped me with hope that there was still a chance for me. I wasn't completely lost.

"Yes, Flower, I'm asking you out and for the record I don't do this very often," he stated.

I rolled my eyes. "So what? Do they just jump into your bed?"

"Most of the time." He chuckled, leaning over like he was really going to kiss me. Ah, what the hell. I could blame the painkillers. "You adore me, Flower, and I can't wait to get rough with you again."

When he started walking away, I was kind of disappointed. Lust was soaring down my abdomen. The sparks were still there.

"Okay fine, I'll give this … whatever this is a go, but you need to take me home. I don't think I can handle anymore excitement today," I told him, not even knowing what I was saying. This date was going to be a disaster, but I was looking forward to it.

"Good, glad that we're on the same page. Trust me, once I'm done with you, Prince Charming will never cross your mind again," he said, with a wink. I was too drugged out to come back with anything witty, and my mind stopped thinking about what was right or wrong.

Zachary dropped me outside my flat an hour later, saying that he would be in touch. I sensed that he wanted to go upstairs and tuck me into bed. I talked him out of it and when his car disappeared in the darkness, I decided to go out. My intuition told me that this wasn't a very good idea, but the craving won— I was dependent on tequila.

When Paul saw me, he came out around the bar, looking pissed off.

"What the hell happened to your face?" he asked, and a few people at the bar looked at me. I looked like shit, but that was part of the job. The local pub was packed and there was a game of poker going on at the back.

"Long story. I had an unpleasant experience meeting an A'rea," I said, when he stopped examining me. He sucked in a breath, and lifted his eyebrow in surprise.

"The A'reas are locked up in pits, Maxine."

"Tell that to the one that tried to use my face as a nail file. She took over the body of the girl that I was going to question in a hotel room. She was sent there to kill her and then she attacked me," I said, flopping on the stool. Paul went back behind the bar, disappeared for a good few minutes and then came back with a brand new bottle of tequila. The craving intensified and I didn't know if I should just take it or smash it against the wall.

"So the Watchers showed up, I presume?" He unscrewed the bottle and poured some into a shot glass. The guy next to me was staring at my wounds. He was half drunk, but that was okay. People needed to satisfy their curiosity.

"Two of them, they took some evidence and made everyone believe that they were supposed to be there. An hour later I had a phone call from Ricky. They asked him to analyse whatever they collected," I added, staring at the shot and knowing that if I drank it there was no going back. Natasha was dead, her body rotten and this was all my fault. I couldn't blame tequila or the fact that my free will was completely screwed.

"Max, I think you should be more careful. I know that you can take care of yourself, but you don't mess with A'reas, and that particular one could have killed you," Paul said, leaning over and giving me one of his looks.

I nodded, still staring at the damn shot glass. The overriding feeling inside me wanted to numb everything, numb Arthur, the fucking secret and everything else. The solution was simple: I had to drink until I couldn't use my brain, then play. The cards were going to be good tonight. There was no doubt in my mind and I had a chance to turn my luck around.

"What's wrong? You don't want it?" Paul asked, looking concerned at this stage.

"If I have this now, then I won't stop. Things got really fucked up the last time I drank," I told him, thinking about the way Natasha had suffered, about Zachary's past and my whole fucked up existence. Things needed to change and tonight was the start.

Paul scratched his head, appearing to be slightly confused. I'd never said no to tequila. Two years ago, when I was still working for the royals, I had occasional drinks during poker games, sometimes things got out of control, but then I knew my limit.

"Do you want something else?"

"No, I need to get my shit together and stop drinking, stop blowing all my cash gambling," I admitted. "Give me a glass of soda and some time to think."

I didn't have to tell Paul twice. A minute later he took the shot away and put the soda in front of me. I drank it in one go. My jaw was aching, my cheek was on fire. Hell, if I really was going to get sober, then this was the best time to start.

Prince George was in London and maybe he was already dead, drained of his blood and soul. I had no other leads, and Alexis had warned me to stay out of this case. I had to start changing my life for the better, for the people in my life that were still important. There were other ways to push this through, but I had to at least try. The burning guilt was never going to go away.

I had made so many bad decisions, exposed the demonic world and pretended that everything was all right.

As I sat at the bar watching other people, it was maybe only the second time since my breakup with Arthur that I hadn't touched magical tequila.

The burning sensation was still at the back of my throat, even after some random human asked me to join him for a poker game. Somehow I found the strength in me to say no. Paul was shocked too and was ready to call Ricky.

I suffered knowing that I was the one to blame for Natasha and possibly Jessica's death.

Now Zachary was part of my curse, and tonight after I went back to my flat, I decided to shift my priorities. I would still look for the prince, but I had to take care of myself first, my life. On top of that I needed to clear my name. Cyril was still around. He was investigating Doomed Cases, and this was my business, my only way of earning a living.

When I dropped on the bed several hours after midnight, stone cold sober and completely aware of my inner demons, I knew that from tomorrow I was going to be a different person.

Chapter Twenty-Six

"Faith is the substance of the things we hope for,
And evidence of those that are not seen..."
— **Dante Alighieri**

The next day I was woken up by my alarm, and I felt worse than I could ever imagine. Every part of my body hurt, and every move was a struggle. I couldn't imagine being stuck at home until I was back to being my normal self. The A'rea had bitch slapped me good and proper, and on top of that my whole face looked like the swollen arse of a baboon.

After coffee that tasted like the swill they served in hospital, I looked through the book of potions that I kept hidden in my bedroom. The red elixir made from the feathers of an angel (yeah, they existed too) was supposed to numb the pain. Normally the bottle of tequila was my usual salve to fix the problem, but I reminded myself that I was trying to turn my life around. I had a little bit of red potion left, and no ingredients to brew another one. It was time to pay a visit to a certain old lady, but even the idea of walking to the tube station scared me.

Arthur was still on my mind, now that my brain was working at full speed and my thoughts were clear. I was struggling to cope with the constant ebb and flow of unexpected emotions. The red elixir started kicking in when I showered. Most of the time it worked like Valium, but it was the magic with something extra boosting my immune system to advance my healing. Suddenly I could function, walk and do the usual nonstrenuous stuff.

Fighting was out of the question, but at least I had some of my strength back. People, mostly humans, were staring at me as I made my way through the streets of Brixton. Mongrels and other demons could smell the charms on me, and the fact that the A'rea's scent was still in my blood made me a bit of a target. Ricky wanted me to stay at home, but this wasn't going to happen. I was bored out of my mind and I needed to stay busy.

"Morning, Maxine, how are you in that…"

Yep, Emma stopped talking in mid sentence when she saw me. She most likely had no idea that I got attacked last night. Humans weren't aware of magical formulas, but I had taken enough elixirs to bring the attention of other mongrels and demons to myself. I always had to pay the price in the end and being called down to hell for using forbidden elixirs wasn't on the list of my priorities. That's why today I needed to stay out of any kind of trouble.

"Chill. I'm fine. I was on the case last night and things got out of hand," I explained, trying to calm her down. She was staring at me with her eyes wide and seemed very concerned.

"Oh my God, but your face. Are you okay? You shouldn't be here in that state. Go home and rest," she said, leading me back to my desk. She was ready to walk with me back to my flat, which was sweet. No one ever fussed over me like this, even when I worked for the royals.

"Emma, I'm fine, just get on with your work. Did Ricky say when he was going to be in?" I asked.

"Maxine Brodeur, you're not fine; you look terrible. Let me at least make you a cup of tea," she said swiftly, never once considering that I didn't need to be taken care of. "And Ricky is on his way. He was working late last night on some new evidence."

I rolled my eyes, and then my jaw started to hurt. Emma was talking to herself in the kitchen whilst she was making my tea. Then she announced that she had to go out for a bit. I just waved my hand, glad that the whole fuss was over. Growing up with nuns taught me that sometimes the best thing to do was to keep your mouth shut as a kid, and it was still true as an adult.

Ricky showed up at eleven a.m. He looked tired and he stopped in his tracks when he saw me.

"For shit's sake, Max, you look dreadful. Your face—"

"Yeah, yeah. I heard it from Emma already. I had to get to the hospital last night. An A'rea nearly ripped my face off, but don't worry. I'm fucking fine, all right?"

He was shaking his head, putting his stuff on the desk.

"This whole case is becoming very complicated. One day you're going to die for that fucker, Maxine, and then what?" he asked. By "that fucker" he meant Arthur. Ricky knew everything that happened to me. He was convinced that I was doing too much, risking my life to find the missing prince who was most likely in hell already.

"Calm down. I won't be going anywhere alone from now on. Zach wants to keep me on a short leash. You better tell me what you found out about the evidence that the Watcher brought in."

He wasn't done with giving me a lecture just yet, but he nodded to me to go to his office. He'd created a spell to deter any intruders from getting inside his drawers. When I looked past the wards, I could see that he was in the process of analysing the potions and hair. The whole setup from the photographs looked a lot like the lab from Jessica's apartment. There was obviously a connection between Natasha and a demon that kidnapped George.

"You finally met someone that talks with some kind of sense. I'm scared, Maxine, petrified that one day you won't make it. I know that we agreed that you should be out in the field and I'm taking care of the rest, but last night was a close call. You were risking too much."

"She could have killed me, but she didn't, so stop going on about it. Tell me, what is it that you found?" I asked, fed up with talking about last night. I was going to be fine, and my friends didn't need to worry.

"Nothing yet. The hair is definitely a human's, but it will take me a couple more days to extract and identify all the ingredients. I'm going to run some tests on all the liquids today."

"Cool, let me know if you find anything," I told him. We discussed a few other possibilities, but I knew that he worked better alone, so after a few minutes I left him to it. He'd taught me a lot about potions and elixirs; the books were useful, but there was nothing better than learning this stuff directly from an expert.

I went to my own room hoping to take my mind off recent events. I had some reading to catch up on and I had to take care of phone messages and reply to emails. Sometimes I also took care of the bills and other paperwork, only if Ricky was busy. My throat was dry and I really wanted to get my hands on some tequila. This wasn't going to happen, because I was planning to stick to my resolution of sobriety. My irritation turned into a frustration just before lunch. I was trying to change my whole lifestyle, and the time was dragging, leaving me free to think of everything I shouldn't.

Emma knocked on my door and I told her to come in. The smell of freshly baked cake and coffee filled the room. Her hands were full, and she started putting various boxes on my table.

"What is all this?" I asked, scratching my head when she placed a fancy coffee pot in front of me.

"I brought in some homemade cakes… lots of them. They make a nice impression to visitors. I left some in Ricky's room too," she said shyly. "I thought that maybe you would like to talk?"

My stomach was rumbling. I realised that I hadn't eaten anything since yesterday. Most of the time I missed breakfast. Maybe this was the best time to start changing my routine. I needed to fuel my body with energy and the cakes looked delicious.

"Talk about what?" I asked, and shoved the raspberry turnover into my mouth. Emma was unsure what to say, her thoughts slightly tangled. The work that I needed to do could wait.

"About what happened to you last night. My mum says that if you're feeling down, talk to someone and have a very naughty cake." She smiled widely.

I started spinning in my chair moving left and right very slowly staring at her, slightly taken back by the fact that she wanted to make me feel better. In my entire short, but eventful life I never had anyone that I could talk to. Most of my friends were guys and we spent time together drinking or playing cards. Getting together with a group of girls and sharing our emotional experiences wasn't my kind of thing. I'd never been a sleepover-pillow-fight chick. Emma most probably had plenty of girlfriends, and today I didn't want to hurt her feelings, so I decided to go with it. The craving for tequila wouldn't just go away and these cakes looked really good. Maybe I could substitute tequila with sugar and get a really fat ass and then Arthur wouldn't be hounding me and then that would be one problem solved!

"Okay, I guess I can try, but I don't think that I'm very good, you know, at talking about stuff in general," I told her.

"Don't beat yourself up over this, Maxine. You saved my life, and I'll remember it forever. Tell me, what's bothering you?"

I thought about her question for a second. There was nothing that was bothering me specifically. I'd made certain decisions that impacted everyone around me whether they knew it or not. I couldn't talk to her about my affair with Prince Arthur. My broken heart would heal eventually.

"The investigation isn't going anywhere. I've made so many mistakes with this case and I don't know what to do. I feel stuck," I confessed. Ricky had to have something in that room. George had disappeared down in the cemetery and the demon that took him had covered all their tracks. "But at the same time I'm not that worried. I know that I should be, but for some reason I'm not bothered."

"Why? Are you thinking about something else?" she asked, and took a bite of a chocolate eclair.

I sighed, knowing that my head was clear. Last night I didn't drink, so my judgment wasn't clouded.

"Zach asked me out on a date and I said yes," I blurted out.

Emma giggled and then started clapping. "OMG, that's fantastic, he's so handsome."

"Yep, that he is," I admitted, feeling a little warmer all of a sudden, "But I don't know if going out on a date with him is such a good idea."

"Why? Because of the case?"

"Yes, we have been assigned to work together, but I don't want to complicate things. My focus should be on George."

Emma was chewing her cake, mulling over what I said. Maybe I really needed to change the way I dealt with things in my life. Humans seemed to understand more; their problems were insignificant, but they had to deal with them on a daily basis.

"In my opinion, you just have to get back to the basics," she announced.

"What are you talking about?" I asked.

"With the case, the investigation. Go over all the evidence once again, and think about what you would do in the very beginning. Maybe you're just overthinking this," she said. "Sometimes I do it too. Before I got this job I was struggling. I didn't know how I was going to get through this month without any money. My ex-husband was supposed to send the maintenance payment, but I didn't get a penny from him."

Only now I begin to realise that Emma used to be broken too, but she always remained positive. Her heart was healed. God, I didn't even know that she was married before.

"Why is he not paying you? Surely you have a child support agency on your side?"

Maybe I wasn't very domesticated, but I knew things like that. A while ago I had a mongrel that wanted to track down her ex-boyfriend. A demon that fathered her child and ran away with someone else. She still had to pay her bills and for that she needed money.

Emma smiled weakly. Part of her soul darkened when I mentioned her ex-husband.

"I had to run in the middle of the night with my daughter. He used to beat me up. Things were tight for a few years, but that's all in the past now."

I clenched my fists. I hated men, humans that abused women. If I could get my hands on that prick I would kill him. Shit, Ricky was right. It was a good thing that I gave Emma a chance.

"But you ran and he hasn't bothered you since?"

She took another bite of the cake and chewed slowly, thinking about her daughter's dance lessons.

"He came around a few times promising that he would change. I had to call the police on him. He couldn't understand that I didn't want to be with him anymore, and when I refused to take him back, he stopped paying me. Things were difficult for a few months, but I managed somehow," she explained. "There is no point stressing over the past. There are some things you will never be able to control, so appreciate what you have. I'm not doubting that you can solve this case, but first you need to take a step back and relax. Go on that date. Zach is a good man for you."

I sat in my chair thinking about what she said for a moment. She finished her cake, got up and left the room. She'd been through a lot and still didn't let this ruin her outlook on life. She picked herself up and carried on. I felt like an idiot, thinking that my addiction could get the better of me.

I could erase Arthur out of my life, but I needed Zach to help me. George was still alive, and I would carry on doing whatever I could, but I needed to cut myself some slack and stop worrying about things that I couldn't control. I picked up the last cake and leaned back consuming it slowly. For the first time in a while I was thinking about myself and felt excited about my upcoming date with Zachary Quinton.

Chapter Twenty-Seven

"The darkest places in hell are reserved for those who maintain their neutrality in times of moral crisis."
— **Dante Alighieri**

The next week I was irritated and pissed off for no good reason. Maybe this had something to do with the fact that I stopped drinking or the fact that I was still recovering, trying to heal as quickly as I could. Tequila was out of reach. I didn't have any more elixirs that would numb my achy muscles and help to heal me quicker. My thinking process was much sharper, but on the downside it was much more difficult to deal with overwhelming memories than before.

I had to admit I had an addictive personality and pumping my body with more magic could cause more bad than good. My relationship with Emma improved over the next few days, and I started paying more attention to what was going on around me. I mentioned to Ricky that we needed to give her a raise. She had sorted out all the files and began advertising our services online. Also the new working phone was ringing off the hook. Most enquiries were related to missing people, things and pets. It was going to take a while before we could start getting more serious clients, but it was an improvement. The past couple of months weren't great. I had been absent a lot, and Ricky had been struggling to run the business when I was skiving.

On Saturday afternoon we decided to close the office earlier than usual. I wasn't getting anywhere with any of my new contacts, and my sources weren't much help either. Ricky had decided to take his work home. Sometimes he was determined to stretch the use of his brilliant mind with a glass of expensive scotch, away from any drama.

When I got back to my flat around three p.m. I didn't know what to do with myself. Zach was taking me out tonight and I still couldn't believe that I'd said yes. My dating experience wasn't very good. I didn't even know what I was supposed to wear tonight. Most days I walked around in worn jeans with an old hoodie. Zach was obviously experienced and he knew what to expect from a woman like me. After staring at my wardrobe filled mostly with combat trousers, T-shirts and jackets, I decided to go shopping. Back in the days when I worked in the palace, I had to wear a livery uniform or a suit. I kept things casual whenever I was out and about. The restaurants, cinemas or whatever other normal people did on dates weren't for us, because Arthur could never officially date me.

My first real shopping trip didn't go too well. I didn't like any of the dresses that the blond sales assistant picked out for me in the huge department store. She kept telling me that I had great legs and I needed to show them off. Every time I put on something I felt underdressed. My aching body and lack of magical tequila was slowly making me lose my mind. Maybe one night of wild and adventurous sex could shift my perspective, but hooking up with the mouthy and arrogant Zach wasn't something that I intended to do tonight. We were going out on a date, only because I needed to tear myself from obsessing over my assignment for at least a day.

Eventually I managed to pick up a black dress with lace on the front. I even bought new makeup to cover the remaining signs of my fight with the A'rea. At seven p.m. I stood in front of a large mirror in my tiny hallway ready to cancel the date. Panic settled and nerves kicked in.

For the first time since the breakup, I realised that I needed a girlfriend. Someone that I could talk to, a friendly soul that could pat me on the back and tell me that I was ready.

I had been sober for over a week now and maybe I was seeing clearly for the first time in my life. Changes were on the way. My phone buzzed half an hour later. Zach was downstairs waiting for me and I was losing my shit, thinking that this date would be a disaster. After a few deep breaths, I opened the door and headed out to meet him. It was time to stop stressing and get on with it.

He watched me as I walked towards him, his dark eyes drifting up and down my body, causing my pulse to jump. Yep, even after what he had been through he still wanted to get into my pants. I put my leather jacket on top of the dress, but deep inside I wished that I could slip back into my old jeans. It was cold outside, and my legs were bare, and it seemed that the dress was cut in a way to expose those parts of the body that weren't for show. I was walking in an old pair of black heels that I bought a couple of years back.

Zach smiled wolfishly when I approached him, not even trying to hide the fact that he was very turned on. Yes, I was much more aware of it now than before.

"Flower, to tell you the truth, I didn't expect to see you dressed like that tonight. You look gorgeous."

He even opened the door to the car for me, which was nice. In all my previous experiences with the opposite sex, there was never foreplay or sweet talk or any nonsense like that. We simply hooked up, but this evening everything was about to change.

"So it's true then, you totally want to screw me in this car?" I asked, and then wished that I bit my tongue. There was something really wrong with me. Hell, I'd never felt so awkward, even when I was sleeping with the most eligible bachelor in the country.

Zach lifted his hands, looking down on my naked thighs.

"Guilty as charged, Flower, but don't worry. As much as I want to bury myself inside you, I want to enjoy you slowly and thoroughly. And a few hours won't cut it," he said, grinning. I felt warmth skittering over the nape of my neck.

"I told you, stop calling me Flower or there won't be any sex to speak of," I said. I hated that nickname and if Zach wanted me to forget about the prince he needed to show me that he was willing to be on his best behaviour.

He smirked but didn't say anything else. This was crazy, my shoulder angel was screaming at me to stop messing with his life. My shoulder devil reminded me I was half demon and in Lucifer's eyes only a second-class citizen, so the rules were less strict when it came to dating a human. This evening I was planning to enjoy myself and act like the past or the future didn't really matter.

Zachary started the car and joined the flow of traffic. After some time his fingers slipped down, brushing the skin on my thighs, gently, barely touching them. Electricity crawled across my body, and that smouldering sexual heat was back. He was thinking about sex, and I was trying to breathe steadily and not melt into a pile of sexually repressed goo. Somehow I managed to ignore his tortures throughout the whole drive and after an hour in traffic Zach parked the car in one of the back streets. My stomach growled loudly. I was starving and I was hoping that he planned to feed me before taking me back to his place. My diet was based on cereals, ready-made meals and frozen food. I thought that I took care of myself the best I could. I'd never had a very good example to follow though. I needed to look after myself better.

"I won't apologise for what I'm just about to do, gorgeous," he said in a hushed tone. I shivered at the heat of his stare, suddenly aware of my own soaring desire. After that one night with the stranger from a couple of weeks back, my libido was on the rise again.

I shook my head, confused, trying to will my heart to slow down.

"Apologise for what?" I asked stupidly. He moved his arm so quickly and then pulled me towards him. The next thirty seconds were lost in sensations that were far from ordinary. Boiling heat rushed through my veins. He kissed me like no other human had before. His lips were tender and demanding at the same time, like he was desperate to lose himself in me. Zachary used both his palms to hold me gently and then devoured my mouth.

I moaned, enjoying every part of him touching me, and my body was slowly turning into a fireball. The passion and sparks flew, zooming between us. By the time he pulled away from me, I was out of breath and flustered. Zachary's breath was erratic too, but the inferno in his eyes told me that this was just the beginning.

Crap, I was in a lot of trouble, acting like a normal human being for a change.

"That's just the pre-foreplay, baby. You have to wait a bit longer for the real deal." He grinned, ran his thumb over my cheek, and got out of the car. I'd made out with Arthur in the limo a couple of times, but we always had to be so careful and in a hurry. This, whatever it was that was going on between Zach and me, was much more explosive.

I smoothed my dress, feeling slightly off balance once I was back on my feet.

"Where are we going?" I asked, looking around, knowing that I had never been in this area. The streets were vibrant, filled with people from around the world. I was too distracted in the car to wonder what he was planning to do this evening. He grabbed my hand and entwined his fingers around mine.

"Part of my family is from Iran, so tonight we are having a Persian feast," he said, leading me to the other side of the street. I felt oddly calm holding his hand, protected and like myself from my pre-palace life years ago.

Zach took me to the corner restaurant, with colourful windows and a name that I couldn't pronounce. After that kiss in the car, my whole body was charged with energy and I was having trouble blocking the human emotions around me. There was a cosmopolitan feel in this area, and I was feeling good being surrounded by people for a change.

"Zachary, my boy, so good to see you. How the devil are you?" shouted a large man that raced towards us. He had dark hair, with salt and pepper streaks on the sides, and was most likely from Iran too. He started hugging the detective next to me, shouting greetings in a language that I didn't understand.

"I'm fine Uncle Azero. Let me introduce you to my date. This is Maxine, we are currently working together,"

Zach said, once he was free. His uncle looked at me and beamed.

"A date, that's impossible… You don't date, my boy, but this creature. She's so beautiful," Zach's uncle shouted. Everyone in the restaurant was staring at us and I was trying to hold it together. The place was quite busy, but most of the customers were foreigners. He hugged me without warning, cuddling me into his large chest. "Maxine, good strong name. She doesn't like to be touched that one."

"I'm sorry?" I asked, baffled when he let go of me, and I could breathe normally.

"Azero, be a gentleman. Maxine is having dinner with me tonight and she desperately needs to taste your khoresh," Zachary said, pulling me closer to his body. "I presume that you have a table for us?"

Azero narrowed his eyes on his nephew and took me by my elbow.

"No need to ask. Tell you what: Zach doesn't know how to treat women right. Let me show you around. The food is good, delicious here, and you look like you could put on a few pounds."

Over the next couple of minutes I was forced to listen to Azero going through his life in the UK, and telling me about his dead wife. After that he let me sit in front of Zach. We had a quiet table at the back. His uncle fussed over me a few more moments, asking about my work and Zach about his mother. He was very loud, outspoken and didn't care that there were other people in the restaurant. He should have annoyed the crap out of me, but I could feel his pride and love for Zach and hoped that I could make him happy. His emotions were so genuine it was hard to be annoyed.

"So you are half Iranian then? I should have guessed earlier on. I had a feeling that your family was from somewhere in the Middle East," I said, once we were finally alone. The restaurant was cozy, keeping in tradition, painted in vibrant red-maroon, blue and sun-gold colours. His uncle had tried really hard to use the antiques, old copper lamps, rugs and carpets to bring out the atmosphere from his home country. It was nothing posh or extravagant, but it felt really warm and homey like you'd be happy to spend the night chilling here.

"Yes, my mother married my father after six months of knowing him. They met in London in the British library. He was British, died of a heart attack when I was four," Zachary explained, putting the napkin on his knees. A moment later, the waitress brought two beers to our table. "Cheers. All alcohol is banned in Iran, but my uncle is trying to adjust to the British culture."

I didn't drink much beer. I always preferred something much stronger, but tonight I was detoxing. My throat burned, but I was planning to stick to my resolution and stay away from tequila.

"So you have never brought any other ladies in here then?" I asked, thinking about the blonde woman from a couple of weeks ago. Zach gave me the impression that he was the kind of guy that always took what he wanted and hooking up with random women was something that he enjoyed doing.

"I don't do dates, prefer keep my ladies in the bedroom, Maxine. I like you, so I'm making an exception," he said, smiling. His dirty mouth was a good distraction.

I was just about to ask him about his mother, when his phone rang. He glanced at the screen and frowned. I guess the fun was over.

"I have to take this," he muttered obviously not too happy that we were interrupted. I nodded and drank some more beer. Zach got up and went outside to take the phone call. A second later Azero appeared back in front of me with a plate with something that looked like crackers and dip.

"Try this, beautiful, it's freshly made hummus," he said, waving the plate in front of me. I reached out and then felt it. The new demonic energy that rippled through me suddenly. A full-blooded demon just walked in and when I looked up I realised that we were somehow connected. And that evening had been going so well.

Chapter Twenty-Eight

"Through me the way into the suffering city,
Through me the way into eternal pain,
Through me the way that runs among the lost."
— Dante Alighieri, The Divine Comedy

He was tall, blond, and for a split second I thought that I recognised him from somewhere. He stared at me for longer than was necessary and then sat at the table in the back, joining a female human. I didn't need to panic just yet. After all, I wasn't that important in the underworld. Maybe he was here for other reasons and I just had to relax. Azero was holding the plate with snacks front of me, so I took a piece of a cracker with hummus, telling myself that everything was fine.

"Any good? It's the special recipe from my grandmother side," Azero asked and his question distracted me from the supernatural creature that was now in the restaurant. My paranoia kicked in, rolling over my body like a cold shower. My life was complicated, but tonight was all about me.

"Good, very good," I muttered with my mouth full. As long as I didn't have Watchers chasing after me, I was relatively safe. "So I'm the first girl that he's brought here?"

Okay, I didn't need to be that nosey, but Zach wasn't particularly forthcoming.

"Yes, his poor mother has been telling him to settle for as long as I can remember, but he never listens. Our Zachary is a wild card."

"Yes, I have noticed," I responded. "How long have you had the restaurant?"

"Since his sister disappeared, over six years now. I treat him like my own boy, but he doesn't come often. He is always busy with his police work," Zach's uncle said, shaking his head like he remembered something from the past. I frowned and leaned over just to make sure that Zach was still outside, talking on the phone.

"His sister? I thought he didn't have any siblings?" I asked. Azero lost his smile for a second and then sat down opposite me, still holding the menu in his hand.

"I don't like telling this story, but you're the first that he brought in here, so I guess it's okay. Zachary has a brother too, but it was his sister that had always been the black sheep in the family. She never used to listen to her mother, was a wild child and things spun out of control. She got pregnant when she was about twenty, very young then. She partied a lot and got herself into trouble with the police and some Turkish immigrant. I don't blame Zafira for what happened to Zara. She brought up her children here, not in Iran, without a husband, so it wasn't easy. Zara left the child with Zafira many times. At first it was a few hours, then days and once she vanished for over a week," Azero said, giving me way more than I expected.

I had no idea that Zach had such a big family. It looked like we both didn't like sharing things about ourselves. Paul was right, he was troubled, even more than I expected. It was strange that he never mentioned his sister.

"During one night Zafira sneaked out for a party and didn't come back. Everyone was used to it, but this time it was different. Zach had just graduated and got into the police force," his uncle continued. "And he had a lot that he had to deal with. Zara had vanished from the face of the earth, and after a couple of weeks Zafira had filed the missing person report. Zach started to look for her, but he wasn't getting anywhere. No one had heard from her. Things were difficult at home too. Zafira was blaming herself and fell into depression. Cornelia, Zach's niece was raised by Zafira, and after her mother's disappearance she stayed with her grandmother for good. Zafira lifted herself up for the little girl. Cornelia is six now and Zach adores her, he helps out as much as he can. He looks after her whenever he can, but I don't think he ever got over what happened with Zara."

I was completely and utterly speechless. This wasn't something that I expected to hear. I thought Zach simply liked keeping his private life away from nosey people like me. His partner's suicide was just the tip of the iceberg. He most likely believed that demons had abducted his sister too. My head was spinning, as I tried to take all this in. Now it didn't surprise me that Zach was so sensitive and believed in supernatural forces.

"I didn't know about her. Zach hasn't spoken about his family at all. Besides, we haven't been working together long," I admitted, feeling like an idiot.

"Zach doesn't like bringing this stuff up. It hurts too much, but he does love Cornelia. He's a hard man, but soft like a cushion inside," his uncle said fondly, thinking how much trouble Zara had brought into the family. I could see he believed that she was long dead.

"Uncle, what are you telling, Max? I've only been gone for what… five minutes?" Zach asked, appearing by our table. His family was important to him, and maybe he just didn't like broadcasting the fact that his sister had vanished from the face of the earth. I was certain that demons had something to do with it and I wanted to help, but I couldn't ask him about her straight away. The date was going well, and I didn't need to ruin it.

"I was telling Maxine about my special dish, the khoresh, so hurry up and order it for her. She is just skin and bones," Azero said, lifting my arm, like he wanted to prove his point. I had no idea what khoresh was, and I didn't want to look like an idiot asking Zach to explain it to me. He chose the food in the end. I finished eating the hummus that Azero brought over earlier on. My stomach stopped growling, but I was still pretty hungry.

I kept thinking about Zach's niece. She was only six and now was growing up without a mother. Deep down I knew that at some point I would have to ask him about her. My own secret was burning my insides, but I'd made my choice. Zach on the other hand was no doubt hoping that Zara was still alive and well. We chatted about the investigation for the next half hour, until his uncle brought the food. It turned out that the khoresh was a stew, made from aubergines, lamb leg and other vegetables.

"Dig in. The chef doesn't prepare this every day, only on special occasions," Zach said, and I did. Everything was delicious, fresh, and yeah, my mouth was on fire by the time I tasted all of the dishes that were brought in. Azero came over every few minutes to check on us. The candle was lit and we ate, talking about my time when I was growing up with nuns. Zach kept asking about my parents. I was having fun, but my phone kept vibrating constantly. I ignored it for as long as I could, until Zach heard it.

"You should answer it. Whoever it is seems persistent," he said, finishing some sort of rice dish that his uncle brought in a moment ago. It was Ricky. He left tons of messages. I didn't want to talk to him right now. Besides, he was supposed to take a night off. At least I was hoping he would.

"What's up?" I asked, not wanting to leave the table.

"Max, what the hell? What took you so long?" he snapped. "This is bloody important."

"What's so important? I bet you're just checking up on me. For your information I'm not in the bar mate, but on a date," I hissed into the phone, wondering how long he was going to treat me like a child.

There was a silence on the other side of the phone.

"A date?"

"What do you want, Ricky?" I asked, going slightly red, because Zach started touching my leg with his.

"I might have found something in the evidence," he said, his tone serious. I shook my head to let Zach know that he needed to stop. Ricky sounded like this was indeed important.

"Tell me," I said, not wanting to discuss the fact that two Watchers had stolen the evidence from the hotel room from the police. Zachary had no idea what could happen if the elixirs got into someone else's hands.

"I found Arthur's hair in the elixirs in the hotel. The mixture was odd, looked like a failed first attempt, so that's why it took me so long to figure it out. Some of the useless substances were filled with his and George's blood too. I had to dig through a lot of books to get the gist of what was inside. Whoever is involved might be controlling the prince from the outside. 'Cherry water' that was the name of the potion. It's a highly possessive elixir that serves only one purpose: to gain control of a human, in this case a very important human," Ricky explained, talking faster than normal.

My stomach contracted and I suddenly felt sick. For some reason Emma's words rang in my head: *just go back to the basics.* What if someone was using George to get to Arthur? Everything was possible.

"Anything else?"

"Arthur might have helped whoever took control of George. The answer is in the palace, Maxine. The answer had always been there, but I backed away from there too quickly."

Zachary was watching me, as the panic settled inside my stomach. I didn't want to believe that I didn't sense that there was something wrong with Arthur. He would have never brought any harm to his brother. Maybe he wasn't himself when he was in that hotel either; maybe the meeting was just an excuse. God, I didn't want to believe that this was even possible.

"Thanks, Ricky. I'm with Zach right now," I told him. "I will check this straight away."

"Arthur might be under the influence of a demon. You should speak to Rodriquez. The demon most likely needed both brothers to create some kind of powerful potion."

I exhaled sharply, massaging my forehead.

"Okay, we will drive there straight away. I'll speak to you later," I said, and then hung up.

"What's going on?" Zach asked suddenly alert.

"We need to head to Buckingham Palace right away. The royals might be in danger, but I believe that most of them are in their usual residences," I said, wondering if Arthur was with Natalie in Kensington.

"My uncle will be disappointed if you leave before tasting a dessert," he said, not taking me seriously. "And if you're pulling any kind of stu—"

"No, I'm perfectly serious, Zach. This lead is solid. There is an intruder in the palace and he might have something to do with Prince George's abduction. We need to check this out now," I pressed, annoyed that he thought that I was playing him. I stood up and picked up my clutch bag.

"Are you coming with me or not?"

"Yes, of course, I won't let you go alone this time around," he said.

Sometimes I hated myself for being a mongrel, hated that I couldn't tell him that the world he knew wasn't what it seemed. We both apologised to Zach's uncle, who didn't seem that offended.

My energy was crackling gently over my skin as we got to Zach's car. Arthur was himself when he trapped me in that hotel room. I would have recognised if there were something wrong. Maybe Ricky was wrong; maybe he made a mistake.

"Put your seat belt on," Zach muttered and roared the engine back to life. The palace was on the other side of the city, but Zach wasn't planning on driving slowly. He maneuvered the car into the flow of traffic and then stopped caring for road rules. He was speeding through the busy streets, overtaking other cars and running through the red lights. I held onto the 'oh shit' handle by the window, hoping to still be alive when we finally reached our destination. My heart was in my throat and I was so grateful that we were both safe by the time he reached the palace gates. My phone kept vibrating in my pocket. Ricky kept trying to get hold of me, but I didn't have time to update him on what was going on.

My abilities were sharpening and working at full speed. The A'rea attack had weakened me, but I was recovering and was able to sense the humans nearby. Even so, I wasn't up to my usual form yet.

The guards at the front gate were difficult. It was late and some young smart arse didn't want to let us in, backing himself up with emergency protocol. Apparently the palace was empty. The Queen Mother and most of the family had left to some party. They didn't know if Prince Arthur was in his quarters or if he was in a different part of the city, in his private residence with Natalie.

We needed to speak to Rodriquez urgently, but the guards had no idea if he was in the palace or not. This whole thing was absurd and after a moment Zach lost his temper. He took out his gun, pointed it on one of the guys and told him to let us in; otherwise he was going to shoot him. Yeah, that worked, only just, but the guards were most likely on the phone to someone inside the palace as soon as we passed through the gates.

We headed straight to the head of security who was based in the west wing. We expected to be greeted by guards, or at least Rodriguez himself, but the corridors were empty. The whole palace seemed deserted. Something wasn't right, and the general sense of dread and pressure was building up in my chest.

Zachary was nervous, suddenly anxious and my own power was going slightly berserk. We barged through the doors of the head of security, reaching abandoned posts. Computers were still on, and there was a fresh coffee on the desk. This didn't look good—why would security leave in such a hurry?

"What is going on in here? Where is everyone?" I asked, concentrating on the people inside the palace, but I wasn't sensing anything. My energy was depleted, and I felt robbed. I was well enough to detect humans or demons nearby, so what the hell was going on?

"Let's split," Zachary suggested, glancing around disoriented. There was only a handful of guards by the gate, and I didn't see that we had any other option. I was truly hoping that Arthur wasn't in the palace, along with other members of the royal family. Whoever was in charge of the security these days needed to be fired.

"All right, I'll go upstairs to the staff's quarters. Call me if you manage to track down Rodriquez," I said. Zachary nodded, loaded his gun and started walking away in the opposite direction. I ran upstairs, taking a couple of steps at a time. My energy began rolling through me faster as I was moving further inside the palace. By the time I reached the second floor I was out of breath and my body was aching; the latest injuries were slowing me down. Ricky's words rang in my ears. Arthur was under the influence of a demon.

I passed a few rooms and headed straight to the main ballroom that was set up for some sort of official banquet. All the lights were off, but there was someone inside. My heart started jackhammering in my chest as I searched for the source of power. The sound of footsteps neared and a deformed face came into a view, blocking whatever energy I was trying to gather.

Every tiny hair on my body rose, air filled my lungs, and fear sunk its claws inside my stomach, freezing me in place. The A'rea was in the ballroom, standing very close, and she arrived straight from the pits.

Chapter Twenty-Nine

"Until he shall have driven her back to Hell,"
— **Dante Alighieri, The Divine Comedy**

The muscles in my legs were starting to burn. Panic punched a hole in my chest as I struggled to breathe. The A'rea was in the ballroom, trying to tap into my demonic DNA. I still had a chance. I could turn around and run, but a second later all the doors were slammed shut, and the floor seemed to roll under my feet. Anticipating danger was part of my instinct, but I had a feeling that this time around, I was in real shit.

She smelled of arsenic and rotten flesh. Her gaze dropped to my chest, and a fresh dose of excitement and anticipation drifted through her veins. Her eyes met mine again and she wasn't moving, just standing several meters away. She wasn't even trying to hide her true form, and her evil soul was filled with only one purpose: to kill. Warmth flared as the smell of metal wafted in the air. I swallowed hard wishing that I had a sword or at least a knife, something that could give me an advantage. I wasn't ready for full fight mode, not yet, but I guess that choice was taken away from me the moment I stepped into the ballroom.

Tonight was supposed to be my night when I didn't have to worry about the case or any member of the royal family. I even went as far as putting a dress on and high heels. I clenched my fists, tormented with anger. At least Arthur wasn't here, so this fight was going to be fair. The seconds rolled on, and the A'rea vanished. She disappeared from my sight for a good few seconds, and then I sensed her zooming around, flying above me.

Then I felt someone else in the ballroom, a demon, and suddenly a high-pitched laugh broke the empty silence.

"Look, Your Highness, look who has come to grace us with her presence," said the voice. I gathered whatever strength and energy I could. Then from the far right corner a woman appeared, and alongside her stood Arthur. Shock held me immobile until the very last moment. The woman was a stranger to me—well, that's what I thought at first, but as she got closer everything suddenly made perfect sense. Alexis Frasier, the demon that acted as judge and jury during my fabricated hearing was in the ballroom. She was in control of the A'rea that circled above me, hissing with desire to consume my heart—yeah, that was pretty much her plan.

"Arthur? Are you all right?" I shouted towards the prince, ignoring Alexis. He seemed like he was out, filled with spells, staring blankly at the space ahead.

"Oh, he's just fine, for now at least. I'm afraid that you haven't been invited to this party. It's a private affair, Maxine," Alexis said, smiling. Only now I noticed that she changed her appearance. Her hair wasn't chestnut anymore, but crimson red. She must have used some kind of complicated potion to cover her demonic soul the first time we met. I had a feeling that she was the one that took George and tried to control Arthur when he was still himself. I should have put it all together sooner, even back at the wasteland. All this time she'd had full access to the palace.

"I warned you to stay away from this case, and I even gave you a chance to leave, didn't I?" she asked, standing tall and proud, like she belonged here, to this world.

"What the hell do you want?" I shouted, thinking through my options. The elixirs and dead hooker in the hotel. Maybe she killed the demon down by the canals too.

"Oh, nothing. I don't need anything from you, my dear. Arthur and his brother George are here to heal me. You will be dead soon anyway. This A'rea is here to finish what the other failed to do," Alexis said, sounding bored and staring back at her nails. I glanced around, sensing another human. Arthur walked past her and stopped in the middle of the ballroom, by the table. George appeared too, levelling his potions with his brother from the west side. They weren't aware of what was going on; their minds were possessed, filled with controlling demonic charms.

I heard a loud squawk and then the A'rea attacked, zooming through the air so quickly that I didn't have time to react. The creature from the underworld wasn't possessing anyone this time around. She was in her true eternal form. From the outside she looked like a human woman with a slightly deformed face and bones, but she had the soul of an evil being, only wanting to cause harm. She had large wings, spanning six feet on either side of her body, made from skin the colour of dark granite, like they were stolen from a dragon or the devil himself, dripping wet with a thick oil-like substance. Whenever she fluttered them around, the noxious liquid spilled down, burning holes in the rug and melting the floor. I dodged to the side, avoiding being splashed, trying to figure my defence strategy.

"Come on, dear Prince, you must do what Auntie Alexis is asking for. I need blood from both you and your brother to repair my soul, to become whole again," Alexis called out, laughing hysterically.

I ran to the other side of the ballroom, swinging my body under the statue of some bearded historic figure. A few drops of a tarlike substance splashed next to me, and the burning smell wafted in the air. The A'rea was hissing underneath, unable to get to me, using her large claws to push the statue down on the floor. I looked over, seeing Arthur. He had a knife in his right hand and his wrists were exposed. George was standing opposite, but I could barely recognise him. His skin was pale, almost translucent. There were bald patches on his head, and his clothes were in pieces. There was a poison in his system that had damaged some of his organs. I could only hope that there was enough time to save him.

I had at least a few minutes to pull my strength back together, when the tiny bit of a substance from the Area's wings dropped on my leg, instantly burning my skin. I tried to get it off me, but my skin was already peeling off, creating a painful agonising wound.

"When I took control of Arthur and asked him nicely to lead Georgie to me, I didn't think that the royals would use a damned mongrel to help them. I thought that young George would be useful, but he became difficult. His blood failed to create the potion that I needed, and his soul wasn't strong enough," Alexis said, walking around Arthur, like she was waiting for something. The knife in Arthur's hand was worrying me. I had no idea what Alexis intended to do.

The A'rea was hissing and squawking underneath me, using her strong claws to destroy the statue, hoping to get to me from the outside. I was unprepared and achy. It was a night when I wasn't expecting to get attacked, and the only elixirs that were now in my bag seemed completely useless.

Alexis's demonic soul was dying, and she was looking to use royal blood to repair herself. I had no idea if that would even work. Both brothers were special, easily manipulated by someone who was in the palace often. I was stupid not to have thoroughly investigated all the people that were fully connected to everyone in the royal family, foolish to think that the answer lay elsewhere.

"Lucifer abandoned me when I wasn't useful to him anymore. I had to pick myself up and start over. It took me years to climb through the ranks, to influence the royals," she said and the A'rea stopped messing around with me. With a loud whizzing sound she pushed the statue off its plinth, the armour crushed into pieces, and the guy's head missed me by about an inch.

I dodged over to the side, got up and tried to run to the other direction, but she was on me within seconds. Her sharp claws ripped the skin on my back and I was thrown across the ballroom, landing on one of the tables. The deep pain sliced across my back, and something thick and warm poured down my spine.

I wondered what happened to Zach, Rodriguez, and the guards. Alexis must have put them all under her control, but how?

The A'rea was fluttering her long powerful wings above me, dropping the deadly poison everywhere. I couldn't escape this time around. The substance was like tiny fire balls, burning deep wounds all over my body. Her deformed face was that of an angel, beautiful pale complexion, and large eyes filled with fire. Pain burst and rushed down everywhere; my skin felt like it was burning. I was trying to breathe, but oxygen wasn't getting into my lungs. Darkness crept over the edge of my vision. The A'rea cocked her head to the side, suspended in the air above me, and smiled.

I felt like I was back in the hotel room again, but this was so much worse. The shadows of my past blinded me for a moment. There wasn't a part of me that didn't scream with pain. My body spasmed uncontrollably; burning pain was splitting my cells, sharper and more intense with every passing moment. I was trying to gather my energy, draining the last bits of strength inside me, but the A'rea was tapping into my demonic abilities.

She landed on the floor and used her leg to kick me. I gritted my teeth, wanting to lift myself up, but my muscles refused to comply. I was going to die in a moment.

When she stood in front of me, staring and penetrating my cells, I prayed for this torture to end. Her poison was filling my body with painful blisters. I hissed for air, for something … anything that could bring me back. I couldn't even get my lungs to function.

The pain eased when she stepped away, lifting her claws, probably because she wanted to finish me off with the last final deadly blow. In a haze filled with agonising pain, I launched myself and rolled over in my last final attempt of escape. Then next to me, the A'rea's claw hit the red rug. It was the exact place where I had lain down only a split second ago.

"Oh yes, spill more blood, my Prince. I need to be like before, strong and powerful," Alexis shouted, dancing around, like she was in some kind of trance. The A'rea was trying to pull her claw off the floor; she was stuck between the two wooden boards. Both brothers were immobile, holding their knives as blood dripped down their faces. I had no idea if they were injured, or where that blood was coming from, but their souls were weak, damaged.

The A'rea squawked loudly, trying to free herself, easing the vibes of her control over me. The blazing fire on my skin faded and I finally could move.

The smell of burning flesh drifted around, but I couldn't just lie down, like I was defeated. I had to fight back. I jumped back to my feet, connecting with my demonic soul again and tapping into Alexis's source of power. This was my only way to pull back, to gain enough strength.

The whole floor began to shake, and the wind whizzed in my ears as I gathered energy from the outside, the earth, and the energy stored in the A'rea herself. Arthur was going to slash his own wrist; he was just about to do it, and George too. Both of them were being compelled to die, so Alexis's demonic soul could be saved.

Light shot across the room in a bolt, hitting the A'rea in her chest. The walls vibrated as a thunderstorm raged outside. She spread her large wings trying to protect herself, but another blast hit her again, straight in her heart. The impact threw her across the ballroom.

The bright and violent energy rolled through me. I flopped on the floor dizzy and disoriented. The A'rea wasn't important anymore, but I hoped that I disabled her for at least a moment.

"It's too late, mongrel. Both brothers' blood is already flowing through me. My soul is being repaired." Alexis laughed, using her hands to smear the blood on her face, like she did during the hearing. I let go of a ragged breath when she stopped and pointed at Arthur. "You, my boy, finish this. It's time."

I let out a hoarse scream, launching myself towards Arthur, the man that loved me as a woman and taught me how to love. He began slashing his wrists, pushing the knife into his skin, releasing more blood. Alexis was laughing hysterically.

Terror formed knots in my stomach, because I felt her demonic soul. It was transforming, filling with new power. I had no idea if it was too late or not, but I reached Arthur and knocked him off his feet. Then the air shifted, turning chilly.

The floor underneath my feet began descending, and everything vibrated. The walls, the furniture in the ballroom, the paintings and statues around. Right in front of my eyes the large hole began to appear, pulling the table and chairs down. The heat sucked in the air from the room, knocking me off my feet. Suddenly there was an entrance to hell right in the middle of the Queen's ballroom, the fiery pits. I felt something whip through the air, the sudden pull of energy that began dragging every living being down to the hole. In my last attempt, I held on to the metal bar that was attached to the wall.

Alexis was now near Arthur, who was lying on the floor motionless only a meter away from me. The sudden shock registered in her features when she realised what was happening.

"No, he can't summon me, not without the prince," her squeaky voice rang in my ears. My body was wrecked and my fingers were slipping away from the metal as the power of hell was pulling me down.

The air whizzed, and smoke began filling the space. Arthur was unconscious and he was slipping away too, when Alexis grabbed his arm, determined to stay away from the pits. She was ready to sacrifice the future king to save herself from being dragged down.

"Let go, you bitch! Let go of him and go back to hell!" I roared, and released my grip, sliding down the floor. I grabbed Arthur's hand and let go of an inhuman roar, spilling the elixirs from my back pocket that I thought weren't useful at first. The elixir made from unicorn tears lifted him above the floor, and he spun in the air on the other side of the ballroom, where the power of the pits couldn't reach him.

The demon inside me rose, and the evil power started dragging Alexis down to the hole.

"Oh no, I'm taking you with me before I die," she screamed. When I glanced down, I saw her creepy smile, her bloody teeth gritted in determination as her hand held my ankle and then pulled. I slammed on the ground, losing my balance. I was lost too. I could no longer fight with the power of hell.

Then time stopped. I could still hear her curses, hear my raspy breath, but part of my demonic soul was connected with hers. My heart plummeted and a scream got stuck in my throat.

Alexis stopped moving and opened her eyes wider. In that short moment, she was feeling and experiencing everything I had gone through in the past twelve months. She was seeing my memories, feeling the pain and the secret that I had been carrying inside me since last year. A dark craving swelled from deep within. I was fighting to untangle myself, but our energies were linked as long as her fingers were wrapped around me.

The fresh burst of pain stunned me. I realised that Alexis was seeing everything that I was forced to give up. Her face twisted in shock. Blood was dripping down from my nose as I tried to conceal my memories from her, tear my soul away from hers.

A moment later the time restarted, and the smell of sulfur nearly choked me. I couldn't let her drag me down with her, so I shook my head, recovering and then kicked Alexis's hand with my right foot. It was like a razor struck me, like I was suddenly aware that she had to be stopped. Her hand slipped and she began falling down to the pits. Her screams rang in my ears when the blistering heat hit me, causing tiny dots of sweat to break out across my arms and neck.

A thunderstorm appeared in the sky. The sound followed. Then the wind howled, and the heat and burning smell receded. Everything disappeared, and the floor was in once piece again. The shattering noise of breaking glass broke the silence moments later. I couldn't see what happened, but I presumed that the A'rea must have thrown herself out of the window in her last attempt to escape. She was weakened, and the Watchers were probably on their way to capture her.

I collapsed to the floor. Arthur was covered with blood. He was strong, so he would pull through somehow. The space where the pits opened up was scorched, the floor charred through the red thick rug. I closed my eyes until I could feel the flow of oxygen through my lungs.

Just before she was pulled down to the fiery pits Alexis had touched me and had connected with me. In that small space of time she learnt everything about me, discovered my deepest secret.

I told myself that no one could survive in the underworld and Alexis was possibly dead. I had won. But that one question was burning me inside—what if she somehow survived the fall?

Chapter Thirty

"And I was told about this torture, that it was the Hell of carnal sins when reason gives way to desire."
— **Dante Alighieri, The Divine Comedy**

I had no idea how long I lay motionless on the red rug in the ballroom, using whatever energy I had stored to rescue George. He was dying, and I was too broken to even lift my eyelids. I would survive, but the young prince was in bad shape. The warmth of healing power drifted down, causing my body to tremble. The pain was settling in my bones though I tried to ignore it, hanging on to the one last positive memory in my drenched mind.

"Max... Max, is that you?" Arthur's muffled voice asked. I kept breathing in and out, wondering if the agonising pain would ever ease. The fact that he was lying there next to me was calming. He was safe at last.

"Yes, I'm here, so you don't need to worry. George is here too," I said, forcing my raw throat to work.

I must have lost consciousness for a while because when I opened my eyes there were people all around me. I heard loud steps and sensed fearful thoughts. Rodriguez was leaning over me, narrowing his golden eyes with apparent concern. Arthur was mumbling, but Alexis was gone, so the charms in his system were fading away slowly. Rodriquez released some of his energy and used it to inject some strength into me. I was grateful, but right now I wasn't the one that needed it the most.

"How bad does it hurt?" he questioned me, as his eyes drifted down over my wounded flesh. The healing warmth rippled away, and I thought that I was still high on adrenaline, because I managed to roll on my side. The smell of burning flesh filled the air, and I didn't need to look at my body to figure out that I was the source of the smell.

"Physically it will take me a while to recover, but mentally I'm fine," I said, struggling to lift myself up. Rodriguez helped me to sit up and for a split second my vision went slightly blurry. Two Watchers were healing young George. I sensed the deep, very complex charms thickening the air. He had lost a lot of blood, and his organs were poisoned, but I hoped that they were going to seal him back together.

The dull pain in my head reminded me of the pits, and Alexis. I was truly hoping that she was dead, although it wasn't as simple as that. I let Rodriguez's healing warmth dance across my skin, sealing some of the worst wounds, but I had a long and very complicated recovery ahead of me.

"What happened here? I was sent to the other side of the city to check on a lead for Prince George."

This wasn't the best time for an explanation. The Watchers were still reviving George. I could talk, so instead of moving I did exactly that. Guards, medics and other royal staff were rushing around, Arthur was taken away, and I went through everything that happened over the past few days. For some reason I thought that it was important to include details from my meeting in the Shoreditch hotel, following Ricky's discovery. Rodriguez paced around whilst I spoke. He was tormented and blissfully furious with the fact that Alexis had been under his nose this entire time.

"She was one of Lucifer's lovers, and when he exiled her out of hell, she started planning her revenge," Rodriquez was saying, smoothing his long beard.

"There was something wrong with her demonic soul. It was breaking, dying off. She was trying to use George's and Arthur's blood for some sort of healing transformation," I blurted out, remembering the incident at the cemetery. Alexis needed a fresh corpse to extract some ingredients for the second chance elixir. She must have kept George in Jessica's apartment.

Alexis was one of Lucifer's lovers, the person that he must have confided in on many different occasions, so why did he exile her from hell? He must have really gotten under her skin if it took her years to plan something so dramatic. There was no way that she could succeed, even if her transformation had gone through.

"In the underworld, the blood of royals is worshipped. She must have used Arthur to get to George. The ritual that she was trying to recreate is very complicated and it required incredible skills. The humans were only there to help her with the planning and preparations," Rodriquez stated. He must have known more about potions than he intended to share.

It worried me that Alexis had gained controlled of the A'rea. She must have some sort of access to the underworld through other sources. She'd used Jessica to control George, to experiment with potions. She'd addicted him to charms in order to have full access to the palace.

I suspected that in the early days, she changed her appearance and somehow befriended Princess Layla. This must have happened when I was absent, because I had never seen her around before. She tampered with Arthur's mind to get control of his blood; she needed both brothers to succeed. I had made many mistakes in the past few weeks. Drowning my emotions in tequila and forgetting about my priorities.

Rodriguez needed to come up with a legitimate story for the Queen Mother and the rest of the family. Something that could explain the extent of the damage all around me.

"The ritual was working. Then the gates opened up, but she wasn't the one that was able to control it? Why is that?" I asked, trying to get some clarification on the source of power that nearly killed me. Alexis was the only other demon in the palace, and the only one capable of summoning the gates. This was the only thing that didn't make much sense.

"Another demon must have summoned the gates, Maxine. I don't know," he said, staring at me intensely. With every passing minute, I felt less and less sane. The pain was distracting me from thinking clearly. I wanted to close my eyes and sleep for as long as it was possible.

"There wasn't any other demon around," I said.

"She had no control over it, Maxine, and from your story, I believe that you might have been responsible for what went down after that," he said.

"I'm a mongrel, half demon. My abilities aren't evolved enough to be able to do something like that," I argued.

He looked like he was ready to disagree with me, but changed his mind when Ricky's face came into view. Princess Layla and Natalie were at the corridors, and I didn't want them to see me in the state that I was in.

Ricky leaned over, dragging his hand through his hair. He was pale and most likely ready to hit something. He handed me some potions without a word. I drank whatever

I could straight away, hoping that they would numb the pain.

"Where is the detective? I thought he was supposed to look after you?" Ricky asked through his gritted teeth when the red elixirs began flowing through my system, slowly making me feeling sane again. Some humans were staring at us, and I needed to remember to conceal the rush of power. I didn't need to be questioned again by the head of Lucifer's faction.

"We got separated, but this isn't the time for a full story. I have to explain everything on the way to the hospital," I muttered, concerned about Zach. Alexis must have used some unknown powers to keep most guards and humans out of the palace. She was much stronger than I thought.

I managed to walk out on my own, but then was transported back on the stretchers in the ambulance. Ricky was ready to use his own energy to get me to hospital, so in the end I had no choice, but to agree.

I updated him on everything. We both suspected that Alexis had more cards up her sleeve. I couldn't tell Ricky that we had connected and she knew what I had been trying to hide from the world. Deep down I was really hoping that she was chained somewhere in hell, with no way out.

"That A'rea messed you up pretty badly, Maxine," Ricky said, holding his head in his hands several hours later. I was in the hospital bed covered with bandages, and high on human painkillers again. My body felt like it didn't belong to me anymore.

I kept going over and over the events from last night, wondering if it was ever possible for me to summon the gates to hell. My abilities were developing, but I always thought it was normal.

"I think you should go home. It's late and you're tired, mate. I'll be fine," I said, closing my eyes for a moment. The problem was that I couldn't sleep; I was exhausted but unable to switch off my racing mind.

He suddenly took my hand and wrapped his fingers around it. Great, he was getting all emotional on me.

"You fucking scared the shit out of me, Max. I thought I'd bloody lost you," he whispered.

"God, Ricky, I'm fine. Go and change your tampon, you girl. You know that I'm not good at any of this emotional crap," I mumbled, telling myself that he was right. I could have died today and that would have been the end of Doomed Cases.

"You're my partner, but also a friend and I know things have been shitty this last year. I just want you to know that I'm here for you."

Okay, this was getting weird. Ricky was one of the most important people in my life. Things were tough and my addiction hadn't made things easy for either of us. The friendship—no matter what, we always had each other and that was never going to change.

"I know, old man, I know … but this case is over, and hopefully we don't have to get involved with the royal family ever again," I said, relieved and yet slightly sad.

"Maxine … shit, are you all right?"

Zachary barged into the room and stopped in his tracks, seeing Ricky holding my hand. He had a black eye and a few scratches on his face, and was still wearing his clothes from earlier on. Ricky pulled away from me instantly and got up.

"Yeah, I'm fine, battered but all right," I said, discreetly wiping at the tear that sneaked out of my eye. "But it's going to be a while before I can have sex again."

I was trying to be funny, but Ricky looked at me like I had lost the plot. Zach walked up to my bed and winked.

"That can be arranged," he said with an amused tone of voice. "The bomb. Rodriguez said that some crazy chick had an explosive and she was trying to blow up the palace with Prince George and Arthur in the ballroom."

I couldn't help but smile. Rodriguez really had surprised me here, but I guess that kind of mess could have only been explained in one way. Zach was going through what happened to him and deep down I wished that for once in my life I could tell him the truth. It wasn't easy being a mongrel, especially a mongrel filled with secrets that had to lie on a daily basis.

***

Several hours later Zach left my side convinced that Alexis had kidnapped young George out of spite. She was jealous, filled with a grudge over what happened earlier on with Princess Layla. Apparently she was excluded from any royal official parties, because the princess had caught her sleeping with the King of Monaco's younger son. Somehow Rodriguez's story held together, but I wasn't sure if I was willing to keep up with my lies. Zach was seeking his own closure, and maybe he needed to know the truth.

Alexis's spell must have affected Zach too. At least a dozen of the other guards that remained in the palace had woken up several hours later, convinced that they were knocked out while searching for the intruder.

I had third degree burns all over my body, a fractured arm and the stitches that were sealing my cheek together had been replaced. Ricky had to smuggle in a lot of elixirs to keep me inside of the hospital for as long as it was necessary.

The next day I woke up feeling like someone had fired a shotgun at me. I told myself that this was the last time that I fought any mythological creatures.

Being in hospital gave me some time to think about everything that had gone on in my life over the last few years. It was something I needed.

When Ricky visited me later he mentioned that George was going to spend some time on the intensive care ward. He lost a lot of blood and needed surgery, so it was going to be a while before he would be back on his feet. I wasn't worried about Arthur. He was in much better shape than his brother.

The burns from the A'rea's wings were healing slower than I expected. Ricky had to experiment with certain potions to patch me back together again, because I was slowly losing my shit. I just wasn't used to lying in bed all day long. I checked out from the hospital after only a few days. Ricky insisted on me staying in his luxury apartment. He liked to keep an eye on me.

I had spent too long sober, and eventually I called Paul. He brought magical tequila when Ricky was out. Yeah, I told myself that I would stop, but I was bored out of my mind and needed something extra to numb the pain. The ex-Watcher nearly broke down when he saw me. I wasn't used to being around emotional men or demons. I promised him a game of poker soon and that kind of lifted him up.

It took three painful weeks of being stuck at home, but I recovered. The only downside was that I was still hooked on magical tequila. It was the only thing that kept me sane during the entire time.

When I settled back in my flat, I thought that things were fine, that I was alive, had a roof over my head and a job. No one could take that away from me.

Chapter Thirty-One

"On march the banners of the King of Hell."
— **Dante Alighieri, Inferno**

"Maxine, it's so good to see you. How are you feeling?" Emma squealed as I walked into the office a couple of days later. I smiled, kind of glad that she was still with us. I heard that she wanted to visit me so many times, but Ricky didn't want her to see me in the state that I was in. We both needed to spare her any further stress.

"Fine, I'm good, healed and ready to rock the next case," I said, sending a wink to Ricky, who was talking to a mongrel in his room. Emma came from behind her working station and hugged me. I was still stunned with her sudden affection.

"I'm so glad. Ricky kept saying that you needed time to recover," she mumbled. "My daughter and I made you biscuits. We were both really worried."

I smiled, happy that someone cared if I was dead or alive. In some ways, she reminded me of my mum. It was an odd nostalgic feeling, and I really needed to get a grip. The past was the past.

"Cool, well, it's all good. You don't have to worry anymore. Have you got any files for me?" I asked, taking a bite of the chocolate biscuit that tasted awesome.

"Of course, a few. Let me get them for you."

I went to my room and sat in my chair, closing my eyes for a second. I felt good, being back. Rodriguez hadn't heard anything from hell. Apparently Alexis had never gotten down to the pits and I had no idea how that was even possible. A lot of demons were currently searching for her.

Every day I hoped that she was securely locked up in the underworld. She knew what I was hiding and, since destroying her dream, I became her number one enemy. It's not like I didn't piss off people on a regular basis, but this was more serious than anything that I'd ever done. She could easily use her knowledge against me.

"Flower?"

I opened my eyes to see Arthur in front of me. I wanted to smile to myself. He wasn't real. I was most likely hallucinating, but this time around I was completely sober. I glanced at Emma, who stood behind him, holding a pile of files in her arms. Her mouth was hanging open and she was staring at the prince, completely startled.

"Your Highness!" I shouted, jumping off the chair, like I just realised that this wasn't a mirage. "What are you doing here?"

"It's the prince… the real prince," Emma kept whispering. Ricky walked out of his room and shot Arthur an unfriendly look. Yeah, he didn't like the fact that Arthur was here. He started pushing Emma back to her desk.

I rubbed my brow, thinking that he looked bloody gorgeous as usual, wearing a casual cream blazer. His hair was longer than a few weeks ago, just the way I liked it.

"I needed to check on you, just to make sure you were all right. Can we talk, Flower? I don't have much time," he insisted and then shut the door behind him. The warmth drifted over my skin, reminding me of our times together. I fought hard with myself to keep away from any royal news and him. I thought a lot about the past, and I couldn't let him ruin the fact that I put everything behind me.

"There is nothing to talk about, Arthur. You're okay, your brother is going to be fine and you shouldn't be here," I told him with my cold tone of voice.

"You saved my life. I came here to thank you. Rodriguez told me everything, Maxine," he said, squatting down on his knees in front of me. I backed away to the wall, panicking.

"Arthur? What the hell are you doing? Get up!" I hissed, ready to use my abilities to tell him that he was making a big mistake. He smiled wolfishly.

"Don't worry, I'm not proposing. I'm only thanking you. Give me your hand, Maxine," he said. I rolled my eyes, annoyed, but my heart was pounding in my chest. I did what he asked, and the warmth scorched over me like a sudden storm. This looked a lot like a marriage proposal. "You saved my skin and nearly died. That was brave and stupid. Now I want you to come back and work for me again."

I had to go over a few times what he said before his sentence made sense. His eyes turned into a mossy shade of green, drifting down to my lips. God, the images of both of us from two years ago were so real. He was asking me to come back and continue doing what I loved most. To protect others.

It took me only five seconds to get it together and pull away from him.

"We both know that's not possible. I can't work for royals. Nothing has changed," I said firmly, trying to breathe at the same time.

"Everything has changed, Flower. I want you back. I told Rodriquez that no one could replace you. This is going to work, trust me."

I sighed, pulling my hair away from my face.

"I'm dating someone now, and I have a full-time business to run, Arthur. Even if I came back, things wouldn't be the same," I said, knowing that lies were only making everything worse, but who cared. Arthur was off limits, and I wasn't going to drag myself down the same road of destruction again.

He looked shocked, angry at first, but he smiled after a moment.

"We both know that you don't date," he responded coldly.

"Well, things have changed. I'm dating Zachary Quinton now and I'm happy, Arthur, so please don't ruin this for me."

He took a sharp breath, staring at me in complete disbelief. He always broadcasted his emotions so strongly, and I knew that he still loved me, but too much had happened between us. We were from different worlds and it was time for him to let me go.

"You're dating that arsehole—"

"And you're engaged to Natalie, Your Highness, so let's leave it at that," I cut him off, pissed off that he dared to mock my choices, insulting Zach. That whole thing was beneath him.

"Flower, please. You don't have any future with that guy. Come back to me."

"I don't have any future with you either. This has to stop. Yes, I did save your life, but I was doing my job. Nothing has changed, Arthur, so stop tearing me apart. We are done," I pressed, raising my voice.

We were so far apart, like we had never been before. Even if I could turn into a human somehow, Arthur couldn't change a thing. His future was already laid out for him.

"So that's it then, you're just going to ignore how you feel?" he asked, when I turned my back to him. I took a deep breath, knowing that there was no point dwelling on our past feelings, or this absurd proposition.

"Yes, I am, and we both know that I can't come back. Go back to your palace, to your fiancée and forget about me, because I have forgotten about you."

My words hurt him, but he needed to hear this in order to move on, to forget. I didn't need to turn around to know that he was gone a few seconds later. My heart pounded insanely fast, my soul filling with black dots of pain, but this was for the best. He couldn't expect me to change my whole life for him.

"A prince, a real prince? Was I dreaming?" Emma shouted, barging into my room a moment later, flustered and pounding with excitement. I smiled, wiping away the last and only tear that I would waste on him.

"Yes, that was Arthur, the future king," I muttered, flopping back on the chair and thinking that I needed a strong drink.

***

I was staring at my reflection in the mirror, telling myself that this time things were going to be different. My new and only dress was in the trash. After the confrontation with the A'rea, I had decided to stick to wearing jeans. The girly clothes weren't for me.

I looked good. My hair was styled nicely. Recently I'd paid a visit to the hairdresser. She used the foils to emphasise my colourful highlights a bit more. This time around I put on dark jeans and a navy top that showcased my cleavage. I threw a leather jacket over my shoulder and then went out.

He was waiting for me outside, smoking in his car. Several hours earlier Ricky asked why Arthur had come over. He couldn't believe that the prince had the nerve to ask me back, to actually think that I would say yes. We were both done with royals, so I told him that he didn't need to worry. It took us a while to calm Emma down though. She was having some kind of asthma attack, and I told myself that in the future, she had to be kept away from any demonic business. I still needed an assistant.

"Hmm, Maxine, you look good … so good that I'm thinking that we should skip this bullshit dinner and go straight to my place," Zachary said when he saw me. He threw his cigarette out on the pavement, eyeing me from head to toe.

I rolled my eyes, feeling extremely sexy. Zach was hot, mouthy and convinced that he could get me to bed in no time.

There were other pending issues, but I didn't want to think about what if. Life was too short.

"Still so sure of yourself, huh?"

"Always. We both know you want me, Flower." He switched on the engine.

"Maybe, but things have changed. I won't jump into bed with you straight away. I'm not that kind of a girl." I laughed, remembering our last steamy encounter.

"Liar. That's all you've been thinking about from the moment we met, Flower."

The end of book 1

Thank you for reading   Demonic Triangle (Doomed Cases Book 1)

Book 2 will be out soon.

If you enjoyed this first instalment, please leave a review.

Printed in Great Britain
by Amazon

36501897R00264